# WARDBREAKER

## Mara Mahan

SKYSHIP FANTASY PRESS

*www.MaraMahan.wordpress.com*

ISBN: 0-9976811-0-1
ISBN-13: 978-0-9976811-0-9

*For  everyone who rambled with me along the way*

# Chapter One

Only the bravest of the brave, the strongest of the strong, and the wisest of the wise could join the Knights of Alinor. Legend held that only heroes could pass through the Stronghold's iron gates.

Kyrin brushed his hair out of his eyes and regarded the enchanted lock that sealed the famous gate, ignoring the rat that clung to his shoulder.

*When I rob this place, I'll go down in history.*

The ward protecting the lock was a thing of beauty, a tapestry of language woven by a master enchanter from lifeless iron and his own inner magic. However, like a tapestry, while the guardian spell had taken great effort, great skill, and great talent to weave, a man only needed to pull the right thread to unravel everything. Kyrin almost had it—he could almost see the common theme. Everything fit together and was related within the spell, and if he could find the flaw, he could take the whole ward apart.

Kyrin drew his prized lock picks from the pocket near his heart. He had hoarded his money for three years to pay for them, skipping meals and going without sleep until he could afford to hire a specialist smith willing to work from his design. Now he never let them out of his sight. The picks were the perfect tools for undoing mundane locks and wards alike, and not a similar set existed anywhere in all of Alinor. At least, that is what the man's face had suggested when he had seen Kyrin's diagrams.

Kyrin had wanted his picks to be perfect, as few things in his life were. All nine of the picks had been imbued with one of the nine elements of magic, and through elegant glyphs carved on a puzzle-like band at the handles, the base powers could be refined and directed. In the right hands, the bands, the glyphs, the magic itself could be twisted and reformed to dismantle even the most devilish of wards without so much as a touch of outside magic. One only needed knowledge, cunning, and a steady hand.

The smith had been excellent. Kyrin probably should have refrained from stealing so much from him afterward, but the temptation of winning back his hard-earned fortune with his new picks had been too much to resist. But no regrets—that day had been Kyrin's first big step towards glory. Remorse was pointless.

*Soon, even the Faceless will revere me.*

"What's the plan, Shadow?" Rat chuckled, scratching at his torn ear with a dirty paw as he dug his tiny claws into Kyrin's shirt. "Stumbling already? Gonna trip over the first hurdle? Drop the dream and go home, kid. Even the Faceless hasn't cracked this egg, and if the Guild leader can't get in, how could a cripple like you?"

"Shut your stupid mouth, Rat, before I make you eat

those words. I'm not like the rest of you streetscum."

"Obviously. The rest of us are human. You… You're just a *shadow* under our feet. Pathetic." Rat's voice rang with spiteful joy as he savored the flavor of each insult.

Kyrin had to sigh. "Yeah? Well how about you switch back to your human form, will ya? It's demeaning, having to talk to vermin like it's a person."

"Funny thing," Rat's voice grew deeper and more manlike as he leapt from Kyrin's shoulder and obligingly shifted his shape, his filthy matted fur lengthening to oily dark hair, his pointed snout and wormlike tail shrinking away as his body bulged and stretched its way back into the likeness of a crouching human, "that's what I said when the Faceless paired me off with you, *partner*. Same word I used too, demeaning."

Kyrin's eyes narrowed and his scowl deepened. "Like you have the guts to talk in front of the Faceless. Last I heard, every time you enter the Inmost Court, you don't to do much more than snivel face-down on the floor."

Rat's pale eyes narrowed. "Yeah? An' what do you know about that, Shadow? Last I heard, you still weren't allowed to show your pathetic face anywhere near the Inmost Court, *cripple.*"

*Again, that word…* Kyrin closed his eyes and willed himself to relax, to keep his voice cold and professional and free from anger. "Rat, I promise you," he said, unconsciously slipping back into the more cultured accent of his childhood, "when this is over and the Faceless finally ends our partnership, I'll—"

"You'll what?" Rat interrupted, cutting Kyrin off mid-threat. "Beat me? Kick me? Make me regret? I'd like to see you try, *dreck*. I'm a shifter, and you're… You're a nothing. A worthless, hopeless, spineless little *cripple* without even a drop of magic in your blood. You're gonna die in there, even if the Knights *are* out!"

"Shut up!" Kyrin cried. Across the street, a set of shutters flew open and a figure leaned out to peer around the deserted street. Kyrin's heart leapt to his throat and he threw himself to the ground. After an annoyingly long moment, the figure pulled the shutters closed again, and Kyrin allowed himself to breathe.

"Rat, *please*," he hissed through clenched teeth, "cut this incessant babble before the Dogs show up. You might be able to shift and scram, but all I've got are my own two feet. Lose me, and the Guild'll fine you an arm and a leg—and you know how the Faceless is about figures of speech."

The partnerships were the Faceless' little joke. Some teams were strategic dreams, legends in the Guild, with powers and personalities carefully selected to complement each other and manage perfect crimes. Others, like Shadow and Rat, were more akin to a waking nightmare—perfectly incompatible and perfectly stupid, holding together only through fear of the Faceless and through a mutual reluctance to face the fines the Guild charged for losing a partner.

Soon, though, Kyrin knew his fortunes would change. No one would dare laugh or call him "cripple" after he robbed the Knights. A hero among thieves was still a hero. Glory was glory no matter where you stood.

Kyrin leaned in for a better look at the ward, repressing a manic grin.

It was a tall gate, made of dark iron—cold, forbidding, and practically unclimbable on account of both the sharpened steel spikes mounted on top, and the powerful ward spells woven into the hard metal. The ringing hum of the hidden magic was nearly audible on this silent moonlit night, and if it weren't impossible, Kyrin would have been willing to swear he felt the deep resonance echo within his bones.

Unless that was just his suppressed anxiety. This gate was the first big hurdle to the ultimate prize.

*Wealth. Power. Respect... After this job, it'll all be mine. I just have to get inside...*

"You gonna admire the thing all night, Shadow? Or are you actually gonna try and crack it?" Rat's slouching silhouette crossed its arms, and the man's booted foot tapped invisibly in the darkness.

Kyrin made a strangled noise somewhere between a sigh and a growl. "Shut. Up. I'm working on it. I know what I'm doing—don't pretend you do."

Rat responded, throwing back some venomous reply, but Kyrin barely registered his words. The heavy iron lock that barred the Stronghold's massive gate had his full attention. Kyrin dared not give it less.

Years ago, in the garden of a wealthy merchant, Kyrin had encountered a ward woven on the ground by shadows cast from magelight. When night fell and the streetlights lit themselves, the garden itself became a trap invisible to all but the experienced eye. Kyrin had missed the signs until it was nearly too late, and he had been forced to burn several pages from his notebook to break the darkness and escape with his life. The scars on his legs still ached some nights, and that twisted darkness often writhed back through his dreams to trap him in chains of bladed black.

Compared to that trap, this lock looked tame. But looks, Kyrin knew, were deceiving.

Rumor held that this particular lock had been forged back in the age when the pictorial script was still common among Alinor's literate population, so it utilized nearly every form of magical defense. Many of Kyrin's childhood textbooks had described the Stronghold's gate as a tangled rat's nest of violate enchantment and misleading wordplay—they had called it the unpickable lock.

"Yet every lock has its pick, and every ward has its flaw…" Kyrin muttered to himself as he bent his neck for a better angle. Though his teachers had repeated that mantra with a different intent, Kyrin lived his life by the simplistic dogma. Nothing was fail-safe, and a way would always open to the creative and determined individual. Kyrin just had to be clever enough to find it.

"I guard the heroes who guard our land…" Kyrin translated, tracing a gloved finger over the ancient words as he mumbled, "Alinor's Knights are safe in my hand…"

"You're making that up." Rat peered over Kyrin's shoulder at the lock. "There's nothing there but squiggles."

"Shut up, Rat. You can't even read plain Common. Don't talk."

"Nope!" Rat chuckled, smirking. "Ordinary folk like me don't need your fancy letters. I got my magic and no cause to *compensate*."

"Shut up. Now where was…? Oh—right. Hand. Let's see… Blah blah blah, something about pure brave heart, land where only heroes tread, poetic nonsense about worthiness…" Kyrin twisted around to read the side of the lock, giving in to his urge to flaunt his skill at Rat.

He finished his reading with a broad flourish. "Basically, the ward is telling us it's a ward, and declaring its intent to never, ever let anyone through who doesn't have the Knight's Key—on pain of a horrific and possibly embarrassing death."

"I coulda told you that, genius. So much for your fancy learning. How's that supposed to get us in?"

"Ah, but you see, Rat," Kyrin explained, letting the genius comment slide, "the important thing isn't *what* the ward says, it's *how* the ward says it."

"What? Get to the point, Shadow."

"The point is, *partner,* that the message the ward spells is less important than the glyphs used to spell it. Everything in the old script is highly contextual, so a symbol that means one thing in one place can mean something else entirely somewhere different. Like—for example, this swirl here means 'hero' But I've also seen it to mean 'shield' before."

"...Eh?" Rat's eyes began to glaze. Kyrin smothered a grin.

"Likewise," Kyrin continued, kneeling down beside the lock and fishing in his pockets for his tools, "a lot of glyphs can name the same word, but all have different connotations. I can think of at least five different ways to write 'hero' off the top of my head, and each has a completely different feeling behind it. The trick is to not only know what a word means, but to also know what it might mean elsewhere, and what it means beneath its first meaning. If you have the sense to read the words that were written the way they weren't meant to be read, the ward'll tell you what it is, what it does, what'll happen if you trip it, and it'll practically give you step-by-step instructions on how to take it apart. So like here—"

"Shut up! Shut up! I get it!" Rat cried, throwing his hands in the air, "You've read a book! Now will you just shut up and take the blasted thing apart? I don't have all night, Shadow! Got better things to do than listen to you talk my last good ear off, you know. Get moving!"

"Yeah yeah yeah." Kyrin had expected Rat to snap after the second sentence, never anticipating the crook would allow him to lecture as long as he had. "Forgive my tryin'a shove some wisdom into that thick skull of yours. Now stand back, will ya? I don't need you breathing down my neck for this. You don't even wanna know what happens if you make me screw up."

For once, Rat obliged without comment. Everyone knew what happened when a ward went off on a thief, and Kyrin knew that, if he failed, Rat would want to be far enough away to watch the show in safety.

But no matter. Now was the time for Kyrin to lose himself in the realm of carven glyphs and mirrored meanings.

Though the gate's spell started out looking like a standard flare-ward—the kind that adorned most middle-class merchant shops in the city—the enchantment soon began picking up undertones of ice and earth, touches added specifically to make unraveling the ward more difficult.

The mix was odd—classically, one would counter fire with water, but here, water was an integral part, negating the negation and tying the whole mess in a paradoxical loop. Kyrin did not know what to think—nothing made sense, and many elements seemed to spring from nowhere for no reason. Whenever Kyrin began to suspect he had found a flaw in one aspect, another sneaked up and kicked him in the pants.

One wrong move, and he would wind up tangled in a web of ancient words to be eaten alive by the old magic at the center. Doubt crept into Kyrin's heart and started gnawing at his core. It would be so easy to step wrong, so easy to fumble and lose life, limb, and pride in one fell blow.

The longer Kyrin examined the thing, the more complex the spell seemed to become. New dimensions threw themselves into the mix at every turn—elements of light and darkness floated into view, with barely noticeable references to ancient history and classic poetry drifting up to join them from the unknowably layered depths of context and meaning. Marks Kyrin had taken as meaningless decoration turned into obscure glyphs— words and words within words. He had never seen the like.

Kyrin closed his eyes to think.

If he had come alone, he could back out without incident, but Kyrin would never live it down if he ran away now, with Rat watching. Kyrin wanted to hand his partner another cause to mock him exactly as much as he wanted a fireball in his face—much for the same reasons. He gnawed his lip and resigned himself to trusting his gut. Kyrin's instinct, his ingenuity, and his willpower would have to be enough to carry him through.

*Wait half a minute... willpower... strength of will... Courage! That's it! That's the key!* Through courage and will, humanity had gained mastery over the elements, over darkness, over light, over magic itself. The old poetry, the history, it all pointed back to human will. Even that old saying: "only a Hero may enter..." What was a hero but a courageous man? Gods—it was all so *easy!*

Kyrin selected the lock pick imbued with the essence of human agency, the ninth element, and twisted the bands around until the glyphs formed a crude reflection of courage and determination. The easy part—the brain work—was over. Now came the tricky bit. If he had guessed wrong, if he had missed something, if his hand slipped, Kyrin would find out—and it would be...unpleasant. Possibly even excruciating. Wards were never gentle, but Kyrin hardly cared.

The thrill was intoxicating. If he had to die, this was how Kyrin wanted to go; pulled to pieces by a spell as he himself pulled it apart.

Here, now, on the edge between success and failure, Kyrin was alive.

Using the tip of his lock pick, he tapped one of the tiny glyphs carved into the surface of the lock, waking it up. The ward started to ring quietly as it came alive under his hand, yawning and stretching like an animal roused from hibernation. Kyrin tapped one word, then another, then another, each stroke confusing the meaning of the magic and confounding the spell long enough to give Kyrin a chance to pick the mundane portion of the lock. Since keys automatically took care of everything all at once, Kyrin had to move quickly to keep the ward from noticing his intrusion. Hesitation was his greatest enemy—if the ward caught him now, he would die.

As soon as the non-magical part of the lock was picked, Rat sauntered back to Kyrin's side. "That all, Shadow? I coulda done that. So much for your one talent."

Kyrin ignored him. Though he had picked the mundane lock, he still had to appease the ward and send the spell back to sleep. One careless slip could still kill him. He pulled his pick from glyph to glyph, gently countering and rearranging the imaginary lines of meaning that lay between the symbols.

Finally, after what seemed an age, Kyrin straightened up and stretched. "Shut up, Rat. Now, you can keep your mouth closed and follow me, or you can go on ahead—I don't care. The other wards won't get me if they're busy with you."

"Not on your life, Shadow," Rat said as he once again shrunk down into his second form, "I ain't going first, and I'm not about to get left behind." Before Kyrin could do more than flail, Rat climbed his trouser leg, scrambled up his shirt, and found a perch on Kyrin's shoulder. "I'm with you, *partner*, and that means we stick together."

Kyrin wrinkled his nose in distaste, but he knew better than to try brushing the vermin off. Though Rat's rodent form was small, his human form was tall, strong, and mean, and Kyrin had no desire to become better acquainted with the man's fist.

Privately resolving to hire a dozen cats when he was wealthy and had a house of his own, Kyrin grimaced and shut his mouth.

Ambition drove his steps. Hatred filled his mind. Kyrin passed the Stronghold's gate and entered the land only heroes tread.

# Chapter Two

If the lock on the gate had been a challenge, the Knights' gardens were wicked. Every turn concealed another trap, and every twist exposed some new danger. Trees extended roots and branches to ensnare Kyrin in a fatal embrace. Patches of seemingly innocent ground opened up beneath his feet to swallow him whole. Flowers caught fire when brushed by human legs, and wards to strike down stationary intruders were woven into every wall.

Kyrin avoided what he could, dismantled what he could not, and ran like heck when neither was an option, all the while tuning out Rat's snide, whispered remarks. Before long, the shadow with the rat on his shoulder made his way to the Stronghold's back door.

Compared to the level of security everywhere else in the garden, the door itself was surprisingly unprotected. No great bars or complex wards prevented its opening. Instead, the door was shut with a simple iron lock—the type young thieves practiced on—and guarded by the kind of simple fire-based spell that could be thwarted by a bucket of lukewarm dishwater.

Kyrin had the door open in moments. As soon as the pair passed the threshold, Rat leapt down from Kyrin's shoulder and again assumed his slightly less verminous form, rising from his four legged crouch with an expression of mild bemusement.

"What d'ya know, Shadow, you didn't get yourself fried," he whispered.

"No thanks to you. Way you kept squeaking and carrying on, I thought you were gonna wake every ward in the city. Miracle we made it at all."

"You *are* crazy, Shadow! Only reason your clumsy skin got through unscathed was because I pointed out all the dangerous crap. Don't you remember? Or did your memory get crippled as well as your magic?"

"Shut up."

"Must've. Explains why those're the only words you seem to know. Don't worry, partner, once we're out of here, I'm sure you'll have enough money to put yourself in a nice home. A comfy little asylum where they only beat you sometimes."

"Shut—" Kyrin cut himself off, biting his lip to kill the expected phrase before it could leave his tongue, "your stinking mouth." He finished awkwardly. "If either of us deserves to be locked up, it's you, ya sun-scored guttertrash. Now stop talkin'—you still wanna get out, dontcha? Heard on the street that the Knights are out, but no one ever said the streets don't lie. Let's hurry up and play this safe. I may be crazy, but at least I'm not crazy stupid."

Yawning lazily to show his contempt for his partner's anxiety, Rat whispered one final line, unable to allow Kyrin the last word. "Listen Shadow, I've been nice—this is your mission, so I've been playing by your rules. But I'm gettin' real sick of all these orders, ya hear? Cool it with the commands, an' maybe I'll be real generous and let you keep part of this haul."

Kyrin's anger flared, but he bit his tongue and clenched his hands. Maybe causing himself physical pain would help keep his mind on the job. If he lost focus, he would punch the condescension from Rat's smug grin, and a scuffle now would jeopardize everything.

Hating his partner's smirk and hating himself for bowing to it, Kyrin led the way into the Knights' Stronghold. The two thieves moved from room to room, from hallway to hallway like a pair of wraiths, leaving no trace but the absence of valuables behind them. Much of what they found was far too heavy to carry, but Kyrin managed to pocket plenty of small, expensive items—more than enough to make the trip worthwhile.

Suddenly, Rat whistled under his breath. "Hey, Shadow, get your hide over here," he whispered, calling Kyrin to a locked door with an imperious tilt of his head.

"Eh? What's the deal?"

"It's locked, idiot. Open it. I don't wanna die if it's warded."

"You're the idiot," Kyrin groaned as he headed over, inwardly delighted that Rat needed his help, "if you weren't so proud of being stupid, you might not—"

"Shut up and work, cripple."

The inevitable acidic curse stung at Kyrin's lips as it escaped his mouth. Rat snickered. Kyrin ignored him, pouring his focus into the door and its ward.

The thing was made from an ancient oak, hardened by fire and time to be tougher than stone. A web of spindly, gossamer-thin glyphs spread across the door's surface, and an expert glance revealed the enchantments to be as old as the ward on the Gate, if not older, with tricks and traps just as convoluted and complex. Whatever hid behind this lock was a treasure. Of that, Kyrin was sure.

"Give me a minute or two—this might take some time."

Rat waved his hand dismissively. "Sure, whatever. Take the whole damn night if you wanna. Not like your life and my fortune is on the line or anything. You wanna hang? Take all the time you want."

"Shut up."

The ward was constructed with the symbols for stone and resilience, for silence and loyalty, interlocked with glyphs for peace, moonlight, and shade. To counter it, Kyrin brought out the pick for water and change, and the pick imbued with the spirit of growth and sunlight. A few minutes of intense analysis and poetic mumbling passed. Kyrin fought to keep his hands steady under anticipation's trembling weight, but eventually the door creaked open. The noise was a triumphant chorus in Kyrin's head.

He stepped back to admire his handiwork, but Rat pushed past without so much as a word of thanks. The smile drained from Kyrin's thin face as he followed behind his partner. However, the unsavory tint left Kyrin's mind the moment he passed the threshold, usurped by unrestrained wonder.

The circular chamber was startlingly bare. Plain walls made from rough, interlocking stones extended up to the domed ceiling and loomed over the featureless gray floor. A low pedestal dominated the center of the room. On the pedestal, Kyrin saw a piece of enchanting so masterful, so amazing, it put his favorite textbooks to shame.

"What the hell is this?" Rat plucked the iridescent white disk from its stand, turning it this way and that in a futile attempt to gauge its worth. Larger than his head, it shone like the inside of a seashell, its pearly exterior throwing back a muted reflection of Rat's unkempt, greasy visage.

Kyrin's awe gave way to irritation. "You'd better be kidding me, Rat. Not even you're that stupid."

Rat's eyebrows shot up as he set down the disk, drawing his lanky form to full height and crossing his arms. "I'm *exactly* that stupid, you little half-wit cripple. So unless you want me to show you again exactly how much I don't give a damn, cut the lecture and just tell me what this shit is worth."

Kyrin shook his head and placed a hand over his eyes. "I don't believe this. I seriously don't believe this. That, Rat, is the blasted Anchor Key—and it's freaking priceless."

"So worth nabbing, then?"

Kyrin stepped closer, reverently trailing a finger over the disk's silk-smooth surface and carefully crafted spells. "No… not worth taking—piece like this is so vital, so distinctive—we'd never find a fence willing to buy it."

Rat cursed. "Blast it—what a waste of time."

"You don't get it, do you? The Anchor Key is the keystone that holds Alinor together! Without it, the city'd—"

"Can't sell it—don't care."

With that, Rat stalked off to continue his raid, leaving Kyrin alone to pay his respects.

"…get torn apart," Kyrin finished under his breath, returning his attention to the miraculous device.

If the gate was a tapestry, if the door ward was a masterpiece, the Anchor Key was a world of beautiful complexities—not a mere image, but a thing, whole and wonderful in and of itself. Now that Rat had left, Kyrin risked taking a moment to look over the object with a professional eye. He had seen drawings, he had read text after text, book after book on the famous wardwork that allowed Alinor to exist in one cohesive piece, but as none of the passages had any clues toward the Anchor Key's location, Kyrin had never expected to get the chance to study it.

This opportunity was a diamond hidden in piles of gravel—the contemporary wards Kyrin snagged off the street to study were about as complex and wonderful as small pieces of string: useful to those in need of an easy solution to an easy problem, but worthless in any situation more demanding than mending a loose button.

Kyrin felt as though his skill had stagnated with the modern wards. There was no challenge—no risk—no room for him to enhance his prowess. But here—here was a piece of enchanting worth studying. Here was a piece worth Kyrin's time.

Holding his breath, Kyrin caressed the Anchor Key's polished surface, gently feeling the nearly imperceptible ridges and whorls of carven enchantment, loving the faint music it made on contact with his skin.

Peace and unity and strength and hope, protection and silence and stillness and rest—interlocking glyphs with interlocking meanings webbed around each other in a brilliant dance, reflecting and refracting ideas through magic to make a marvelous spell.

Kyrin took out a tiny notebook and began to sketch.

A beautiful minute of research slipped by, penstroke by quiet penstroke, until the perfect peace shattered, mutilated beyond recognition by Rat's harsh whisper sidling in through the cracked door.

"'ey, Shadow—you having a good time in there or what? Quit making love to that glorified soup plate and get out here—you ain't fillin' your quota until my month's paid off."

Kyrin sighed, his pencil halting mid-glyph. "What I take is mine, Rat."

"Yeah, yeah. Sure. Same goes for me—especially when I'm taking from you."

"Go take a hike in the Outlands, why don't you? Find a cliff and jump off it."

"Nah, I got business in this life yet. Now git your butt out here, yeah?"

Rat's tone allowed no argument. Kyrin reluctantly obliged, leaving the Anchor Key and the realm of enchanting behind to chase his fate as a thief.

Throughout the rest of the Stronghold, the pair found nothing but good luck. Kyrin chanced upon a wonderful little figurine enchanted to walk around when its glyph was touched, and Rat seemed to have a knack for locating gems and jewelry. Gold bracelets set with emeralds, knives enchanted to never grow dull, necklaces charmed to protect the wearer—all found a new home in the pair's pockets. By the time the partners had explored the first floor and found the stairs to the second, Kyrin's numerous pouches were stuffed to the brim with all manner of enchanted paraphernalia and valuable oddities, and Rat had acquired so many ornaments that he clinked when he walked and glittered in the barest gleam of moonlight.

Although he knew it was childish and unprofessional, Kyrin allowed a broad grin to slide across his face. This place was a paradise—the Knights had brought every imaginable variety of treasure and wealth back from their journeys abroad. None of it was warded, and almost nothing had been locked away.

Kyrin had only ever seen more wealth in one place that night he had dreamed of a world turned gold. Even though only a fraction of this fortune could ever fit in his pockets, Kyrin knew the guild would soon see his worth. After this take, no one would ever laugh at him again. No one would dare to call him cripple. Soon, things would get better. They had to.

Kyrin glanced around the dark hallway, keeping an eye out for new, exciting finds. Moonlight streamed through the large glass windowpanes, clearly illuminating the ornate imported carpets and the ancient suits of battered armor dotting the premises. Every Knight who served Alinor within these walls left a suit of armor behind in his memory, and the Knights had a legacy going back centuries.

Once upon a time, Kyrin had dreamed of earning a spot for his own armor within these walls. Once upon a time, he had longed for a place among these ancient heroes. Real life had forced him to wake, though, and now Kyrin was just as happy to rob them blind. Life goes on, and priorities change. Infamy was just the other side of fame, after all.

Lost in his thoughts, Kyrin paused a moment to gaze out the window overlooking the Stronghold's entryway. From up here on the second floor, the garden seemed peaceful—not at all like the deathtrap he had only barely evaded. Dignified old trees whispered in the warm breeze, and the uncombusted flowers bowed their heads under the weight of the starlight. A series of bumps and clatters marked Rat rummaging in the next room over, but Kyrin paid no heed to the noises. He turned his attention back towards the railing and gazed down at the floor below.

To either side, a rich curved staircase spiraled down into darkness, golden handrails shining brightly under the pale moonlight. Overhead, a chandelier dripped and glittered, gleaming like a waterfall of crystal suspended from the ceiling.

In his mind's eye, the hall filled with Alinor's nobility. Kings and princes, lords and ladies richly clad in jewel-like colors lined up to beg his aid, offering great sums of money if he could only…

Only what?

Kyrin shut his eyes and shook his head to dislodge the half-baked fantasy. He had no special talents. Nobody wanted him. Even the Guild barely tolerated his presence.

"No more," Kyrin breathed, regaining his customary scowl, "After tonight, I'll be livin' the good life."

Turning his back on the empty hall and his empty dreams, Kyrin brought his gaze back to the window, intending to get one last glimpse before returning to his robbery. However, his firm determination met a sight it was quite unprepared for—a sight that melted Kyrin's bones and turned his blood to ice.

The Knights of Alinor were returning early.

Five armed figures strolled up the warded gravel path, completely unaffected by the magical traps as they laughed and playfully ribbed each other. For several heartbeats, Kyrin could do nothing but stand and stare in horror.

Returning early…

The Knights of Alinor had come home early!

*Dammit!*

Unfreezing all at once, Kyrin dashed into the room Rat was still in the process of pillaging, tripping over his own feet in his effort to reach his partner in time.

"Rat!" he gasped, hearing and hating the fear in his whispered cry, "Rat! Where are—"

"What—?" The other thief poked his head out of the door, a ridiculously ornate crown balanced upon his greasy brown hair. "What's the deal?"

"Knights! Knights here! Now! Back! Let's go!"

Rat paused, freezing for one eternal second as the words sunk in—then he was gone, off down the hallway with Kyrin tailing behind. The second floor provided no means of escape. The windows were warded, and Kyrin did not dare risk taking time to open one. His only hope was to make it out the back door before the Knights entered through the front and saw them.

The thieves had all of a minute or two, if they were lucky.

The pair dashed down the staircase, leaping the carpeted marble stairs three at a time, praying not to trip and die. In his haste, Rat lost his crown.

Merciless empty hallways beckoned to Kyrin in his flight. They leered at him, promising escape and threatening him with dead-end capture. Kyrin had taken care to try and learn his way around these maze-like hallways beforehand, but fear now wiped the pattern from his mind.

*There's a door around here somewhere—there has to be. There has to be a—*

The front door creaked open quietly. The Knights' laughter drifted through the opening, terrifying echoes of life in the safe and secret darkness. Even more frightening was the sudden silence that followed after.

Kyrin could almost hear the warriors' whispering: "Someone's here." "Intruder" "The Stronghold's been breached." "Find him." "Justice."

"End this."

"Kill him."

*Notgoodnotgoodnotgood!* Kyrin's heart seemed to pound out the words in time with every frantic footfall, and his every gasp of panicked breath seemed a scream in the silent Stronghold. He was vulnerable—a mouse in the lion's den—and knowledge of his weakness only made his terror worse.

A door appeared in the wall, materializing through the twilight glow of magelight with promises of salvation and hope in Kyrin's hour of need. Momentum stole his balance and fear banished his coordination, but Kyrin managed to yank the door open and dart inside.

"Rat—" Kyrin hissed to his companion as loudly as he dared, "here—hide!"

Rat darted to Kyrin's side, his ill-gained jewelry clinking and jangling like alarm bells in the taut stillness. Kyrin hissed in annoyance, biting his tongue as he eased the door shut behind him.

Silence bloomed.

Holding his breath, Kyrin listened to the soundless darkness. He strained to hear through Rat's heavy panting, through the layers of silence to the Knights who hunted beneath its cover.

Were there... whispers? No—surely that was only Kyrin's overactive, overstressed imagination. Were those... footsteps? Surely not.

With the agonizing slowness of one afraid to disturb the air, Kyrin inched further into the closet, hoping to hide his human shape amidst the mass of hanging coats. If he could camouflage his limbs—distort his silhouette with the suspended cloth, he might be overlooked if the Knights came knocking.

Following a similar train of thought, Rat stashed all the plunder that would fit into his various pockets and pouches. Like all clothes worn by shifters, the pockets were enchanted to change with the wearer, but any item left behind would stay behind—and here, a loss of potential profit could result in loss of life.

Rat shifted and ran up a coat sleeve. Kyrin adjusted his footing and pretended not to exist.

The world went still. Kyrin hardly dared to breathe.

The innumerable seconds ticked by slowly, indistinguishable from the lengthy—

WHAM!

The door burst open, nearly flying off its hinges. Kyrin flinched. A man blackened the doorway. Tall. Broad. Gleaming armor. Mace in hand.

Kyrin held his breath.

The mace hit the wall—too near Kyrin's head. Although the Knight swung blindly, his stance was certain. The thieves were in the closet. Their fate was sealed. The man's cocky grin promised it.

Rat broke cover, darting from his sleeve to flow across the floor like a shadow fleeing light. The Knight caught the motion and swung after Rat, but his mace was a moment too slow to squash the tiny target. Kyrin leapt forward and punched the man in the face. Startled and unbalanced, the man stumbled, caught off guard by the lucky blow.

Kyrin shouldered past him, then ran—rational thought trampled by primal terror.

Silhouettes danced everywhere, their wild rhythm punctuated by sharp barks of fierce laughter. From the corner of his eye, Kyrin saw a lady Knight—a dark-skinned woman with long auburn hair tied back behind her head—scoop Rat up from the floor and dangle him by his tail.

"Now what have we here?" She purred through Rat's shameless pleading, examining him as one would inspect a rare, but slightly revolting curiosity, "Little shifter in over his head?"

Kyrin ducked around a corner to catch his breath. If he waited to dash, maybe he had a chance...

The lady Knight tossed Rat across the room, ignoring

the thief's panicked screams. A tan young man with a pale scar crossing his left eyebrow effortlessly darted in and plucked Rat out of the air. Flames danced between the fingers of the scarred man's other hand as he waved it beneath Rat's terrified form. "Think I should toast him?"

The Knight with the mace emerged from the closet, wiping a smear of blood from beneath his nose. He hefted his weapon and turned his head, scanning the shadows.

*Dammit...*

Hang Rat. Forget the fines. Kyrin broke cover and sprinted down the hallway.

Another Knight appeared as if from nowhere—a blond guy, only slightly older than Kyrin. He stepped out from a doorway and grabbed at Kyrin as he ran past. Kyrin panicked, elbowing the guy in the gut before diving and rolling away, slipping through the man's grasp to win another moment of freedom.

Kyrin gasped in a rough breath, pushing himself to run faster. He turned a corner randomly and willed the hallway to hide him. A shining new figure stepped out from a side door. Kyrin crashed into her. He scrambled back to his feet, barely feeling the sting of his scrapes and bruises as he ran.

He knew where he was now. The exit was only a few yards away from the next turn. Kyrin just had to run a little farther, and then—

His feet stopped. Kyrin fell, his chin slamming into the cold marble floor. Pain spiked throughout his body. Kyrin could not move—not even his eyes would blink at his will.

She knelt beside him, the pale girl in the silver armor, and Kyrin's arms and legs forced him to rise. Ordinarily, the pain he felt would bring him to his knees, would leave him recovering on the ground for at least a few moments more, yet now Kyrin's muscles moved him to stand.

The girl placed a gentle hand on Kyrin's back as if to steady him, and the two of them walked calmly back to the other Knights in their hall as if nothing in the world was wrong.

Kyrin raged. His limbs would not obey him, and every unwilling step stabbed his injured chin and punched his wounded pride.

*Blast it.*

Kyrin wanted to run—to flee, to curse, to rest—but he had no choice but to walk.

So much for fame. So much for glory. *Stupid magic, making things complicated...*

The girl sent Kyrin to face the Knights. He marched forward like wind-up toy facing a firing squad.

The Knight with the mace smiled, adjusting the elaborately enchanted gauntlet on his left arm before running a hand through his red hair. "Good job, Sal, you got him. Almost thought he'd get away there for a second."

*Me too,* Kyrin thought bitterly.

"Nope!" the girl chirped, flashing a white-toothed smile of her own, "I told you, I've been practicing splitting my focus! I've got this guy under my complete control!"

The Knight nodded. "Don't overdo it—you don't want to exhaust yourself. Just keep him still—that'll be enough."

The pressure on Kyrin's mind relaxed. He fell to the floor, wincing as shocks of pain ran up his body. He swore once, quietly, just to prove that he could, before casting a hate-filled glare up at the triumphant heroes.

Rat, meanwhile, groveled pitifully at the feet of the

dark-skinned lady Knight, crying and sobbing and squealing for mercy despite his now-human form.

"It was him—it was all him—Shadow's the one—please, please don't kill me—Shadow's the one who broke your ward—I told 'im not to but he wouldn't listen—he made me do it, I swear—" Pathetic sounds burbled from Rat's lying lips, culminating in a strangled sob when the lady Knight kicked his prone form.

"Shut it," she barked as Kyrin fixed his fury on his worthless partner. "What say you, Tryn? Guild's overstepped its bounds this time—how 'bout we send 'em a little message?"

Both Kyrin and Rat paled, picturing a future that ended with their heads mounted on spikes above the Stronghold's gate.

"No no—nonono *please*," tears coursed down Rat's face, carving pale, glistening tracts through the dirt on his cheeks, "It was him!" A dramatic finger flung towards Kyrin's magic-bound body, "It was all him—his idea, I didn't wanna come! He made me! I didn't have a choice!"

"You *lying bastard*—I'm gonna *kill* yo—" Kyrin's own teeth clenched down on his tongue, his anger cut off mid-threat. His will was powerless in the face of the girl's puppeteer magic.

"See?" Rat groveled, clutching pitifully at Tryn's legs, "He said he was gonna kill me—he said he'd kill me if I didn't come! It's not my fault, good sirs, it's not my fault—find it in your noble hearts to spare me!"

Kyrin wanted to vomit, and from the looks on their faces, the Knights felt the same.

"Brysson—" the Knight with the mace wrinkled his nose as he extricated his feet from Rat's grabbing fingers. "Check our 'innocent' friend's pockets, will you?"

"You heard him," the scarred Knight lazily conjured a

ball of orange flame and let it play about his hand, "empty those pockets, shifter, it seems Tryn's thinking about letting you go."

Babbling incoherent thanks, Rat emptied his most obvious pockets and pouches, all the while proclaiming his innocence and blaming Kyrin. Eyebrows raised and glances exchanged at the volume of treasure produced from Rat's pockets, yet none of the Knights made comment.

"That everything?" Brysson summoned a second flame and grinned.

Rat nodded; apparently scared out of his wits, but Kyrin knew the assent was a lie. Rat still had enough stashed by to gain a healthy profit, but Kyrin had no way of exposing this deceit.

"Well, thief," Tryn's voice carried a certain, peculiar finality, "we're gonna let you go."

"Oh—thank you, *thank you*, Sir, I—"

"Quiet—I'm not finished. We're letting you go so that you may carry a message to the one you call Faceless. Tell your master that though we've turned a blind eye to city affairs—our domain is the Outlands and we respect that it's the Dogs' job to chase you lot around—if you or your Guild pals come anywhere near our hold again, we might just decide to take a civic interest, ya hear? You've already got the Dogs on your tail—do you really want the Knights hunting you as well?"

Rat gibbered, his words deserting him.

The lady Knight leaned in, her teeth bared in a hunter's grin, "Let me give you a hint: the answer's 'no.'"

Rat nearly fainted.

"And as for your friend here—"

A muted growl cut Tryn off. Kyrin's rage, of its own volition, clawed its way up his throat, only to get trapped behind his sealed jaw and bespelled tongue.

Tryn hardly missed a beat. "I'm sorry—not friend, apparently. At least, not anymore. Your accomplice here, well, he's going to stay with us for a while. Until the end, probably. You, shifter, get to play the messenger, but there's still the whole matter of us. You two wronged us, therefore I feel some form of r... uh... re..."

The red-haired Knight trailed off mid-speech, unable to find the word he wanted. An awkward silence drifted lazily through.

"Reaction?" The puppeteer girl offered tentatively.

"No, that's not it..."

"Retribution?"

"Closer, but no."

The blond guy who had nearly grabbed Kyrin in the hallway near the door chimed in. "Recompense?"

"That's the one!" Tryn declared, triumphantly snapping his fingers, "Thank you, Dain. As I was saying—I feel some form of recompense is in order, therefore we're taking him as payment for the trouble you caused, the wards you tripped, and the trinkets that you undoubtedly still have about your person. After all," Tryn paused for effect, a Cheshire grin flitting across his face, "you're gonna carry our message, but we still need to make our own point, just in case."

*Marvelous,* Kyrin thought through his rising hate, *lovely. Father would be so proud. I'm going to die a failure.*

Rat, meanwhile, was entirely unconcerned with Kyrin's fate, so long as he did not need to share it. Tears spilled from his face as thanks poured from his throat—the man did not spare so much as a glance towards the partner he was leaving to die.

It made Kyrin sick—a feeling the Knights seemed to echo. The blond guy, Dain, whispered something to the puppeteer girl, Sal, who chuckled derisively.

Tryn yawned. "Alright, our journey is done, the intruders have been apprehended, so I think we can declare this quest officially over, yeah?"

Briea, the lady Knight, nodded. "Yeah. All that's left... You. Vermin. Come here." She wielded her pointer finger like a blade. Rat did not dare refuse. He slunk closer, looking for all the world as if he should have been moving backwards. She grabbed the front of his shirt, lifting the lanky man off the ground despite her lesser height. "Shift. Now."

Kyrin had never seen Rat transform faster than he did in the face of Briea's growl. Kyrin wished he were free so that he could enjoy his partner's terror more properly.

"Alright—now Dain, open a window."

Dain did as ordered. Rat whimpered. Without wasting another breath, the lady Knight turned and hurled the tiny criminal out into the garden like yesterday's garbage.

Had Kyrin's tongue not been bound, had his own life not been at stake, he would have laughed.

Tryn ran his hand wearily down his face. "I hate it when adventures make house calls..."

"Same here," Brysson agreed with a yawn, "Let's hurry up and find our little house guest proper accommodations—I have been far too long parted from my bed, and I'm starting to miss its company."

"Indeed!" Sal laughed as she manipulated Kyrin to stand, "I must say, it'll be nice to have a few days where nothing is actively trying to kill us."

"You can say that again." Dain clapped Kyrin's shoulder companionably as he examined the thief's face, confident in Sal's ability to hold Kyrin still. "Hey... do I know you?"

With naught but a silent glance, Kyrin managed to

convey the complete and total idiocy of that statement. A noble Knight—the top of the social ladder—knowing a no-good thief on the bottom?

*Yeah, right.*

Dain dismissed the idea as well. "Whatever. Anyway, Sal, you can let him go and get yourself to sleep—gods know you need it."

"You sure?"

"Yeah, I can handle our prisoner here for a few minutes without your magic—I am a Knight, after all."

"A squire, you mean," Brysson corrected, carelessly binding Kyrin's wrists behind his back with a bit of cord, "It'll probably be a few more adventures 'til Briea sees fit to let you take the Trial."

"You're not my senior by that much—" Dain chuckled, peering over Brysson's shoulder to ensure the knots were properly tied, "I'll be catching up to you sooner than you'd think. Sal, too—one of these days the two of us'll pass that Trial and get ourselves knighted as well, and then we'll see who gives all the orders and stuff!"

"Tryn will." Sal's blank-faced contribution made both young men turn in momentary confusion as Kyrin stood in simmering silence between them, a mere prop on the stage to be talked around and ignored.

Tryn turned his head at the sound of his name. "I will what? What are you three doing? Take our visitor to the cells already—I'm going to bed." With that, the man walked off, stumbling slightly as sleep already began to overtake him.

Sal giggled. "See? There goes our glorious leader, commanding as ever. But anyway, seriously. I'm going to release our buddy here, so you two be ready in case he decides to do anything stupid."

"On it." Brysson laid his hand upon Kyrin's shoulder.

The iron will keeping Kyrin upright faded. His strings were cut, and gravity once again had grounds to claim him. Although he would have given the world to stand strong and unfazed, a hero among thieves, untouchable even under arrest, Kyrin's own legs betrayed him. When Sal's will deserted him, Kyrin's knees turned to jelly and his balance failed.

The Knights caught him as he sank, but Kyrin almost wished that they had let him fall.

"You alright, buddy?" Dain's cheerful, almost friendly tone did nothing to soothe Kyrin's injured pride.

"Go hang yourself." Kyrin's tongue, at least, was fully cooperative.

"Nah," Brysson grinned as he roughly hoisted Kyrin to his feet, "Dain wouldn't do that. No, I think *we'll* be hanging *you*."

Chuckling cheerfully, the two young Knights bid Sal goodnight and hauled Kyrin away to his stony new home.

The floor was cold. The stone was bare. Warded iron bars cut dark stripes into the block of pale moonlight that shone from the tiny window up above. Kyrin sat in the corner of his cell, his arms crossed over his chest, his head bowed.

*So much for glory. So much for fame.*

All that was left to look forward to now was... Death? Probably.

*Oh, what fun.*

Kyrin slid down, sinking further towards the ground. His chin touched his chest. His eyes squeezed shut. Kyrin ground his teeth, frowning at the cruel fate that led him here. A wave of gloom welled up from the depths of his stomach.

Always, some ill fortune swept victory from Kyrin's fingers just as he was about to grasp it. Always, some insurmountable barrier barred him an inch away from success.

*Am I cursed?* Kyrin wondered as he swallowed a surge of bitter despair, *Was Father right? Am I really..? No.* Kyrin shook his head to chase away the memory, *It was Rat. Rat's fault—not mine. If I'd have been alone, I could have pulled it off. If Rat hadn't broke cover—if Rat hadn't squealed and stabbed me in the back—it's all his fault—all of it!*

The old familiar anger comforted Kyrin. The cold flame of hatred seemed a useful tool to burn away despair. Let the rage flow, the warmth bloom—let the fire grow to consume all else—that was how one stayed strong. That was how a person could exist under the world's crushing weight. Sadness, self-pity, weakness—Kyrin would burn them all away and temper his soul to steel.

Kyrin leapt to his feet and began to pace, fueled by the anger that drove him to live. He glanced out the window. Small though it was, he could just make out the moonlit blades of grass above. Barred, warded, and small, it was of no use to him.

The door, too—too solid to be broken down, too enchanted to surpass, too... too locked to be opened. Normally, it might present some challenge—the ward seemed well-made and the lock seemed well-forged—but nothing a few good minutes work with his picks could not solve. Normally, Kyrin would almost enjoy the thrill. Normally, he would relish another chance to prove himself—but normally, Kyrin's picks would be in his pockets and not in an evidence chest elsewhere in the dungeon.

The Knights had taken them. They had taken

everything.

Having no constructive outlet for his rage, Kyrin kicked the door. His booted foot hit the impassable oak with a satisfying thud, sending a painful flash up Kyrin's leg, through his body to his bruised chin. Swearing through his clenched teeth, Kyrin kicked the door again. And again. And again.

A steady stream of profanity trickled from Kyrin's mouth as he hurled himself bodily at the door, beating at it with all the strength at his disposal.

Not enough—no effect.

Kyrin pounded the door with his fist one final time as he sank to his knees, his anger spent. A hot tear of frustration rolled down Kyrin's cheek as he rested his forehead against the cold oak. The door may as well have been stone for all Kyrin could move it. Not that he had ever had any hope, there. A prideful, desperate fool had as much chance breaking out of the Knights' prison as a fly did escaping a sealed glass jar.

Kyrin ferociously wiped the tear from his face, as if trying to scrub the weakness from beneath his skin. He took a deep breath, climbed back to his feet, and carefully, calmly, went back to his corner to sit.

Kyrin saw no escape from his cell, he saw no alternative but to face justice for the crimes he had committed. He was guilty—it was true. He could not escape his fate, so Kyrin figured he would face whatever came with his head held high—no shame, no regret, no remorse, and no fear. Squeezing what comfort he could from the prospect of going out in style, Kyrin eventually dropped away into an uneasy sleep.

*Darkness. Rushing water. Cold—terrible cold. Kyrin could not see—could not breathe. He was drowning, dying, he was—*

*Click.*

Kyrin's head shot up as the door to his cell swung open. He blinked blearily, resisting the urge to rub the sleep from his eyes as he glared at his visitor.

The puppeteer girl, Sal, stepped through the door, bringing with her a bowl of oatmeal on a tray. Golden sunlight streamed through the barred window to highlight her soft brown hair and illuminate her sparse freckles.

Kyrin scowled and turned his face away.

Sal smiled sympathetically, setting the tray on the floor as she herself sat down cross-legged a few feet away from Kyrin's corner.

He almost felt insulted—one lone girl, hardly older than he was, waltzing in here unarmed and unprotected without a touch of fear. If it were not for her blasted magic, Kyrin would have no problem overpowering her and fleeing to freedom—maybe even snatching a trinket or two in the process. As things were, though, Kyrin knew she would have him under her spell the moment he lifted a finger.

"Sorry if I woke you." Sal tilted her head, trying to catch Kyrin's eye as she inched the tray closer to him. "I didn't realize you were still asleep. It's nearly noon, and I thought you might be getting hungry."

Kyrin remembered his last meal—an apple and half a loaf of bread he had nabbed from a street vendor yesterday afternoon. The offered breakfast, though plain, was warm and—

*No. Not gonna fall for that.*

Kyrin clenched his jaw, refusing to meet Sal's hazel eyes. Breakfast or no breakfast, Sal was only here because she wanted something—and Kyrin was determined to withhold it.

As if on cue, Sal spoke again. "You don't mind if I ask you some questions, do you?" A moment passed as she paused to allow for an answer that was not forthcoming. "Let me rephrase that—I need to ask you some questions—would you please answer?"

Still no response.

Sal sighed and waved her hand.

"Yes ma'am." Kyrin's own voice betrayed him, words tearing themselves from his throat and lurching out of his mouth without a moment's hesitation. His stomach twisted. His head spun. Kyrin bit his lip and squeezed his eyes shut as he internally cursed the world.

"You see," Sal continued as if Kyrin's answer had been natural, "I *can* make you speak, but it isn't terribly easy for me, and I imagine it can't be very pleasant for you, so I'd rather avoid having to do that if at all possible. So will you please cooperate? It'll be easier on all of us."

The only sound in the cell was the hissing intake of Kyrin's breath as he fought the urge to snarl some biting curse. Going down might be inevitable, but submitting without a fight would be an insult to what little honor Kyrin still possessed. It was out of the question.

"…Okay then. Please don't make this harder than it has to be. So—first question. We'll start with something simple: I'm Sal Puppetmaster, Squire to Tryn Boneweaver—you?"

A pause—no answer. Sal's eyes narrowed with the effort of charming Kyrin's tongue to answer.

"I am the Shadow, partner to Rat, servant of the Faceless." Kyrin bit his lip as soon as the hated words passed, hating the magic and hating himself for his inability to fight it. Hate was Kyrin's byword, and he fell upon it gladly. The next question—he would not answer.

"So the guy who turned into a rat... was Rat... and you're Shadow. Wow—that's not generic at all. Such creativity your Guild has."

Kyrin bit back a sharp comment.

"Anyway," Sal continued obliviously, "so if Rat's a rat-shifter, are you a shadowmancer? What's your magename? Who are you really?"

Again, Sal paused, giving Kyrin the chance to speak of his own volition, but again, he refused to take it—instead preferring to brace himself for the inevitable battle of wills.

Sal waved her hand. Kyrin fought. His brain felt caught in a vice, his ears rang, his mouth tasted of metal, but still, Kyrin fought. He ignored his churning stomach, he ignored his prickling skin—Kyrin simply bit his lip harder as his body turned against him.

And yet, Kyrin could not fight forever. Air—he needed air—Kyrin opened his mouth for one gasping breath—and the strained words flew out before he could stop them.

"I am Kyrin."

"Okay, Kyrin, very nice. But what's your magename? Please don't make me push you harder—I can tell that you're in pain."

Kyrin said nothing. Breathing was too much effort. Before he could steel himself, Sal applied the magic again.

"I have no magename." The words slipped out almost without hassle, although Kyrin's stomach still twisted as the sound crawled out from his unwilling jaw .

"What? What do you mean? Everyone has a magename! Where do you classify? Are you an elemental? A psychic? You don't look like a shifter..."

Kyrin bit his lip and tasted blood. "I... have no magename... for I have no magic."

"No magic? But that's—" the word "impossible" hung in the air unspoken. Under a puppeteer's string, no man or woman could ever tell a lie.

Kyrin bit his tongue, almost wishing he had the nerve to bite it off and silence himself forever.

"Did you lose it somehow? In an accident of some sort or something? Is that even possible?"

"No. I never had it."

"But… If Rat's called Rat because he's a rat, why are you called Shadow if you can't do anything with shadows?"

Kyrin nearly bit through his tongue. This conversation pained him in every possible sense, and the prospect of bleeding out through his mouth seemed almost a relief by comparison. Kyrin's anger, his envy, his self-loathing pride, all flared up in perfect sync with his pounding heart and lurching stomach.

"I am called Shadow," he struggled not to say, "because without magic, I am less than half a man. I only exist as a byproduct of those who are great—I am what is left when greatness is extracted. I am called Shadow because I am nothing more than a shadow at the Faceless' feet."

"That's… awful. You don't believe that, do you?"

"No!" Kyrin wanted to shout, "Of course not! What kind of idiot do you take me for—to think I'd believe such blasted rot?" but Sal had neglected to release her magic, and Kyrin's tongue was still not his to command. All that came out was a single, emotionless "yes."

Sal had nothing to say. She cleared her throat awkwardly. "Well… um… moving on. Next question: I'm supposed to ask you what the Faceless offered you for this job—what was at stake, and why you felt compelled to take it. Your answer may affect your sentence."

"The Faceless offered me nothing."

"Then who?"

The pressure on his mind increased, but Kyrin had no answer for the question. For once he was able to maintain his silence.

"Who compelled you to break into our Stronghold, Kyrin?"

"I did."

"What were you after?"

"Glory."

"Is that all?"

"Yes."

"I see... Well, thank you, Kyrin, you have been very helpful. Your cooperation has been appreciated," Sal said without a trace of irony, "now, please, enjoy your breakfast."

The girl stood up, spared her prisoner one final glance, and left, meeting with Dain in the hallway.

"Did you get that?"

"Wrote down every word."

The two Knights walked away, discussing quietly, and Kyrin was left in his cell—nothing to do but bury his face in his arms. The breakfast waited. Although Kyrin was hungry, he did not have the heart to eat. Somewhere in the outside world, untethered and unhindered, a bird sang its mocking tune.

# Chapter Three

Days passed. Nights followed. Kyrin's confinement continued. Although he was fed regularly and treated well, Kyrin longed for the sky and the wind and the thrill of roaming the city rooftops. In the mornings, he would pace, and in the afternoons, he would sulk, stewing in his own bitterness and drowning his despair with anger and hate. Nights passed restlessly as Kyrin fought off dreams of the past and nightmares of the future.

"Psst! Shadow! Hey—Shadow!"

Kyrin awoke to a whisper from the moonlit window above his stiff cot.

"Rat?" Rubbing his bleary eyes, Kyrin stood up on his cot, balancing on the tips of his toes to press his face against the cold metal bars. Never in a thousand years had Kyrin thought he would be glad to see his partner. "How did you..?"

"Knights haven't fixed the ward-gate yet, so I just figured I'd swing by and see my old buddy."

"Yeah?" A sliver of hope crept into Kyrin's voice. Perhaps the Faceless had finally seen his worth—perhaps someone had arranged a rescue!

"Yeah, an' I've got great news."

"Yes?"

"I just thought I should let you know," Rat lazily

changed his form, growing until his human face and its sadistic grin were clear in Kyrin's view, "I have a new partner now."

The phrase Kyrin had once dreamed of hearing now struck his heart cold. "What?"

"Yeah, the Faceless paired us up this morning. Real great guy, too. A copytongue, so there's a lot of potential, there. It'll be a nice change."

"You bastard." Kyrin's voice was flat, his anger cold. "You pathetic little bastard. You came all this way here just to taunt me. You had nothing better to do then come out here and mo—"

"Nope! Nothin' better to do at all, ya little cripple," Rat laughed, insultingly cheerful, "You're entertaining enough."

"I'm gonna kill you—I'm gonna fr'ckin' kill you!" Kyrin made a grab through the bars for Rat's throat, but the man merely grinned and leaned out of reach.

"You're gonna need one helluva plan, Shadow, if you're hopin' to kill me. Gonna have to act fast, you know."

"Shut up." Kyrin growled, still straining to claw out Rat's eyes.

"Oh, you know it's true, though." Rat took Kyrin's wrist and twisted it, bending it farther than it should have been able to go before shoving forward with enough force to send Kyrin sprawling, "you got three days to live, Shadow. Official word as of this morning. You got three more days 'til you're fitted for a new necktie."

"Shut up."

"You're gonna dance the hempen jig, Shadow. Ain't that great?"

"Shut up!"

"They're gonna stretch your neck and hang your sorry

skin!"

"Shut up shut up shut up shut up shut up!"

Rat laughed. Kyrin wanted to scream.

"Anyway, Shadow—much as I love chatting with ya, I'd hate to wear out my welcome here," Rat said, flashing a toothy grin, "After all, this is *your* cell, not mine—it's not my place to intrude."

"Go to hell."

"Why don't you save a spot for me? Three more days and you'll have premium pick."

Rat stood up and swaggered off before Kyrin had the chance to find his tongue. Once again, the blasted vermin had stolen the last word. Once again, Rat had won.

Kyrin crawled back to his corner and hid his face in his hands.

Not long after, morning came. The sun rose. Kyrin's spirits fell. A day passed without incident. And another. And then a third. That final night, Kyrin felt as though he were already dead.

The Knights had given him food, but he had not eaten. He was not hungry. They had come to speak with him, but Kyrin had not cared to talk. His heart still beat, but that was all. Hope seemed pointless. Kyrin was a dead man breathing.

As he sat with his head in his hands, Kyrin became gradually aware of a faint sound, a subtle ringing vibration on the far edge of hearing. Like the peal of a golden bell moving backwards through time, the melodious tone started in silence and grew slowly louder, seeming to emanate from the prison stones themselves.

Kyrin raised his head and shook it. The sound remained. Kyrin covered his ears. The noise dimmed. Acting on a confused hunch, Kyrin pressed the back of his hand to the ringing wall. The faint vibration made his skin crawl.

Kyrin snatched his hand away and scrambled to his feet, nearly falling over in his haste to reach the barred door.

"The stones!" he cried, shaking the door as hard and as noisily as he could, "The stones are singing! The stones are singing the stones are singing the stones are singing the stones are *singing!*" He rattled the bars and shouted himself hoarse as the walls' volume rose, until finally the scar-faced Knight—Brysson—staggered down the stairs, blearily rubbing his eyes.

"Whassa matter?" the Knight yawned, conjuring a small flame to light the dungeon's darkness.

"Get me out of here! Can't you hear it?" Kyrin cried desperately.

"Hear what?"

"The stones!"

Brysson yawned again. "What about 'em?"

Kyrin stared. Was this man deaf? Was he stupid? The singing stones grew ever louder—Kyrin's ears felt fit to burst, yet Brysson was unaffected.

"You're kidding!"

"Look, buddy, I know you're desperate, but you should have thought about that before robbing us. Playing crazy isn't going to get you out of your date with the hangman."

"I'm not playing, dammit!" Kyrin sputtered over the rising tide of noise, "And I'm not crazy either! Can't you hear it—it's everywhere—the walls—the walls are—"

"Okay, okay—I get it, I understand. The stones are singing—got it. Now sleep, will ya? At the very least, let me sleep. You might not have much to do tomorrow, but I—oh, I'm sorry—that was callous." Muttering to himself about his need for sleep, the Knight retreated back up the stairs—leaving Kyrin to drown in the golden sound.

Kyrin sank to his knees and put his hands over his ears. Out in the city, the bells tolled eleven, and then later, midnight, but Kyrin could hear nothing over the singing stones.

Suddenly, the sound surged. Volume increased twofold. Kyrin screamed, but his voice was lost to the overwhelming, all-encompassing noise. No sight, no sound, no taste, no touch was left. Sound was the world, and the world was pain.

Had Kyrin been able to hear, had he been able to see, he would have noticed Brysson dashing back down the stairs to come to his aid, to check the cause of the screaming. Had Kyrin's eyes been of use, he might have seen the wards sealing his prison begin to glow faintly. Had Kyrin's ears not been filled with the awful, all-consuming tone, he would have heard the crashes, the cries, the explosions. All Kyrin knew was the sound—and the sudden silence.

He took his hands from his ears in grateful shock and sank down, relaxing and recovering for a moment on the cold stone floor as his hearing returned.

Gradually, as his breathing deepened and his heartbeat slowed, Kyrin began to register the distant cacophony in the Stronghold upstairs. Now that his ears could properly function, Kyrin could catch the subtle sounds of battle muted by stone.

Kyrin stood and staggered towards the door, hoping to call for Brysson and learn the situation, however when he leaned against the bars—the door swung open. The wards had burst, overloaded by some strange magic. The lock itself had shattered from the blast.

Worrying about the source of this sudden luck was

pointless. The alternative to seizing this dubious chance was a definite hanging, and Kyrin preferred to avoid that.

He slunk out of his cell, slipping through the door as soundlessly as a shadow. He crept forward, only to trip over Brysson's prone form. The scar-faced knight lay sprawled across the floor, apparently unconscious.

Kyrin knelt beside Brysson and checked his pulse. Yeah—the guy was alive... The magical overload would wear off after a minute, and then Brysson would be left with a bad headache and a worse mood.

Kyrin cast around. This was a dungeon—there had to be... *Ah! There.* He grabbed some cord and some cloth and returned to Brysson's side, gagging and binding the man with practiced skill. As Kyrin secured the knots at Brysson's wrists, the man's eyes fluttered open, then shot wide.

Kyrin made a shushing motion, patting the Knight's shoulder companionably. "Sorry about this, buddy," he whispered, giving the cord one final tug, "just doing what it takes to get by. I know you'd do the same for me."

In the face of Brysson's silent, hateful glare, Kyrin could not help but smirk. Every so often, it was good to be the one calling the shots.

Kyrin stood, dusted himself off, tied back his hair, and gave Brysson one tiny salute before continuing on in search of his lock picks. Without them, he was as good as dead.

Thankfully, the Knights, in their arrogance, had not bothered to lock his possessions away. Kyrin found his prized picks thrown carelessly upon a shelf, along with his other tools and oddments. He rescued them quickly, pausing only a moment to polish a beloved silver handle before stuffing the lot in his pockets. Kyrin then ascended to the main floor of the Stronghold to face whatever chaos awaited him.

Cautiously, he opened the door and listened intently for danger. The harsh music of battle was louder now; the mysterious explosions and brazen cries were now distinguishable from the strange background hum that persisted in Kyrin's ears.

Kyrin crept out from behind the dungeon door and knelt beside a suit of armor, his heart pounding in his throat. He closed his eyes, willed himself to relax, then ran. Hug the shadows, step lightly, keep your breathing silent—these were the rules upon which his life depended, and Kyrin followed them to the letter. The only other option was... not an option.

The hallway connecting the dungeon stairs to the rest of the Stronghold was mercifully short, yet Kyrin could not escape it quickly enough. His heart counted out the sharp rhythm of the passing seconds as if his life depended on their number. Anxiety threatened to strangle Kyrin as he slunk from the safety of the shadows and stepped into the light of the next room.

A stray fireball flew past Kyrin's head and exploded across the back wall. Kyrin hit the floor, biting back a startled curse. A woman's laughter cut across the clash and clatter of conflict, high and pure, completely at odds with the darkness and danger of the scene. Too giddy to be Sal, not harsh enough to be Briea—Kyrin could not immediately identify the giggle's source. Until another fireball burst on Tryn's hastily raised shield.

The thrower was a girl—slender and shapely, with pale golden hair and fair skin like porcelain. She seemed to glow as she summoned another orb of orange flames, and for a moment, Kyrin had to stop and stare. This girl was beautiful, stunning even as she hurled death and sowed destruction. Her smile was brilliant, despite her fatal intent. Kyrin's heart pounded—lost in awe as much as fear.

*Something about her...* Kyrin thought as the girl lazily conjured another fireball, *something about her is*—

Briea entered the fray, charging the girl. The invader threw her fireball—and missed. The lady Knight ran faster, shifting her form to that of a great lioness. Briea leapt, fangs bared, claws outstretched. The girl's dark eyes widened, she faltered—then winked out of existence. Briea landed on empty air, roaring her wrath, shaking the Stronghold with the force of her rage.

Once again—the happy laughter echoed. Kyrin gaped. *This girl—she—she...*

"Witch!" Briea's anger was palpable. "Return and fight! I'll tear you to bloody pieces!"

"Sal! Behind you!" Tryn's cry to his squire snapped Kyrin back to reality. As Sal whirled to face the witch, Kyrin crawled across the ground, hoping that the confusion would cover his escape.

The witch grabbed Sal's throat. Sal dropped her sword. Kyrin ducked beneath a table.

"Where is it?" the witch inquired sweetly, drawing a small knife and pressing it into Sal's back. "And don't any of you other guys move closer—I can stab her a lot faster than you can grab me."

Sal stood stiffly, "I—I don't know what you're talking about." Here in the dark, with her enemy behind her, Sal could not establish the line of sight necessary to work her powers. Her magic was useless. Kyrin wasn't sure if the emotion welling within him was triumph or pity.

"Don't play dumb with me—I know you know. The Worldwork Gauntlet—I want it. And the Anchor Key—I want that, too."

"I don't—" Sal's protest degenerated into a muffled

scream. Even from his position under the table, Kyrin could see the witch's hand—the hand at Sal's throat—glow red with heat. Kyrin winced in sympathy.

"Sal!" Tryn cried, gripping his mace tightly, not daring to step forward and risk the witch's wrath. Dain was in much the same state, although from beneath the table, Kyrin could only see the squire's legs.

"There! There—that way!" Sal gasped, gesturing frantically down one of the many dark hallways.

The witch grinned like a child receiving an unexpected gift, before releasing Sal and happily skipping off in the indicated direction, warping forward every few steps.

Sal fell to the ground. Tryn rushed to her side.

"Briea!" the man barked, instantly taking charge as he checked Sal's vitals, laying his own hand on her neck, "I'll heal her—you head off the witch! Dain—go find Brysson—he went to check on the prisoner—make sure he's alright!" The lioness dashed off, a fierce grin on her feline face, and Dain ran down the dungeon stairs. Tryn's hands began to gleam with a cool blue light as he closed his eyes, concentrating, and cast his medical magic.

Kyrin took his cue to move. He sneaked out from under his sheltering table and dashed down the hall as quickly as he dared. All the Knights were accounted for, and all potential threats seemed safely out of the way—at least for the moment. Soon—soon, Kyrin would be home, and he would have only the Faceless to deal with.

Only the Faceless... That was like saying the fish that falls from the pan has only the fire to worry about. Kyrin hoped that he would not burn.

Forgetting for a moment his pounding feet and dire flight, Kyrin's mind jumped back to the witch girl. She had thrown fireballs, yet she could teleport. She had two magics—she was double the norm—while he was half.

Kyrin wanted to hate her. He wanted to loathe her and her power, but rather than envious, rather than wrathful, Kyrin was curious.

*How can one person have two magics? How don't they clash? How does a family—*

The sight of the front door thrilled Kyrin's heart and drove all other thoughts from his mind. Freedom. Kyrin instinctively stretched out his hand and ran faster, determined to reclaim the sky. The city streets called him to their multitude of unsuspecting passerby with loaded pockets, the rooftops beckoned with their high vantage points and marvelous views.

Home was not far—just a few steps away.

An instant before Kyrin could seize the Stronghold's door and flee out into the night, the witch warped into his path, disrupting his escape. The two ended as a tangled heap of limbs upon the floor, inconveniently sprawled and knotted.

"Watch it!" Kyrin growled instantly, roughly disentangling himself.

Dark eyes wide and glittering, the witch climbed to her feet as well, retrieving the white disk of the Anchor Key from where it had fallen. "I couldn't see you," she muttered perplexedly as she placed a delicate hand over Kyrin's heart and looked into his confused green eyes, "I can't sense you at all..." Suddenly, her head whipped around, a mere instant before the Knights came into view.

"There they are! Stop them!" someone cried, "At least catch *one* of them!"

Like an iridescent soap bubble or a half-remembered dream, the witch vanished without a trace. Shaking off his bewilderment, Kyrin turned, yanked the door open, and fled out into the moonlit world.

# Chapter Four

The nighttime streets of Alinor were no place for the faint of heart. Thieves, muggers, drunks, murderers—anyone might lie in wait around any corner for the unsuspecting victim.

Kyrin took little pride in his place among these criminal ranks, however, once he had cleared the Stronghold and disguised his scent for the Dogs, he did not hesitate to lift some cash off a few other late-night wanderers out past curfew. Kyrin only barely found enough to pay this month's rent, but it was enough to keep him from having to dig too deeply into his savings.

At least, he hoped it would be enough. Due to his imprisonment, Kyrin was already three days late on his payment. He half expected to go home to find that his landlady had cleared out his room already and found some other, more reliable renter.

*I'm sick of all this scraping.* Kyrin thought as he stashed his stolen coin and stuffed his shame far out of sight, *I'm sick of the damnable rent and the leaking roof and the incessant drafts… If my family was—*

Kyrin shook his head, forcing his mind back on the present. He didn't need them—or their money. Kyrin could make it on his own. Sure, once upon a time, things had been better, but times had changed, and Kyrin had changed with them.

He swept a few loose strands of hair off his face and out of his eyes and made his way down Aspen Road to the dingy little alleyway that hid the door Kyrin knew as home. It wasn't much to look at, just a wooden door in a brick wall with a set of tarnished brass numbers next to it, but the beds were cheap and the landlady never asked about more than the rent, so Kyrin made do.

He opened the door with a sigh and slunk inside, hoping to get upstairs without encountering anyone who demanded interaction. Unfortunately, Kyrin was not that lucky. Mrs. Raph Blackbill, the dreaded landlady, caught him on the stairs, her face suggesting she had found more welcome surprises stuck to the bottom of her shoe.

"Oh. It's you. I heard you'd been locked up."

Kyrin reached into his pocket, withdrew his rent, and dumped the money into her outstretched palm.

She counted it carefully, noting the extra coin Kyrin had thrown in to buy her silence. Satisfied, Mrs. Raph nodded once. "Next month'd better be on time, boy."

Kyrin muttered an indistinct reply and pushed past her, carrying on to the room he called his own.

The walls were bare, and the old white paint had cracked and flaked in the corners near the floor and ceiling. The floor creaked and groaned like a morbid chorus no matter how cautiously Kyrin placed his feet, and the only furnishing aside from his unkempt three-legged bed and the old crate that propped it up was an ancient, battered wardrobe stuck awkwardly in the corner. Although the room was basically empty, Kyrin hardly had enough space to stand.

However, sleeping in a closet was fine for a man who

lived his life on the streets. All that mattered was that Kyrin had a place to lay his head.

At least, that's what he told himself.

Trying not to trip over the crate that kept his bed level, Kyrin lit a half-burned candle stub and opened his wardrobe. Inside, an eclectic mix of tattered cloth, broken wards, and partially dismantled spells found shelter. Kyrin pushed them aside to dig out the sturdy wooden box that had been hiding at the bottom beneath the detritus.

This box, like everything else in Kyrin's life, was plain, unadorned, and strictly functional. The only marks even remotely resembling decoration were the spiraling glyphs clumsily carved into the box's featureless lid. They were the simple sort, a mild spell thrown together by an apprentice enchanter just learning the basics of the craft, but the simple guard was all Kyrin had been able to afford, though even a feeble ward such as this was more than enough to confound the average, uneducated, law-abiding citizen.

Kyrin drew a pick from his pocket and disarmed the ward almost without thinking. The key had vanished years ago, probably dropped somewhere, but it hardly mattered. If Kyrin could not break into his own box, he felt he deserved to lose the savings within.

Kyrin ran his fingers gently over his life savings. All the money he possessed that had not been given over to the Faceless' tax collectors, stolen by Rat, or spent on the bare necessities of life sat inside this small wooden box. By the faint glow of his one candle, Kyrin counted his coin. So what if he already knew the sum by heart?

Someday, after he made it big, Kyrin would save enough to buy passage on a traveling caravan and start a new life in some far-off settlement, away from the grime of the city and the cruelty of the Guild. Someday, when he got sick of fame, he would get an honest job that a man could be proud of—he would make an honest living and get a nice house of his own. Someday, Kyrin would raise enough money to purchase the means to a decent life, but the pathetic state of his funds assured Kyrin that the day he dreamed of was still several somedays away. After he deducted the money he owed to the Faceless for the inconvenience of his arrest, Kyrin figured they added up to an extra couple of decades.

Forcing back a tide of bitter regret, Kyrin put away the pathetic amount that was his to keep, undressed himself, and flopped wearily onto his bed. His harebrained gamble against the Knights had cost him much, but at least he had managed to win back his life. His morning no longer held a hanging.

Tomorrow, he would do better. He would get back in the game. Tomorrow, Kyrin would get his life in order.

*Pale hair floated ethereally around a pale face. Beautiful dark eyes stared silently out from behind a veil of gray rain. The witch stretched out her slender hand, beckoning for Kyrin to come nearer, calling him away from the edge of his pier. He shook his head, but she smiled at him—she had a dazzling smile—and she beckoned again. His heart fluttered. Kyrin opened his mouth to speak, and—*

Kyrin awoke to the melodious sound of Mrs. Raph having a row with another patron downstairs. Apparently, the man was a week late on his rent. Kyrin rolled over and attempted to reclaim his dream and return to sleep with his pillow over his head, but the flattened bag of secondhand fluff did little to muffle the noise. Rather than dull, the sound only seemed to intensify—as if the two arguing downstairs were specifically aiming to disturb his slumber.

Since reclaiming sleep was impossible, Kyrin had nothing else to do but get out of bed. Failing to disentangle himself from his ratty sheets, he rolled from his mattress and fell to the cold floor with a heavy thud. Kyrin groaned and hauled himself up, accidentally catching his foot on the crate and stubbing his toe.

Cursing mornings and all they entailed, Kyrin ran an exhausted hand down his face. His clothes were on the floor where he had left them, but his boots had to be fished out from under the bed. Everything he owned was dirty, full of holes, and had definitely belonged to someone else at some point—someone entirely the wrong size. Someday, he'd be able to afford new clothes—proper clothes that fit, and belonged to no one but him, but until then… Kyrin had to be content looking like a peasant and a beggar—like a no-good thief. He dreaded the day these rags wore out and he had to drop some precious coin to buy himself some shoddy replacements.

Dreaming of the day he could afford to leave behind his rags and wear whatever clothes he wished, Kyrin dressed himself, pulled on his boots, and tied back his hair. Now, he had to be ready to face the present.

He opened his door as quietly as he could manage and edged down the hallway, past the rooms inside which his neighbors presumably still somehow slept, and down the steep, narrow staircase to the kitchen below. Raph was still yelling at her debtor, using language even Kyrin, with his curse-stained mouth, was shocked to hear. Not wanting to get involved, Kyrin ducked behind a counter and tried to sneak past, but he was a moment too late.

"You! Boy!"

Kyrin stood up guiltily, trying to act as though he had not just been caught attempting to hide.

Pinning her beleaguered renter in place with a sharp glance, Mrs. Raph marched over to Kyrin and grabbed the front of his shirt, unhesitatingly pulling him down towards her pointy nose.

"Dogs're looking for you, boy," she hissed softly under her breath, her gray hair frizzing out around her head like a colorless nova, "been out on the streets asking questions. Showing pictures. Offering coin for information. A good bit of coin."

Before Kyrin could decide if her words were a warning or a threat, Mrs. Raph released him and stomped back over to hassle the other unfortunate before the man could slink away.

*Great,* Kyrin thought as he stepped out into the alley, *I knew something like this was bound to happen, but still. Blasted Dogs didn't used to be so quick on the mark. Bet it'd have been different if those damned Knights weren't noble.*

Kyrin eyed the street distrustfully. Anyone might be out to get him. He raised his hood to hide his face and quickly scaled the wall.

While a man on the rooftops was far more suspicious than a man on the ground, he was far less likely to be spotted by the passerby down below. Plus, the roofs between Aspen Road and Merchant's Way offered a much shorter, safer path than the twisting city streets. The ground route would take him directly past two of the city's Doghouses, and that was not the best road for a man in hiding.

From the roof, Kyrin could see every creature on the streets below, and he had a full view of the sky above. A falcon wheeled in the blue abyss. Probably a shifter. Possibly with the Dogs. Kyrin tugged his hood down and lowered his face.

Down below, among the everyday citizens of Alinor,

Kyrin could make out several pairs of policemen walking their beats—more than usually roamed in this part of town. The Dogs really were out in force today.

*What a pain...*

Kyrin moved from roof to roof like the shadow of a cloud, eventually descending in an alley off Merchant's Way. Fifteen minutes had passed since he had left his door. After he straightened his clothes, it was a simple matter for Kyrin to rustle up an illegal breakfast from a couple of lax vendors and pad his pockets with whatever coin he could lift from the unwitting passerby.

Despite the morning's youth—the sun had hardly risen above the city walls—Merchant's Way was already crowded and ringing with cheerful energy. Salesmen waved and shouted, hawking their wares, while servants bustled about, looking to win bargains for their masters. Various tantalizing smells drifted from various stalls—the spicy tang of foreign seasonings imported from over the Thousand Seas, the sweet aroma of fresh-baked pies and pastries, and the ever-present odor of salt and sea mixed together to become the breath of the Alinorian market. Off a little ways away, near the giant fountain impossibly sculpted from polished granite, a juggler began to draw a crowd, tossing colorful balls high in the air as he danced acrobatically through floating rings of glittering water.

Kyrin frowned. *Show off,* he thought, biting into a piping-hot pastry he had obtained from an unwary baker. Although the fragrant, fruit-filled tart was the best thing he had tasted in days, Kyrin could not relax enough to enjoy it.

Dogs sniffed at every shadow. The law was hunting him, and Kyrin could not run forever. His only hope of safety was with the Guild—assuming the Faceless saw fit to take him back.

Hardly tasting the last bite of his stolen breakfast, Kyrin wiped his hand on the fabric of his pants and obsessively adjusted his hood. He glanced around, searching for a familiar face. A handful of Guild members always hung around Merchant's Way. No matter the hour, criminals always found some coin to grab, so the odds seemed in favor of Kyrin finding at least one ally amidst the sea of people.

There, at the fruit stall—the man with the scarred face and the open smile—Kyrin had seen him before in darker settings. His was the face of the Guildsman.

What was his name? Oh—yes, he was the Claw, the ironskin, partner to the dragon-shifter, Ducky. The pair was known throughout the Guild as one of the Faceless' favorite teams—the Dragon and the Iron Claw—no pair of thugs were more brutal, no team was more deadly, no murderer was colder or more effective than the friendly looking man selling apples to the innocent shoppers of Merchant's Way.

Kyrin wandered over, wondering how any man could keep two such incongruous personas separate and out of the law's reach. His pulse raced as he attempted nonchalance.

"Hey," Kyrin greeted hoarsely, acutely aware that this man before him could tear out his throat bare-handed—and probably would, if the Faceless gave the word.

"Good morning. Can I help you, lad?" Claw rubbed a cloth over a brilliant red apple as he spoke, admiring the fruit's rosy gleam in the morning light.

"Yeah." Kyrin selected an apple and passed Claw the appropriate payment, as if this were any ordinary exchange. "I could use some help. I have pressing business with the family, but I haven't been given a key.

Think you could lend me yours?"

"Ah—I see." Claw glanced beneath Kyrin' hood, nodding quietly to himself. "I might be able to lend a hand. What's so urgent?"

"I was bit by a dog, I need to show my face so my family knows I'm alright. As a son, I'm… I'm indebted to do so." Kyrin knew his lines did not make much sense when considered mundanely, but he hoped that he had dropped enough key words to get his point across without seeming unnecessarily suspicious.

Thankfully, Claw seemed to understand. Stupid men did not get far in the Faceless' Guild.

"Yeah, okay, I'll see what I can do." He smiled kindly, his pale scar curving oddly around his grin.

Kyrin nodded and mumbled thanks as Claw bid his assistant—undoubtedly a lesser Guild member—to watch the shop. He then led Kyrin away.

Despite the cheery melody Claw whistled as they walked through alley after twisted alley, Kyrin could not forget the rumors he had heard—of men torn limb from limb to be left in various gutters around the city—of debts the Faceless had redeemed in blood—of all the damage pair of iron hands could do. When Claw finally turned and amiably addressed him, Kyrin nearly jumped out of his skin.

"So. You're the Shadow kid?"

"Yes."

"Try again."

"Yes… Sir?"

"Better." Claw's tone was still easy-going and calm, but here, out of the city's sight, the man's eyes gained a steely, dangerous glint. "How old are you, boy?"

The suddenness of the question caught Kyrin off guard. He had to fight to keep his face impassive and his voice free of fear as he answered, "Seventeen, Sir."

"Seventeen, eh? Awfully young age for someone to try knocking over Alinor's Stronghold, don't you think? Especially for a shadow's man like you."

Kyrin's eyebrow twitched as he held his face still and kept his temper cool in the face of the obvious jab at his pride. "Age is just a number, and shadows blend into the dark... Sir."

For a moment, Kyrin thought his last moments would be spent with his entrails wrapped round his neck, but Claw only laughed. "Good answer, kid! I like you. Let me tell ya, it's a good thing you sought me out—the Faceless put out the word earlier—if you hadn't found me, I might've had to find you."

Kyrin nearly swore, but somehow he managed to hold his tongue. "I'm glad not to have put you to the trouble," he managed.

"I'm glad too—I only just got the blood out of this shirt, and I'd hate to have to wash it again so soon."

Kyrin choked, coughing and spluttering as if the casually spoken words had tried to strangle him.

Claw chuckled, scratching self-consciously at his scar, "I'm kidding, only kidding. Don't worry so much, lad. I would never kill you without orders."

"I'm so relieved," Kyrin murmured, unable to resist the sarcastic reply, "I'll really be able to rest easy now, knowing that."

"Great! Now hold still a sec."

"What?" Kyrin froze as Claw drew a thick band of cloth from his pocket and gestured toward Kyrin's eyes.

"Gotta blindfold you, you see. Faceless'd have my hide if I let someone find the Inmost Court who wasn't supposed to."

"Right." Reluctantly, Kyrin donned the blindfold. He

hated having to put his faith in the shifty man with the too-sincere smile, but he had no alternative.

"That's the spirit! Now, come with me…" Claw rested a hand on Kyrin shoulder, and the two of them moved on. Every street and every corner of his familiar city seemed labyrinthine to Kyrin in his unaccustomed blindness. Once, there were some stairs, and another time there was the sound of water—but mostly there was nothing. Nothing, save for the monotonous tread of booted feet on hard cobblestone, and Claw's annoyingly tuneful whistle.

Kyrin tripped and fell on his face several times throughout the journey, as he was unable to watch the uneven ground. He half suspected Claw was pushing him down and spinning him around on purpose to disorient him further. The other half of him suspected that the two of them were just hopelessly lost.

Whatever the case, it was too late to worry.

After what seemed an eternity of stumbling around, Kyrin's ears finally caught the muted threads of distant revelry. Someone somewhere was having a good time, but the laughter's harsh tone suggested that most of the mirth was at someone else's expense.

"We there yet?" Kyrin dared to ask.

"Yes and no," Claw replied, "we may have reached the court, yes, but I'm not actually supposed to let you see anything 'til you're before the Faceless himself. You understand."

"Yeah," Kyrin lied, summoning as much dignity as he could muster beneath the opaque cloth binding his eyes, "makes perfect sense."

"Now, hang tight another minute, Shadow, I gotta talk to some people. Do some things. Just stand there for a sec, okay? Don't move—I'll be right back. And most importantly, don't touch the blindfold."

Although it was impossible to tell for certain, Kyrin assumed that Claw had left him alone within a crowd. Turning his attention to his hearing and his sense of smell, Kyrin formed a general picture of his environment.

The partnered scents of cheap alcohol and heavy stew wafted in the air, along with the jovial chaos of a noisy, happy group. Someone sang a butchered version of an old love song, while, in perfect disharmony, someone else sang a different one. Periodic cheers of elation and groans of heartfelt despair—punctuated by a strange rattling—suggested a dice game, while bawdy, rhythmic chanting presented the picture of a drinking contest—one which Ducky was apparently winning.

*Say what you like about the Guild*, Kyrin thought as he struggled to stay calm and collected in the face of the blind, bewildering energy, *no matter the hour, these criminals are never dull.*

A moment later, Claw returned, and Kyrin imagined the odor of cheap drink intensified slightly. A guiding hand was placed once more on the boy's shoulder.

"C'mon, kid—I told the Faceless you turned up."

"Lead on." Kyrin nodded, absurdly proud that he had kept the tremor from his voice.

Claw chuckled. "Watch your step."

Claw lead Kyrin past the crowd, through the blanket of sound, and into the heart of the Inmost Court. Kyrin heard a door creak open—then slam shut, locking out the noise in favor of a foreboding silence. Surely it was only a coincidence of the imagination that this new room seemed so much colder, that Kyrin's heart beat so much faster. Surely it was only coincidence that his hands began to shake.

An emotionless, tuneless voice laden with unnatural, bell-like undertones rang out from somewhere above and before Kyrin. "Free his eyes," it commanded. Kyrin's blindfold fell.

After the cloth-induced blindness, the pale, flickering magelights on the walls dazzled Kyrin. He blinked hard, resisting the urge to rub his watering eyes as his sight returned.

He found himself standing before a dark throne of twisted, blackened metal, upon which sat a faceless figure draped in shadows and dressed in deepest night. The lord of the Thieves' Guild stared blankly down at his lowly vassal. Kyrin's heart froze, colder than stone.

*Kyrin, I strip you of your name.* His initiation. That was the first—and the last—time Kyrin had encountered the Faceless. *Henceforth, you shall be known as the Shadow, for that is how you are to me. Henceforth, you are my creature, and I shall protect you. Welcome to the family.*

In Kyrin's mind, the memory burned.

"You've been busy, Shadow," the slender man on the twisted throne intoned, resting his masked chin on a gloved hand.

"I have the money, Lord," Kyrin said, stuttering slightly as he reached into one of his hidden pockets. He drew out a purse and set it on the ground.

"Marvelous," despite his featureless white mask and magically disguised voice, Kyrin got the sense the man was smiling, "you have been a good Guildsman, Shadow, always loyal, always acting to bring fame to our humble hall."

"Thank you, Lord." Such praise—Kyrin was unsure if he should preen his pride or hide beneath a rock.

"Yes, you have done much to enhance our

reputation—many would say even entering the Knight's Stronghold uninvited is an impossible task—yet you have proved them wrong. You, Shadow, have personally led the Knights to acknowledge our Guild!"

"Yes, Lord." Kyrin stood awkwardly, not knowing whether he should kneel or bow, yet intensely aware of Claw still guarding the door behind him.

"But," the Faceless continued, gesturing for Claw to toss him Kyrin's money, "on the other hand, at least I get three times the money off your head."

Kyrin's hope, the shriveled, atrophied thing only beginning to flutter its feeble wings, plummeted. "Three?"

"Yes, Shadow, three." The Faceless held up the appropriate number of fingers as he spoke, counting off. "The first was Rat paying me for your death. The second was you buying back your life. The third is the handsome price the Knights placed on your handsome head. More than it's worth, certainly, but there's no accounting for taste. They even want you alive, Shadow—I hope they have something fun planned. I hear there are men in the palace dungeons who can keep you alive for years—though you'd wish yourself dead, of course. But no matter. Claw!"

"Yes, Lord?" The ironskin stepped forward as Kyrin stood dumb.

"You've a reputation for civic-minded honesty. Escort our little Shadow home to his new keeper."

Claw bowed slightly. "Yes, Lord."

Kyrin stood silently. A wide, lazy grin spread across his face, lost and confused as to how it got there. Kyrin knew he should be angry—he knew he should be furious, insulted, betrayed—yet for some reason, Kyrin found himself content.

He waited, curiously disinterested as Claw bound a pair of wrists behind Kyrin's back. He watched, unprotesting, as a gag sealed a mouth. It was his mouth, and they were his wrists, but Kyrin could not bring himself to care. He felt detached from his own body, but he was warm, he was happy, he was—

*It must be magic,* thought the last rational part of Kyrin's mind, *blasted sorcery—my emotions aren't even my own...*

Bound, gagged, and irrationally pleased, Kyrin toppled. Claw picked him up as effortlessly as he would move a bag of fruit, and walked away whistling.

Bone-white mask impassive, the Faceless opened Kyrin's purse and began to count.

# Chapter Five

The sun was high when Kyrin awoke, though he was in no position to see it. The prison's gray stone floor was cold against his cheek, but Kyrin did not care.

Nothing mattered anymore. The Thieves Guild, the refuge for all whom society would not accept, had cast him away, tossing him aside a defective tool—worthless, replaceable, unneeded.

Kyrin sighed through his gag and wished he could swear. He had once claimed that he would be the best, that he would show them all—Kyrin had once vowed to be a hero among thieves—but that was before the thieves had thrown him to the dogs. The Faceless had sold him. He had thrown Kyrin away.

*Maybe a hanging is the best—*

Footsteps rang through the dungeon. Kyrin sat up. A new determination sparked—he still had a chance to prove himself strong. The hanging had not yet happened. The Knights had not yet killed him. Kyrin could still die a hero's death. Hide the panic, hide the shame, hide it all behind a mask of anger and pride.

Heroes could be angry, but no coward ever won glory.

Glory… Now, here in Kyrin's tiny cell, the word mocked him, but Kyrin ignored it as the warden came into view. Her sandy blonde hair hung around her chin, and her green eyes glinted impatiently in the dungeon's dim light.

"Seriously? No one ever bothered to untie you?"

Kyrin frowned as the girl—she looked hardly older than twenty—unlocked the door to his cell and undid his gag.

Not knowing how else to react, Kyrin glared and swore.

The warden raised her eyebrow. "Cool it, Sunshine, I'm just trying to be decent, here."

"Shut up."

"I didn't have to do this, you know."

Kyrin's lip curled. "I never asked you to."

The warden gave a dramatic sigh. "Sheesh, Sunshine, hang a girl for trying to show a little humanity."

"Stop calling me that."

"Maybe if you ask me nicely, Sunshine," the girl said, grinning.

Kyrin rolled his eyes. "Shut up."

"I can put this gag back, you know."

Kyrin held his tongue and clenched his teeth. She had a point, annoying as it was, and he could not argue.

Kyrin had heard other Guildsmen say that the worst part of prison was losing the sky. They were wrong. Nothing could ever be worse than this helpless fury.

"Anyway," the warden continued heedlessly as she exited the cell and relocked the door behind her, "now that you're awake, I should tell you—the Knights will be here in an hour to collect you. Just so you know."

"How much?" Kyrin asked, fidgeting with his still-bound wrists.

"Excuse me?"

"My head. What was the price? How much're they wasting on me?"

The warden leaned herself against the wall outside Kyrin's door, apparently prepared to hang around and talk all day. "I don't quite know. A good bit, I recall, but I don't remember the reward being *too* extravagant." She grinned. "Otherwise I would've been out looking for you myself."

"I feel so loved," Kyrin stated dryly, twisting his fingers around to feel the knot restraining his hands.

"You should. For a very, very short time, you were the most popular man in all Alinor."

Before Kyrin's mind could catch up, his mouth spat out an instantaneous demand for silence.

The warden grinned, flicking her straight yellow hair from her eyes. "You need to learn more words, Sunshine, those two are getting awfully worn out."

Kyrin groaned. "By all the gods, cease your incessant tormenting! You have me, yes! I'm here, yes! I know that, you know that—we all know that! So will you quit with the pestering and leave me to rot in peace?"

"Nope, afraid not, Sunshine. It *is* my job to guard this place after all, and you're the only other person here—so you're stuck with me for the rest of whatever's left of the hour."

"Oh joy." Kyrin turned his back to the door to signal the conversation was over, but the warden remained, examining her fingernails. After a moment, she spoke again.

"So, Sunshine, is it true you don't have magic? Because that's what I heard. Sounds a little silly, if you ask me. Everyone's got magic."

"Ha ha," Kyrin tonelessly spat through his teeth.

"Oh—you don't? You really don't? Wow…" She trailed off, and Kyrin was glad of the quiet. After a moment's deliberation, she began again. "Did you—"

"No, I didn't lose it."

"Are you—"

"Yes, I'm sure."

"And you were—"

"Yes, born without it. Are you done? Only I had this conversation last time I was in prison, and I'm really not in the mood to have it again."

"You know what, fine." The warden raised her hands in a gesture of defeat. "You want to be like this, you can be like this. I was just trying to make what could be the last hour of your life a little more civil before the Knights come by to take you away for whatever the heck you did to them, but I guess you'd rather just be treated like streetscum. I shouldn't have suspected you of decency."

"No. You really shouldn't have."

The policewoman vanished—she could teleport, just like the witch—and Kyrin was left with the strange satisfaction her hatred brought. Kyrin was a criminal, it was what he deserved. Why had she bothered to think differently? The only potential within him was for failure.

From the moment of his crippled birth, Kyrin had been a failure.

The rest of the hour passed slowly, but Kyrin did not mind being left alone with his thoughts. If he could make himself properly miserable, death might not seem like such a tragedy.

*If my birth was a mistake, would my death make it right? I don't have any place in this world—maybe leaving it will be a good thing. Maybe—*

*No. Augh, no—I can't do this. I don't want to die. I'm not ready. I'm still not ready, blast it. I'm not gonna die like this!*

Irritated by his failure to convince himself to let go of life, Kyrin blew upon the pale spark of rebellion burning within his core. Anger had driven him this far, perhaps it could drive him a little farther.

"Hey! Hey Dog!" Kyrin threw himself towards the bars of his cell, his bound wrists throwing off his balance and sending him crashing clumsily against the enchanted metal. When the girl popped into existence before him, Kyrin nearly fell over.

*Blasted Voidwalker...*

"What do you want? I thought you were just planning on sulking until the Knights showed up." The warden stood with her arms crossed over her chest and her head cocked to the side. Though she sounded bored and frustrated, Kyrin could see the curiosity in her green eyes.

"Shut up," Kyrin growled, "do you wanna hear what I have to say or not?"

"I don't know, do I?"

"Yes, you do."

"Well, then go on, Sunshine," the warden said, yawning as she waved her hand dismissively, "speak your piece."

"You're lucky I hate the Guild right now more than I hate you, Dog."

"I'm honored. Now, are you gonna say something important, or can I get back to what I was doing? The Knights are going to be here any minute, and once you're gone, I'm going to have to get back on patrol."

Kyrin sighed, biting back a curse. "The man who brought me here—what did he look like?"

"What? How is this—"

"Just answer me."

"Well, he's got short, dark hair and brown-ish eyes. Tall, broad, square-ish features. Friendly looking—he sells fruit in Merchant's Way. I buy apples off him sometimes. They're some of the best."

It was hard for Kyrin not to roll his eyes. "Did he have a scar across his left cheek?"

"Yeah. I was getting there. I asked him about it once—he said he got it when a creature from the Outlands—I can't remember what—wandered into his orchard."

"That was a lie."

"What? Is this some kind of petty revenge for—"

"Shut up. That man is Claw, of the Thieves Guild. He is the Faceless' favorite enforcer. He got that scar when Cutter—that rogue bladesman who killed all those people a few years back—forgot to pay the Guild quota."

"Wait—I remember that case—the whole city was in panic! And then the murderer was found torn to shreds an alley—we thought some mad Outlands monster had gotten him!"

"Nope. That was your friendly fruit man out playing tax collector. Believe me, don't believe me, I don't care. Just don't forget what I said, Dog."

The warden passed him an appraising glance. "You know what, Sunshine, maybe you aren't so bad."

Before Kyrin could respond, a man dressed in brilliantly polished guard's armor came down the dungeon stairs, his face clean-shaven, dutiful, and set like stone.

The warden saluted. "Captain!"

"At ease, Voidwalker."

So this was the captain of the Dogs… The hound-shifter's family had led the guards of Alinor for generations, and had given the force their distinctive name. Kyrin had heard rumors about this idealistic lord—they said when he had inherited his position, he had vowed to clean up Alinor and eradicate the Guild—but Kyrin had never seen him. As a career criminal, he had generally preferred to avoid encountering watchmen.

Under the eye of the Hound—as the captain of the Alinor Guard was historically known—Kyrin was removed from his cell and led upstairs, where three familiar figures in rich, polished armor awaited him.

"Yes." Tryn nodded stiffly. "That's our man. Sal, deliver payment."

Sal stepped forward, a box presumably filled with money in her hands. Kyrin could not help but notice the hand-shaped burn still visible on the pale skin of her neck. A nod from the Hound sent the Warden up to accept the reward. She shoved Kyrin forward to be caught and restrained by Brysson.

"Always an honor to assist the noble Knights of Alinor."

"Always a pleasure to work with you and your diligent Watchdogs."

The odd, tense formality between Tryn and Hound reminded Kyrin of the eternal rivalry between the Knights and the Dogs. Although both defended Alinor— the Knights subduing the Outlands and the dogs patrolling behind city walls—both sections were in constant competition to prove themselves more competent than the other.

Kyrin's mouth twisted into a wry grimace. The chilly, polite animosity reminded him of his childhood home.

After filling out the proper paperwork to complete the transaction for Kyrin's life, the Knights escorted their charge to a group of three large, long-haired, vaguely feline creatures saddled and waiting for them out in the city streets. Kyrin frowned. The Knights hardly ever rode their chimeras for anything less than an emergency—the monsters were too large and too dangerous to try and navigate through the chaotic mess of human life that swarmed within the city's narrow streets.

Tryn mounted the blue chimera, his face impassive. Sal swung herself onto the sea-foam green one, and Kyrin was placed behind Brysson on the chimera with the deep purple stripes and the slate gray horns.

Kyrin gnawed his lip, anxiety growing in his gut. He had not thought his execution to be of such vital importance, nor had he expected the Knights to ride when the Gallows Tree was only a short walk away. Tryn did not seem the type to tolerate such inefficiency.

Perplexed, Kyrin waited anxiously to see what would come, and the Knights rode on.

# Chapter Six

The Gallows Tree was a place of nightmare, a graveyard of hope and a carrier of many a man's final breath. Tall and forbidding, it stretched its age-darkened branches to the sky as if reaching to ensnare the heavens in its dismal tangle of condemning branches. So many doomed souls had met their ends dangling beneath those twisted limbs, and lives—like leaves—fell often from those blackened boughs.

Kyrin's heart leapt into his mouth when he saw the noose swinging gently in the faint breeze under the Gallows Tree. The rope's mournful creaks were the sighs of lawful death. The single hempen loop encompassed all eternity.

A crow cackled derisively from atop a nearby building, thirsting for the blood of Guildsmen. Kyrin wondered if it was one of the Faceless' spies, sent to bring news of his just execution. Oh, how Rat would laugh...

So occupied was Kyrin with his apparent fate, he hardly noticed that the Knights were quickly leaving the Gallows Tree behind.

"Waitwaitwait—what?" Kyrin said, finding his voice

for the first time since returning to the Knight's custody, "What are we doing? I mean, I'm in no hurry to hang, but I thought we were—"

"Shut up," Tryn replied shortly, a distant look on his rugged face.

Kyrin swore softly, muttering under his breath, "That's supposed to be my line."

Brysson snickered, and spurred his chimera onwards.

Not only did the Knights ride past the Gallows Tree but, to Kyrin's amazement, the chimeras carried them past the Stronghold, past the outer gates, past the city walls themselves to a seemingly endless stretch of farmland where Briea and Dain waited with loaded packs and chimeras of their own.

Kyrin did not know what to think. The walls were the boundaries of his known world, and he had never before set foot outside them. After a lifetime trapped within Alinor's dirty, claustrophobic streets, it was almost frightening to see wide-open expanses of green pasture and blue sky. Kyrin risked a glance over his shoulder and caught his breath. Behind them, Alinor's high walls were vanishing, receding into the hazy distance.

"Seriously—what's going on here?" Kyrin asked, struggling to sound brave, "Where are you taking me? You won't just dump me in the Outlands, will ya?"

"A tempting thought, thief, but no. That's not our way." Tryn replied without turning around.

"Then why—"

"We want your girlfriend's head on a spike, thief," Briea pulled her chimera up beside Brysson's and shot Kyrin a sharp-toothed smile, "and you're gonna help us get it."

"Not to mention we need the Anchor Key back." Sal

added.

"What?"

"Oh, don't play dumb," Dain chimed in, "you can't honestly expect us to believe it was pure coincidence that you disabled our gate and got caught just in time for the thing holding the city together to get stolen—at just the right time to allow you to conveniently escape. That was a bit too clean to be an accident, buddy."

"Yes—no—I mean… What? That's not—she's not my girlfriend!" Kyrin finally managed to stutter, much louder than he had intended, "That night—it was the first time I ever saw her, I swear! I'd never seen her before! I just saw my opportunity when the wards burst, and I took it!"

"Nonetheless," Brysson said, glancing over his shoulder to look at Kyrin, "it's true that in the time before the witch's coming, you were shouting and screaming and generally freaking out as if something were eating you alive. Even if you deny it, you and this witch have a connection of some kind, and we fully intend to discover and exploit it—no matter the cost to you. If dragging you across every land from here to hell is what it takes for us to reclaim what's ours, we're damn well going to drag you through every land from here to hell. Like it or not, thief, you're coming on a quest with us."

Kyrin was almost too numb to swear. The games he'd played as a child, his idle imaginings, they all came flooding back to him. Oddly enough, his fantasies of adventure had never included handcuffs or death threats.

"Ha." Kyrin barked, letting irony roughen his tone, "off on a quest with the noble Knights—looks like all my dreams are coming true."

"You'd better believe it, thief," Tryn stated, urging his chimera to go faster, "and if you don't close that mouth of yours, your nightmares might come to life, too."

Feeling far out of his depth, Kyrin took a deep breath and closed his eyes. The witch's face appeared to his memory, beckoning him forward just as she had in his dream.

*Maybe this is what I need... I just have to stay calm. No panicking. I'll just... finally follow my own advice.*

Kyrin opened his eyes and shut up.

Silence reigned as the Knights rode forward. The only sounds were the soft pad of the chimeras' soft paws against the green earth, the rhythmic swish of their fluffy, snake-headed tails, and the faint clinking of the Knights' gear and armor. Though birds twittered in the otherwise empty sky, their song seemed strangely muted. Kyrin cleared his throat just to break the bizarre peace.

Kyrin knew that being a prisoner was probably better than being dead, but the fear of the unknown refused to stop gnawing at his stomach. He and the Knights were still within the bounds of Alinor's famous protecting wards—they were still within the realm of the safe and the canny—but once they passed the border and entered the Outlands...

Gradually, the rolling emerald farmland shifted to dense orchards and fields of dark trees, and Kyrin could bear the silence no longer.

"I've never seen so much green in one place..." he muttered, still gazing around at the trees on all sides.

Brysson was the only one to hear him. Tryn and Briea both rode ahead, scouting the terrain, while Sal and Dain had fallen behind, chatting amiably together. Brysson, with Kyrin tied upon his chimera, rode in the middle—keeping his prisoner safe and under watch.

"You ain't seen nothing yet, thief," the Knight

murmured back, "we've only just begun."

Kyrin absorbed the statement quietly. "Right… Just where exactly are we supposed to end up?"

"With the witch."

"And where is she?"

"I'm sure we'll figure that out."

"You gotta be kidding me… Have you at least got a plan for when you find her?"

"Nope," Brysson responded, swaying easily with the back-and-forth motion of his ambling chimera, "we're probably just going to wing it or something. That's really why we're bringing you along, remember."

*Because I totally know what to do,* Kyrin thought sarcastically, *No plan, no destination…* "We're all gonna die, aren't we." Kyrin's tone was flat as he absorbed his childhood heroes' apparent incompetence.

"Doubt it. I mean, we never have before." Brysson's nonchalance did little to reassure his captive.

"That's what I said when they told me I'd get caught if I tried robbing the Stronghold," Kyrin growled, "right about now, my wrists are wishing I'd thought that one through."

"Ah—but see, the biggest difference between this and that," Brysson twisted around in his seat to look Kyrin in the face with a roguish grin, "is that we're not you."

Kyrin cursed venomously. Brysson turned back around, chuckling at the criminal's helpless anger.

From behind his place on Brysson's chimera, Kyrin heard Sal's bell-like laugh. He knew that her mirth was likely in response to something Dain said, and not a reaction his aggravation, but still, the sound was irksome in its joy. It seemed little more than an annoying reminder of Kyrin's unhappy fate.

*Things could have been different, had I been born normal…*

Kyrin shook the thought from his head with a barely repressed snarl. Self-pity was weak, and he was done with it. Regret was pointless, and dwelling in the unchangeable past held him back from embracing the future. If Kyrin could not face tomorrow with a haughty scowl, then he felt he might as well be dead.

Hours passed. The sun began its slow descent to the horizon, lending a russet glow to the world. Shadows extended their dark fingers back towards Alinor, and the green leaves seemed to glow golden in the dying light.

Tryn called a halt, his red hair shining like fire under the setting sun. "We'll camp here for the night," he declared as Briea dismounted and began to brush down her pastel pink chimera.

"Figured it was about time," Brysson remarked casually to Kyrin as he urged his chimera the last few yards forward towards Tryn.

Kyrin said nothing. Instead, he peered forward through the trees, squinting his tired eyes at the land beyond Tryn's chosen campsite.

A mere handful of yards from where the Knights now stood, the great orchards of Alinor ended and gave way to tawny sand as abruptly as if someone had sketched a line across the ground. The space, which logically should have been occupied by more trees, instead was home to a veritable ocean of sand, studded randomly with tall, irrationally placed standing stones—blood-red towers flung by giants into an empty, arid landscape.

Unable to understand what his vision showed him, Kyrin turned his head back and forth, back and forth from the lively green to the bone-dry brown. A hot breeze rasped against Kyrin's face, blowing back a few escaped strands of his black hair. The air smelled baked, impossibly devoid of moisture.

Kyrin hardly noticed Sal's chimera step up beside Brysson's.

"Well, looks like we've reached the end of our home domain, eh, Brysson? My, how time flies. It seems just yesterday we were setting off on our last quest."

Brysson sighed. "Yeah, it really does, doesn't it? Man, I feel like the road is more our home than the Stronghold now, what with one thing and another."

"Same, same," Sal said, grimacing, "I almost feel bad for Tryn—he was so looking forward to spending some time at home for once…"

Brysson nodded. "Yeah, I noticed that his mood took a turn for the worst these past two days. I figured he was just worried about how we'd get the Anchor Key back without the Gauntlet, and what'll happen to Alinor if we fail."

"There's that too, of course."

Kyrin remembered the ornate piece of gold-colored armor Tryn had worn the night of Kyrin's capture. The elaborate enchantments had caught Kyrin's professional eye, but at the time he'd had more important things to worry about. Now, though, Kyrin recalled that the gauntlet in question had seemed different than the rest Tryn's armor. It was more elaborate, far older, and now apparently absent.

*That must be what the witch took…*

"What's so special about this gauntlet?" Kyrin heard himself ask suddenly.

Both Knights glanced at him, expressions suggesting that they had forgotten Kyrin's presence.

"Why do you care?" Brysson asked lazily as he climbed down from his place in the saddle.

"Professional interest," Kyrin replied as the chimera knelt down and Brysson unceremoniously pulled Kyrin to the ground.

"What are we talking about?" Dain intruded, setting down an armful of firewood and cheerfully flicking his blond hair from his eyes with a tilt of his head.

"Wow—we hardly stop five minutes, and already you're being productive!" Sal said, only just dismounting her chimera. "Kyrin here was just asking about the Worldwork Gauntlet."

"He was, was he now?" Dain laughed, helping Brysson arrange the gathered wood into a proper pile, "what have you told him?"

"Nothing, yet," Sal admitted. "Hey—By the way... when Briea gets back with whatever food she scrounges—do you think I could try my hand at cooking again?"

"No!" Both Brysson and Dain shouted in unison, startling Kyrin with their sudden forceful volume. Sal's face fell.

"Well, maybe you could cook something for him," Brysson conceded, jerking a thumb towards Kyrin as he lit the fire with his magic, "He deserves that and worse. But after last time, Sal, I respectfully ask that you leave meal prep to Tryn."

"Yeah," Dain agreed, standing up and brushing dirt from his knees and hands, "I'm with Brysson here, no offense, milady. Anyway—we were talking about something, weren't we?"

"Oh, don't you 'milady' me, Dain! And yes, yes we were. Kyrin asked about the Gauntlet."

"All right, yeah, what about it?"

"Uh... What's it do?" Kyrin felt even more out of place. Not only was he a thief among heroes, but he was an outsider among close friends.

"It shifts the domains for us," Dain answered,

oblivious to Kyrin's unease.

"What?"

The Knights exchanged a chuckle.

"You know—I forgot how ignorant city people are," Sal remarked, shaking her head.

"And to think you used to be one of them," Brysson chided, feigning exasperation.

"Don't you worry, thief," Dain laughed, "I'm sure you'll understand tomorrow."

"Fine. Whatever." Kyrin sighed, irritated and confused. "Keep your secrets. Play your games. But would you, oh noble heroes, allow me the use of my hands again? They've gone kind of numb. And my arms are sore. Am I really so much of a threat that I have to be chained all-hours like a monster?"

Kyrin's plea seemed to strike Sal's sympathy. She glanced at Brysson, who shrugged.

"Hey, Tryn?" Sal called.

"Eh?" the man looked over, interrupted midway through rechecking the supplies.

"Prisoner wants his hands free, what say you?"

Tryn paused to consider. "All right, fine. Keep a close eye on him, though, and make it clear what'll happen to him if any of my stuff comes up missing."

"Alright."

"And remember to tie him up again before we all take rest—we're still close enough to home that he might risk slipping off."

Brysson glanced at Kyrin before supplying "I don't think he's *that* stupid, sir."

"I don't know—" Tryn snickered, returning to his work, "he did try to rob us, after all."

"Good point."

"I'm right here, you know," Kyrin's snapped as Sal

worked to untie his wrists, "I haven't gone deaf or anything."

"You know, thief," Dain stated mildly as he sat down beside the now blazing fire, "if you wanted our respect, robbing us was the wrong way to go about getting it."

"Shut up."

Sal halted her work at the tight knots, regarding Kyrin with a cool, even stare. "You do realize that we're by no means obligated to untie you, right?"

Kyrin ground his teeth, letting his silence speak for him.

"I think you owe Dain an apology."

When Kyrin did not speak again, Sal removed her hands from the knots that held him. "You can't be serious. Just say you're sorry and you can have your hands back!"

To apologize was to admit defeat, and to admit defeat was to acknowledge weakness.

"Ugh—fine. Be that way, if it makes you happy." Sal said, taking a seat for herself beside Brysson's fire.

"Thank you, I will."

Kyrin's dry wit earned a sharp look from Sal and a laugh from Brysson. "You know what—I'm almost starting to like this guy."

Dain chuckled, "I guess he is good for a laugh, if nothing else."

Refusing to be cowed by the mockery, Kyrin turned his back to the warm fire and faced the lifeless, barren desert. The sun was low now, dipping nearly below the horizon. The standing stones' black shadows streaked the yellow sands like ink spilled across new paper. Kyrin watched, lost in thought, as the stars slowly winked one-by-one into the endless sky. There were more of them than he'd ever seen in all his life.

A short while later, Briea returned in the shape of a lioness, a large bag of fruit and root vegetables slung over her back. As Kyrin stared uselessly over the domain's nonsensically neat border, the Knights fed their chimeras, and Tryn made soup. When it was done, Sal brought Kyrin a bowl, setting it gently down on the grass behind him.

"Well, here you go," she said as Kyrin shifted awkwardly around, "Tryn made it, and it's good. Although I'm not sure how what you planning on eating it with your hands tied behind your back like that. And I'm honor-bound not to untie you until you apologize, so…"

"So I'll just have to find a way." Kyrin's tone was as flat as the featureless desert.

"Suit yourself." Sal returned to her companions around the merry fire, leaving Kyrin to sit alone in the darkness outside the happy circle of light.

The thief cast a thoughtful eye at the shallow bowl of soup. Even in the dim twilight, Kyrin could see the healthy chunks of carrot and rich potato. The scent made Kyrin's mouth water and his wrists ache.

He could not apologize and beg to be untied—Kyrin's pride balked at the very thought—yet it was just as demeaning to bring his face to his food in the manner of a dog. Kyrin's swore under his breath, wishing he could curse his dilemma away, but he had no such luck.

As the soup cooled on the ground, Dain began to sing, although Briea quickly silenced him with a shout and a thrown shoe. Kyrin sighed, his head drooping wearily to his chest as he privately bemoaned his fate. Stiff and weary, Kyrin rolled his shoulders and stretched arms as far apart as he was able—and was pleasantly surprise to find he could move them farther than he had thought.

Though Sal had failed to untie him, she had succeeded in loosening the knots at his wrists—possibly enough to allow escape.

Kyrin pulled and twisted, contorting his hands into all manner of uncomfortable shapes, until at last the loop of cord lay loosely in his palm. He set it aside and, with trembling fingers, lifted the bowl of soup to his lips. It tasted like victory. Tryn was a good cook.

Sal's eventual cry of "Wait a sec—who untied you?" was music to Kyrin's ears, and his reply, a calm, triumphant, "I did," was the sound of satisfaction. No two words had ever given Kyrin such an inordinate amount of happiness.

"Are you surprised?" Tryn yawned, "He *is* a thief. Just tie him up better next time, and let's get to sleep. We've got a long journey ahead."

Following Tryn's advice, Sal stepped forward with a new length of cord. Kyrin cooperatively presented his hands to be bound again, hoping that Sal would take the bait and tie his wrists in front of him, rather than behind his back.

She did. Kyrin suppressed slight smirk. While he was still far from free, at least with his arms in front, Kyrin could still perform basic tasks.

As the Knights lay down beside their warm and furry chimeras to sleep, Briea took the first watch, and Kyrin rested with his back to the fire, gazing once more over that strange, incongruous border at the silent sands beyond. This day, he reflected as the stars twinkled above and a cold, sandy wind caressed his face and made the fire dance, had not gone as planned. Already, the morning— waking up in his room, sneaking past his landlady— seemed like part of another's life.

*But hey,* he reasoned as his eyes began to close in their

own accord, *at least I'm not dead yet. And maybe, if I play my cards right, I can still come out of this with some gold in my pocket... Assuming Raph doesn't clean out my room when I don't come back... blast it...*

Comforted only by the small fact that he still retained possession of his lock picks, Kyrin slipped away into a restless sleep.

*Pale magelight glimmered on the rain-soaked streets. Heavy droplets churned both the ocean and the path into a silver sludge. Thunder crashed, and the sea roared like a monstrous creature, hungry and violent. A frigid wind howled, screeching through the rigging of the sleeping merchant ships, loud enough, mournful enough, to scare even the ghosts away. Kyrin clung closely beside his father, placing his feet carefully on the slippery wooden dock. He had to be careful, or else—*

A bird screamed, heralding the dawn with its bloodcurdling cry. Kyrin jumped, sitting bolt upright, startled from his dream. He looked around frantically, trying to remember where he was, and... Stopped, staring in disbelief.

Yesterday, Alinor's orchards had ended abruptly in a desert, but now a massive swamp sat beyond the line of grass, blotting out the sky with its twisted, towering trees and luxurious sprawling growth. Over the domain line, the ground vanished, transforming into deep, sticky mud and treacherous murk. The straight, tall, respectable fruit trees gave way to massive, mutilated mangrove trunks. Twisting roots clawed the untrustworthy earth and chained it in place.

Kyrin stared, watching the brimstone-scented fog roll thickly out from under the plant life's dark shadow. He gazed uncomprehendingly at the tangled mass of living vines that had somehow usurped the lifeless, wasted desert. Unable to understand the scenery's new face, Kyrin turned towards the Knights. They had already begun to pack up camp and ready themselves for the day's journey.

Kyrin cleared his throat. "Am I crazy—or was the swamp a desert yesterday?"

Dain paused midway through harnessing his orange-furred chimera and gave the question due consideration. "Yes," he answered finally, after a moment's thought.

Kyrin ignored the thinly veiled jab at his sanity, keeping calm as best he could. "So—if this was a desert yesterday—where did this swamp come from?"

Dain shrugged, returning to his work. "Where does anything come from?"

Not knowing what to make of this, Kyrin glanced at the dense greenery that had appeared overnight. "We're not going to have to go through there, are we?"

"I think Tryn said we might. I'm not sure—I'm still only a squire, remember. I haven't got my Key yet."

"Your what?"

"Hero's Key—it's the thingy that proves you're a Knight and opens the Stronghold's Gate. Hey, Brysson—you've got one, right?"

Brysson blinked blearily and staggered upright. Although the long, silky-smooth fur of a chimera made for an excellent pillow, Kyrin noted with detached amusement that no matter the cushion provided, sleeping on one's feet did not look comfortable.

When Brysson was properly awake, Dain repeated his question.

"What? Yeah," Brysson yawned, giving his chimera an affectionate pat as he fastened on the last strap, "I've got my Key."

"Show the thief." Dain prompted eagerly, moving closer.

"What? Why?"

"Because I wanna see it again, too."

Brysson let out a sigh of good-natured exasperation and strolled over to where Kyrin sat, kneeling down before him and drawing a gleaming silver pendant from beneath his shirt. Dain's usual grin broadened slightly at Kyrin's expression.

The pendant was beautiful—a delicate arrow shaped from shining steel hung from a thin, polished chain. No matter how the faint, sulfurous wind pushed it, the arrow's shining head always pointed the same way— through the swamp to whatever lay beyond. Kyrin could see tiny golden glyphs shining out from the cold metal, weaving a subtle enchantment into the pendant. His lips moved slightly as he examined the intricate spellwork— from what he could tell, the enchantment was a clever one, set to lead the arrow's master to his goal, no matter what that goal might be. The perfect trinket for a questing Knight in an uncertain land.

"What are you doing, thief?" Brysson raised a suspicious eyebrow, noting Kyrin's silent speech.

"Oh, I'm... trying to read it." Kyrin's voice came as if from far away as he stared fixedly at the pendant, attempting to manage a detailed study in the brief moment he had.

"Read it?" Brysson frowned, stowing the Key beneath his shirt once more, "You don't read it—it points the way you follow it. It's not a book."

"I know—" Kyrin began, trying to find the words to explain, "I was just—"

"What do you three think you're doing?" Briea's voice, clear and commanding, cut through the air like a blade.

"You Knights shouldn't be getting so friendly with the prisoner—you realize that once this quest is through, he'll be going back to the Gallows Tree."

"Yes ma'am!" Dain and Brysson jumped guiltily to their feet. Kyrin continued to sit cross-legged on the ground. As a prisoner, no one expected him to move.

"Brysson," Briea continued haughtily, "you go talk to Tryn—he wants to discuss our route with you. Dain, you need to come with me—you are still my squire, and you have duties to perform if you ever want to earn your Key. And you…" she looked down at Kyrin, seeming a loss.

The thief shrugged, and offered, "I'm just here."

"Yes, you are. And if you wish to continue just being there—" Briea seemed too caught up in keeping everyone on task to think up a good threat.

"Just… stay here?" Kyrin tentatively finished for her.

"Yes. Don't you dare move." Briea glared, before stalking off to finish preparations.

A good ten minutes later, all the Knights were armed, fed, and mounted, and Kyrin was stuck behind Dain in the saddle. The Knights had decided to take turns carrying him, and Dain had drawn the short straw.

Tryn turned his chimera around to face his loyal band of followers.

"Okay. So the Keys are pointing us this way, and looks like we're going to have to pass through this blasted swamp. Now—without the Gauntlet, I can't guarantee the danger level of this place, so literally anything could be in there—and the quest has only just begun. We don't have the time to warm up, and we don't have the resources to slip up. Without the Gauntlet, I have no idea how long we'll be out here, or what we'll have to face before we get the chance to resupply. Anything might happen, and if I've learned one thing since starting this job—it's that anything probably will. If we have faith in our Keys and in our steel, we just might make it through this in one piece. That's what we did before the Gauntlet, and by the Brother Gods above, that's what we can do again now.

"So, Knights of Alinor, defenders of the realm, protectors of the weak and champions of humanity—are you ready?"

"Aye!" Briea, Brysson, Dain, Sal, all greeted Tryn's speech with resounding approval.

"Then we go questing!" the red-haired Knight roared, raising his mace to the heavens.

A good show, Kyrin thought as Tryn wheeled his chimera around and urged it into the swamp, but it did little to inspire Kyrin's confidence.

"Here we are, we're going in blind, try not to die," Kyrin translated under his breath as Dain's chimera made the transition over the domain border and into the odiferous mud of the outland swamp.

Dain was the only one to hear. "Yeah, words of encouragement if I ever heard them. Now, I'll advise you don't speak again until we get the lay of the land, thief. Something unpleasant might hear you."

Kyrin glowered, the Knight chuckled, and the chimeras trudged on.

The longer the company rode through the swamp, the more Kyrin hated it. He hated the putrid, stinking muck that stained his clothes, he hated the foul-tasting wind that kept pushing his hair into his eyes and his mouth, and he hated the biting, whirring insects that swarmed out from every rotten log to sting at his exposed flesh. The air hummed unpleasantly with unknown life, and the opaque, stagnant waters rippled threateningly around the chimeras' furred legs. No one seemed incredibly happy, but none of the Knights seemed to hate the swamp like Kyrin did. They had no problem being surrounded by water.

*I bet their gear is enchanted,* Kyrin mused as he glared distrustfully at the murk. *Blasted Knights. The mud just slides right off them.*

Aside from the occasional muttered direction, the Knights rode in silence, paying close attention to every chirrup and squawk of the local fauna.

"Brysson," after the long pause, Tryn's voice came almost as a shock.

"Yeah?"

"While we're in here, I want you to watch the sparks, all right? We don't know what's in the air, here. We don't need to accidentally ignite any flare-ups."

"Alright, yeah, gotcha."

"Good. And Dain?"

"Yessir?" the blond squire perked up. Kyrin got the sense that he'd been waiting for someone to call on him to help.

"You're a treetalker—tell me what they're saying."

"Well," Dain closed his eyes and stiffened, sitting immobile on his chimera as he focused all his attention on his auditory magic. "They're saying... I think... I'm not sure, but I think they're trying to warn us of something..."

"Can you give us some exact words?"

"Yeah, I'll try, but... You know how trees are. These ones especially—they're almost... Laughing at us."

"I wonder why?" Kyrin muttered quietly.

Dain ignored him. "They're saying... *Beware the song from under murk, Beware the dark where hunger lurks... Beware*

*your friends or else you'll die, Beneath our roots your bones will lie."*
Dain cleared his throat and opened his eyes. A bird flew up from the ground and through a mote of golden sunlight, its earth-colored wings frantically beating the air.

Brysson chuckled. "Well, that's not morbid at all."

"Any idea what it means?" Sal asked, giving her chimera a comforting pat on the neck.

"Nope," Dain replied, "but I don't much like it."

"Me neither," Tryn murmured, glancing distastefully at the deep, muddy water all around. The chimeras were submerged up to their knees, and Kyrin wondered for a moment how the Knights planned to wash the mud out of their mounts' fur.

"Ask the trees what they mean—see if you can't get some answers!" Briea demanded, anxiously flexing her hands and tapping her fingers on her chimeras' saddle.

"On it." Dain closed his eyes again, and Kyrin noticed a faint, barely audible hum in the air—not unlike what he had heard before the witch's coming. He shook his head. Dain's eyes opened. The noise receded.

"They won't explain. They just keep repeating that rhyme over and over again. I get the feeling—"

A tree branch detached from the lofty canopy and splashed into the mud near Dain's chimera. The creature jumped, snarling at the sudden noise—throwing Kyrin from its back into the saturated terrain.

"I get the feeling they don't like us much," Dain finished lamely.

"No kidding," Tryn sighed as he dismounted and waded through the waist-deep bog to where Kyrin had fallen.

Kyrin floundered up, desperately spluttering curses and spitting mud. Tryn grabbed the back of his shirt and hauled Kyrin to his feet. Kyrin wiped the cold gray muck from his eyes, gasping for air even as he muttered blasphemy.

"You alright, thief?"

"I'm tied up and covered in blasted filth in the middle of a stupid magic swap surrounded by creepy sinister poet trees—do I look alright?" Kyrin fought to keep the pitch of his voice from rising.

"Yes." Tryn grinned slightly, "you look just fine to me. It's also starting to look as if you might be more trouble than you're worth."

Kyrin glared, realizing the impossibility of maintaining dignity when bound, covered in mud, and held upright by one's enemy.

"No snappy retort? My, and I thought you kept your wit sharp. How silly of me."

"Shut up," Kyrin growled, "I'm not—" he broke off suddenly, his green eyes glazing slightly as a new sound hijacked his attention and drove his mind into a wall. "Do you hear that?"

"Hear what?" instantly, Tryn was on guard, alert and ready for action. He evidently remembered Kyrin's behavior on the night the witch struck.

"It sounds like... Music."

"Music? Everyone—weapons ready!" Tryn cried, throwing Kyrin roughly over his chimera's broad back before leaping into the saddle and raising his mace. "The trees say songs—the thief says music—in a place like this, I doubt very many people are making merry. I think... My guess is we might have a basilisk on our hands!"

"Dammit," Briea swore, shifting her form halfway between lioness and human, sliding out her wicked claws as her hair lengthened and turned to fur, "that's *just* how I'd hoped to start my day."

Tryn called out sharply to his squire, "Sal—you

remember your training, right?"

"Yeah! Basilisks: don't look or listen to them unless you have a thing for geology, don't go swimming, and avoid the teeth and tail. I remember that they don't much like fire or bright lights, but they do go mad for blood. And apparently they're poisonous."

"Good girl—right on the mark. So stay alert, people!"

Flung carelessly across Tryn's chimera, Kyrin could not decide whether to panic or rage. A monster roamed nearby, a creature Kyrin had heard about solely in legend and seen only in books and nightmares.

Basilisk, the stonesight devil, bane of the marshes— Kyrin had heard the stories. Listen to its entrancing siren song, get lured to looking into its crystal eyes—and risk facing the rest of eternity as a granite statue.

*No thank you,* Kyrin thought as the unnatural magic grew louder.

Unlike real music with tune and beat and rhythm and design, the sound haunting Kyrin's mind was an odd conglomerate of bell tones and piercing notes. Though it set his nerves on edge and made his skin crawl, Kyrin found the cacophonous discord strangely beautiful. Like shards of broken glass reflecting a painted sunset, the unearthly notes sent fractured rainbows and disjointed patterns of light ricocheting through Kyrin's mind.

He bit his lip, drawing blood as he fought the noise and attempted to focus. Were the Knights faring as poorly as he? No—their expressions were drawn and dutiful, and their weapons were steady in their grasp.

"It's getting closer…" Kyrin mumbled through a face-full of chimera fur.

"Hear anything?" Tryn asked Briea tensely.

"No…" She flicked her leonine ear sideways, cocking it towards the wind, "wait—yes—Yes! I can hear the music! It's near!"

"Where?" Dain cried, anxious to start the battle and win the day.

"Shush, Dain," Brysson cautioned, "close your mouth, and we might be able to figure it out."

At that instant, the swamp erupted. Water, muck, and algae flew everywhere, tossed into the air by the massive creature's lunge. Kyrin could see only a flash of scales and gleam of teeth—and then Brysson was gone, knocked from his chimera and vanished into the murky waters. His chimera began to scream, and the other Knights' mounts followed suit as the horrendous monster thrashed around, diving into the deep.

*They're drowning out the basilisk song,* Kyrin realized. The melody was still hiding beneath the surface, like the creature itself hid beneath the murk, but the music no longer held its siren threat.

*If it ever had...* Before Kyrin could pursue the rogue thought further, the basilisk leapt again, scattering the Knights and their chimeras and separating Kyrin from Tryn's saddle.

Before he splashed a second time into the swamp, Kyrin got the fleeting impression of peach-tone scales dyed gray by dirt, of crystal blue eyes gleaming malignantly in the dim, uneven light—then nothing.

Cold, dark mud closed around him, suffocating Kyrin in its clammy embrace. His heart pounded. The mud clung to his face and filled his mouth—his nose—his—

*Wait... crystal blue eyes?*

Kyrin suppressed his panic and struggled to break the surface of the swamp, clawing at the air. His lungs heaved, his heart pounded, but beyond his own desire for life, beyond his need for simple breath, Kyrin had another purpose.

Kyrin had seen the basilisk's eyes, yet he had not turned to stone. Something was wrong here—something more than the twenty-foot monster attacking the group. It was not right—this was the wrong twenty foot monster.

"I 'aw 's eyes!" Kyrin spat through a mouthful of mud. None of the Knights heard. "I saw its eyes!" he repeated loudly once his lips were clear.

"What?" Tryn as he blindly smashed his mace into the monster's scaly back, "Get down, thief! Shut up! You wanna be a rock?"

"It's not a freaking basilisk you moron!" Kyrin shouted again, staggering forward through the mud, "I saw its eyes! I saw them and I'm not a blasted stone! Listen to me you idiotic half-wit—this isn't right!"

"Damn right it isn't," Briea snarled, caked head to toe in thick ooze. "I've fought basilisks before—they sing, they bite—but I've never seen one of the musical alligators jump like this before…"

"That's because it's not—"

The false basilisk leapt up again, straight at Sal. Now that they knew it was unnecessary to hide their eyes, all in the party could see its ragged flesh-colored scales and blood-red maw flying towards Sal's face at breakneck speed. Quicker than thought, Tryn shoved his squire aside, catching the basilisk on his shield—where it exploded.

Tryn fell backwards into the swamp. The basilisk burst into an amorphous mass of seething shadow, each fragment diving down into the deep murk like shooting stars forged from darkness.

Kyrin gaped, his mouth hanging open. He glanced at the Knights—they seemed shocked as well.

"That… wasn't a basilisk." Sal managed eventually.

"Guess the thief was right," Briea shifted back to her fully human form, wrinkling her nose as she wiped the filth from her hands and face. In the chaos, the Knights' chimeras had fled—taking with them all of the Knights' carefully packed supplies.

Tryn cursed quietly. "Guess we're on foot from now on. Chimeras should make it back to the city okay without us—they have their own magic. So don't worry Sal—I saw that look on your face."

Sal shrugged sheepishly. "Fluffy gets lonely when I'm not around."

Briea ran a frustrated hand down her face. "If I told you once, girl, I told you a million times—its name isn't Fluffy, it's—"

"Where's Brysson?" Dain interrupted suddenly, looking around.

The Knights all paused.

"You didn't see?" Kyrin stood, dumbfound.

"What happened to Brysson?" Tryn demanded flatly.

"He was knocked off his chimera when that *thing* first leapt out of the water."

"We have to find him." Sal said, her tone leaving little room for argument.

"He fell into the blasted water with that flame-cursed monster!" Kyrin cried.

"Sal's right," Dain agreed, "we have to find him. We don't leave companions behind. Right, Tryn?"

Tryn sighed wearily, "Hate to say it, but the thief might be right here…"

"No!" Both squires cried out simultaneously.

"We can't lose Brysson!" Sal insisted, floundering frantically through the mire to where she had last seen her friend.

"I won't accept this." Dain's face was set.

"You might have to." Briea was blunt, detached as she gazed up through the treetops at the blue sky above.

"People die, Treetalker." Kyrin's voice was cold. He could not help it. "People die and there's nothing you can do to change that."

"Shut up, thief!" Dain shouted, desperation clear in his tone. "Sal and I won't give up—Brysson's our friend and you don't give up on your friends."

Sal nodded emphatically. "He's okay—I know it. I'm sure he's not dead."

"Idiots—both of you." These people had imprisoned him—his hands were still tied—Kyrin felt he should have been glad that one of them had died. He should have been glad that one less bastard in armor survived to torment him. He should have been glad.

Sympathy was unacceptable.

"Sal…" Tryn's voice sounded strained. Briea was silent.

"No. I'm a puppeteer! I know things! He's alive. I'm sure of it. I know things."

"You can't be—"

"I *am* sure!"

"But even if you are—"

Dain interrupted, "I'll ask the trees." The golden haired squire closed his eyes and focused. Again Kyrin thought for a moment that he heard the faint, bell-like sound he associated with the witch.

Dain opened his eyes. "*The deep hunger has claimed the fire. Another soul sleeps in the mud. Wake him not beneath the mire, for the beast may yet draw blood,*" Dain recited slowly, "*the hunger is the fire's chain. To slay the one is to kill two. To bring the necessary pain, you must find if your friends are true.*"

"What's that mean?" Sal asked, anxiously rubbing her face with her hand.

Dain shook his head and shrugged. "I don't know.

"I don't like the sound of this "to slay the one is to kill two" line," Kyrin mused aloud, shifting into wardbreaking mode, "the rest seems pretty straightforward but—"

"Man, these trees don't have anything uplifting to say, do they?" Brysson waded up to the group. He was covered with sludge from head to toe, his sleeve was torn, and he was bleeding from a small gash in his forehead, yet the fire Knight seemed very much alive.

"Brysson!" Sal hugged him. "You're okay!"

"Where were you?" Briea asked sharply, relief shining through her stoic frown.

"We were about to tear down this whole swamp looking for you," Dain added.

"Sorry to have worried you all—I took a hit when the basilisk jumped up, but I'm okay now."

Brysson's voice sounded somehow strange, but Kyrin could not put his finger on the cause.

"Here, let me look at your head. You're bleeding." Tryn gestured for Brysson to come near.

Brysson touched his wound with the heel of his hand. "Oh, so I am. But it's nothing—I'll be fine. Save your energy, Tryn, we're gonna need it since all our chimeras ran off."

Kyrin narrowed his eyes and chewed on the inside of his cheek. "Talk again."

*Another soul sleeps in the mud, you must find if your friends are true...*

The words echoed in Kyrin's mind, bouncing around and buzzing against his psyche. This was not right—if Dain—if the trees—were speaking the truth, then this could not be Brysson.

"Speak," he commanded again.

"What's with you, thief?" Brysson chuckled, "I'm back—I'm okay. It's over. We can move on."

The man before him spoke in Brysson's voice with Brysson's words—yet beneath his tone, despite his meaning, Kyrin could hear the clamorous, sinister bells of the "basilisk."

"You're not that fire jerk."

"What are you—"

"Shut up," Dain intruded, "just because you want to see him dead doesn't mean he is—that's not how the world works."

"Oh, so basilisks don't turn people to stone anymore and just explode when they bump into stuff? Did none of you question that? I'm telling you—this isn't him. Can't you hear the difference?"

"What difference?" the not-Brysson seemed amused, as if having its validity questioned was somehow funny. "I'm honestly starting to suspect that whatever happened back with the witch was a coincidence after all. You're just crazy, thief."

Tryn seemed thoughtful. "What's your logic, thief? 'Cause if your only argument is that you don't like the sound of his voice, well, that ain't much to go on."

The not-Brysson snorted derisively, "You can't seriously believe this crap?"

Tryn waved a hand dismissively. "Of course not. I just want to hear—I'm curious."

"Suit yourself. Carry on, thief. I want to hear this too."

Kyrin took a breath, "The trees said so."

"What?" Dain, who had been watching the exchange in a state of mild bewilderment, jumped in. "They never—"

"Shut up, I'm trying to save your sorry skin, Treetalker—gods know why. The trees freaking said it—I guess you're just too thick to understand."

"When did they—"

"Shut up, I'm getting there. The first bit of your sinister tree verse—refers to the hunger. What do you think that means?"

"I don't—"

"The monster, you moron! Can you at least understand what it means by 'the fire?'"

"What? I can't—"

Kyrin ran a frustrated hand down his face. "Gods—how can a Knight be so stupid?"

"Fire—you mean Brysson, don't you?" Sal interrupted before Kyrin could launch into a full-blown tirade.

"Finally! Thank you! Someone has half a brain! The trees said the monster's taken your pal hostage. 'Beneath the mud.' 'May yet draw blood'—I doubt he's dead. 'To deal the necessary pain, you must find if your friends are true.' This guy," Kyrin paused for effect, wishing his hands were not bound so that he could point accusingly at the faux Knight, "this guy is clearly a fake. This guy is our monster—it's flaming obvious."

Contemplative, incredulous, disapproving, there were many adjectives to describe the Knights faces the moment after Kyrin's declaration, however none could adequately capture the look of satisfied disdain on the false Brysson's face.

"Clever." The mimic conceded, bursting into fragments like a lightless firework.

"Brysson!" both squires cried in unison as their friend exploded into a shower of dark.

"Apparently not," Tryn growled, adjusting his grip on his mace.

"It's a kelpie," Briea swore as she shifted back to her semi-bestial form, "I *hate* kelpies."

"What is it—some kind of shifter?" Kyrin stepped back, hoping to slink out of the spotlight before he could get involved in the fight.

"Hell no!" Briea seemed offended by the notion, "Kelpie! Monster! Not shifter—a blasted skin-changing thing that steals men's faces and then eats their entrails! Drags you to the bottom of the pond and you're never seen again—not a decent honest two-form human shifter! Shifters don't eat people!"

"By the gods, I hope Brysson's okay." Sal nervously shifted her grip on her sword.

"He'll be fine," Tryn assured, his green eyes flicking back and forth as he scanned the swamp. "we'll kill the thing before anything worse happens, we'll get the real Brysson back, and everything will be fine. I know it."

As if in response, a black cloud rose up from the swamp, enveloping Kyrin. He screamed. He could see nothing through the whirling vapor, he could hear nothing over the rushing roar of uncanny wind. Something heavy and unrelenting forced Kyrin beneath the surface of the mire, holding him under the mud. Though he kicked and punched and writhed, Kyrin could not break free. Cold fear welled up through his bones. A sharp pain flowered on his forehead, followed by a strange tickling sensation.

*Suffocating—dying—drowning—*

Darkness closed in on Kyrin's mind. In the last moment before he lost consciousness, the constricting power released him. Kyrin pushed himself back to the surface.

He spat out mud, gasping and panting and fighting for breath. The sulfurous air had never tasted so sweet. Hardly noticing his freed wrists, Kyrin let his hand drift to his pained forehead. His fingers came away bloody.

"Damn," a voice said. Kyrin frowned slightly. The voice was his, but he had not felt his lips move. Kyrin raised his head and looked himself in the face.

A few feet in front of him, a pale young man with glaring green eyes and a loose black ponytail stared at Kyrin with an expression of irritated bewilderment. His cheap clothes were torn and soiled with sludge, and a thin stream of scarlet blood trickled down around his left eye. Kyrin staggered back, shocked despite himself. The other young man did the same.

"You—you are not me!"

"You stole my face!"

"Kill the blasted monster!" one of the Kyrins pointed at the other as the Knight stared. "That's not me!"

"Aw—shut up!" the other Kyrin pointed back, "that one's the fake, I'm the real one! This is ridiculous!"

Briea threw Tryn a glance, "Can we just kill both of them?"

"I wish it could be that easy…" The Knight replied as the thief argued with his doppelgänger, "unfortunately, I still feel we might end up needing him."

"Go die in a ditch, fake!"

"I'm not the fake, freak!"

Tryn stepped forward, his mace gleaming wickedly in the patchy sunlight. "All right, we're going to get this sorted out—here and now."

Both Kyrins paled simultaneously.

Kyrin—the real Kyrin—spoke up, "I know it might be hard for you, but don't do anything stupid, Tryn."

The Knight hefted his mace, purposely drawing all eyes to the heavy weapon. "I wasn't particularly planning on it. Now, I *would* start trying to ask questions only the real you would know—only I don't know you well enough, and I think it's obvious the kelpie can somehow steal memories as well as looks, so that would be rather pointless. Agreed?"

The false Kyrin touched his bleeding face, "the blood…"

Horrified, the real Kyrin clapped both hands across his wounded forehead. "You're saying it drank my blood and sucked memories out of my head? That's beyond disgusting!"

"You drank my blood? That's… ugh," the false Kyrin stated almost simultaneously, seeming nauseous.

Tryn looked from one Kyrin to the other, his brow furrowing as he attempted to logic his way through the conundrum.

"Kill the fake! Now! Stop that blasted freak!" The false Kyrin commanded.

"I think… Our guy is the one on the left?" Sal supplied in a feeble attempt to be helpful.

"No, no, our thief is definitely the one on the right," Dain said, crossing his arms over his chest as he pondered.

"Well I can't tell," Briea declared, "they both just smell like stink and swamp to me."

"Everyone—stop talking—background chatter won't get Brysson back." Tryn's tone was firm.

Guilty silence bubbled up with the swamp gases. Kyrin clenched his teeth angrily.

"Yes, rescue your precious Knight, kill the freak, and tie me back up. My survival is irrelevant."

With equally biting sarcasm, the mimic Kyrin added, "I don't matter. No, just retrieve your precious companion and leave me to die, why don't you?"

"While you two do make a compelling argument," Tryn looked from one to identical other, completely at ease, "I'm afraid I can't do that. Annoying or not, we're not leaving you behind."

His gaze ended on the fake.

The creature stepped forward, hopeful relief in its eyes. "So you're not completely stupid after all. I told you that I'm the real one, I—"

A thorny branch caught the things arm, slicing a thin red line into its borrowed skin.

"Ow!" Kyrin cried simultaneously, "what—" he rolled up his sleeve to find an identical crimson cut on its own upper arm. He had not moved, he had not done anything—yet the kelpie's wound had somehow become his own.

"Tryn! 'To slay the one is to kill two!' If you kill it now, I'll still die anyway!"

"Oh—yeah right. That's ridiculous! Tryn—don't listen! It's trying to confuse you!"

Tryn lowered his mace uncertainly. "Well, it's working. This is getting weird."

Kyrin's mind raced. What was the point of getting them both killed? What was the monster's motive? Unless... Unless while in his form, it would not actually die. If Kyrin died and the monster merely feigned death and switched its form, the Knights would lower their guard, and Kyrin's body would be left to the monster.

The thought made Kyrin sick.

There had to be a way—there had to be something they could do to get rid of the blasted skin changer, but what? Desperately, Kyrin bit his lip and tried to think. The fake Brysson—something had seemed off about him. Maybe if Kyrin's forehead would stop stinging, he could figure out what it—

"Wait—Tryn!"

"Oh what now?" Briea snapped, breaking her promise of silence.

"Shut up! I'm not talking to you! Tryn—the cut on its forehead! The fake Brysson didn't want to heal it!"

"That's ri—"

"Idiotic!" the fake declared, interrupting, "there's no way that's relevant!"

Tryn gave Kyrin a look, "that's right. Completely irrelevant. This kelpie, it spent this whole time trying to confuse me—but I'm done with that. It won't mislead me any longer."

Raising his mace again, Tryn waded slowly towards the real Kyrin. Behind his back, the kelpie's borrowed face showed a spark of dark delight. Playing along, Kyrin stepped back.

"No—it's not me—you're making a mistake!"

Tryn roughly grabbed Kyrin's head, his palm "accidentally" coming in contact with Kyrin's cut.

"I make no mistakes."

The false Kyrin smiled. For a moment, the real Kyrin feared he had read the Knight wrong—until a cool, soothing blue light filled his brain, followed by a sensation of well-being.

The kelpie screamed. Cut off from its form's source, it could no longer maintain its guise. Kyrin watched its face—his face—contort and writhe as it tried to stay tangible. He could see through its skin to the swirling black abyss beneath as the thing struggled to maintain his shape. Kyrin felt as if he were in a nightmare, watching himself die.

Suddenly, a silver thorn sprouted from the false Kyrin's chest. Red blood dripped down, and the kelpie's scream ceased abruptly, as if bottled. It melted away into the swamp, a pitiful, malformed mass of half-dissolved flesh and lumpy crimson blood, revealing a dirty and rather annoyed Brysson standing behind it.

"Hey, guys. What'd I miss?"

"Brysson!" Sal ran to embrace him, nearly tripping and falling face-first into the murky water. She held her friend at arm's length. "It is really you this time, right?"

"I think so. What you mean by this time? Have I ever been anyone else?"

Dain laughed, clapping his friend on the back. "It's good to have you back, Brysson. You alright?"

"Yeah, I'm fine. But what's with the thief? I could've sworn I just stabbed him."

"Well, thanks for that," Kyrin muttered.

"No problem. But really—what's going on?"

"Kelpie," Briea explained, in her usual concise manner, "it stole his face. Yours too, for a bit."

"Ah. I see."

"Yeah," Dain added, "for a good while we thought you were dead. Sal was freaking out."

"Oh, and you weren't?" Tryn teased, raising an eyebrow.

Dain shushed him, waving a hand airily. "I was a little worried. That's all."

"Hey, Knights. I hate to break up the happy reunion, but can we get a move on? That thing might've had friends, and our supplies all ran off. I'd rather not die here because you're all too busy hugging it out."

"As much as I love the attention," Brysson laughed, "the thief's right. We can clear everything up as we walk. Which way are we going, Tryn?"

Tryn took out his Key and watched the silver arrow swing. "Looks like we're going this way. I had a thought—I know a place where we can get more supplies, and maybe even some information, if we're careful. World willing, it shouldn't be too far out of the way; the domain's always on the edge of vision, when I look.

Generally it shows up when I need it."

Briea nodded. "I love places like that. I had this field once—it was a great place, 'til those hell-spawned dragons moved in and destroyed the place. Of course, that was before I became a Knight."

Sal grimaced sympathetically, "I hate it when that happens."

Kyrin rolled his eyes, "You hero types are weird."

"We save the blasted city every other week, and we keep Alinor from being overrun with monsters— including dragons—" Brysson scraped mud from his arms and his face as he spoke, "after repeatedly putting our lives on the line to save your ungrateful neck, I think we've earned the right to be a little goofy if we want."

Kyrin ran his fingers through his hair and sighed. "Whatever."

The group trudged through the swamp for hours, avoiding crocodiles and snakes and giant poisonous frogs and all manner of overly large insects. Briea claimed that no adventure was ever complete without such nuisances, but Kyrin had his doubts. Far too many things with the wrong number of legs were trying to eat him.

Sometimes the damned water was as high as Kyrin's chest, and other times, it was only to the soles of his boots, but all the while, despite the sticky terrain and the inhospitable creatures, the Knights somehow kept their spirits high. Kyrin wanted to collapse and sleep and die, yet the Knights smiled and laughed and sang as though they were on a leisurely stroll through their garden.

Remembering the flaming flowers of the Knights' garden, Kyrin suppressed a grimace. That comparison actually made a lot sense. These people were obviously insane.

"Hey—Dain—come look at this! Sal's voice rang out from up ahead.

"Look at what?" Dain pushed on ahead, moving past Kyrin as Tryn and Briea walked obliviously onward.

Kyrin floundered after him, "Hey! Wait for me!"

Dain did not stop.

Up ahead, Brysson and Sal waited by a strange pillar. As Kyrin approach, it started to look less like a pillar and more like a giant green cup that had been dipped in red and speckled with white, sticking out of the ground.

Sal glanced back, "Hey—Dain—I think it's a plant— you should try talking to it!"

"Alright, I'll see what it has to say."

Insects hummed around the cup's vast mouth as Kyrin, Sal, and Brysson waited for Dain's report.

"It says it's hungry," the treetalker said eventually.

"What? Plants don't eat!" Sal exclaimed.

Brysson gave the plant a suspicious stare. "This one does, apparently."

"What the heck does it eat?" Kyrin wondered aloud.

"Anything that falls in," Dain supplied helpfully.

Brysson glanced at the thief, smirking unpleasantly as he mused, "Hmm… We could save the hangman some rope…"

Kyrin gave the young man a cold look as he backed away, placing Sal between himself and the fire Knight. Brysson laughed.

"What else does the thing say?" Sal asked.

"It says it's bored," Dain answered.

"At least this one isn't quoting poetry at us, this time…" Kyrin pointed out under his breath.

Brysson chucked. "That is true, that is true."

"It says it misses the good old days…" Dain trailed off.

"Oh?" Sal wondered, "Why?"

"Apparently, back in the day, a city used to be here, and…"

"And?"

"And apparently this used to be a hot spot for human sacrifice…"

"Oh… Lovely. I don't have a clue what to say to that."

"I do," Brysson stated firmly, "this plant is freaking creepy. I don't like it."

"With ya there," Kyrin murmured, "let's get outta here."

"It also says…"

"Says what?" Sal's morbid curiosity kept her firmly tied in place.

Before Dain could relay the plant's words, massive, twisting vines snaked their way out of the damp earth, wrapping themselves around everyone's feet. Kyrin jerked into the air like a fish on a hook. He could only scream as the carnivorous flora dangled him over its sticky-sweet maw.

The Knights fared just as badly, each of them bobbing and flailing as they went through the swamp's humid canopy. Sal yelled, hacking at the grasping root with her knife. Dain yelled, berating and bargaining with the plant to let them go free. Brysson yelled, ordering everyone to shut up as he tried to figure out if it was safe to throw a fireball. Kyrin yelled, adding his voice to the din on general principle.

Tryn and Briea came barreling into the clearing, weapons held high, claws at the ready.

"Gods above—what in all lands do you four think you're doing?" Tryn shouted as Briea roared and attacked the vine dangling her squire aloft, "I turn my back on you for five minutes—five flaming minutes—and you have to go and get yourselves attacked! Are you stupid? You're supposed to be Knights! Get down from there!"

Sal hacked ferociously at the vine, her normally light, fluffy hair spattering her face with strings of dark mud as she sawed her way to freedom. The deep green tendrils thrashed and flailed, battering at Sal's knife hand, but she held her grip. She chopped through the vine and plummeted to the thick, marshy ground.

She took a few moments to recover her breath before speaking. "Sorry, Tryn."

Dain was unable to reach his knife, and the carnivorous plant would not listen to his pleas, but with Briea's assistance, it was not long before he, too, had returned to the earth.

"Brysson—you're a full-fledged Knight now," Tryn called up, "you've got to get yourself out on your own. Grab the thief, too, while you're at it."

If Brysson replied, his words were lost to the wind. Kyrin, from his place directly over the plant's pitcher-like mouth, could hear nothing but his beating heart and rushing blood.

Brysson managed to free a hand from the vine's viselike grip. He summoned a ball of brilliant orange flame and clapped his hand to the side of the plant's green flesh. Startled and pained, the plant writhed, dropping Brysson as it wrapped even tighter around its last remaining prize.

Kyrin screamed, convinced his ribs were cracking from the pressure. Surely he was dead.

The fire Knight sighed, casting a second ball of flame at the center of the spotted plant. With an eerie, otherworldly shriek, the voracious flora dropped the thief and withdrew its grasping roots. Kyrin landed heavily in the thick mud, cursing the day he was born.

Ignoring him, Tryn began to scold the younger Knights.

"I'm disappointed in you three. Especially you, Brysson. You've been promoted. And Sal—I thought you were smart enough to know not to poke funny plants here in the Outlands."

"I'm sorry, Tryn."

"You could have been killed!"

"It's not like it was a hard fight," Brysson mumbled.

"Hard or not—you still have to be on your guard out here! Did that kelpie thing teach you nothing? We can't afford to be impulsive!"

"Sorry, Sir."

"Right now this third-rate criminal we're dragging along is laughing at us thanks to you."

"What—I wasn't la—who're you calling third-rate? I was one of the best!"

"Shut up; I don't care. My point is: we *all* have to take this quest seriously. If we die along the way—if we fail to retrieve the Anchor Key—Alinor will fall. The district domains will separate, and the civilized world will come to an end. We are the Knights of Alinor. We are the only ones standing between our people and the chaos of the open world. Without us, the Kingdom will fall, and lives beyond count will be lost amidst the shifting lands. I thought you all understood that, by now."

Guilted into absolute sobriety, Sal, Dain, and Brysson shuffled their feet and murmured apologies. Kyrin was impressed, and, for once, grateful to be an outsider among the group, if it meant escaping Tryn's disappointed gaze. Kyrin felt the Knight's tone could have shamed the Faceless into giving up crime, and as a failed burglar, Kyrin needed no more of that.

He had quite enough shame already.

The swamp ended as abruptly as it had begun. The dark mud ceased as if afraid to ooze further, giving way to pure, undisturbed, crystal white snow. The effect was almost blinding, and the numbing chill did nothing to help.

"Alright, Brysson," Tryn said, grinning as the group shuffled over the domain line, "in that swamp, I told you to watch the sparks, but here and now, this is your time to shine—and I mean that in the most literal sense possible."

"Oh joy," Brysson chuckled with good-natured sarcasm as he focused his power and began radiating heat, "I'm the second sun. Just try and keep me from burning myself out, alright you guys? I know I will if you don't remind me to take it easy every now and again."

"Will do." Sal nodded, smiling.

Dain knelt down to adjust his boots. "This is not gonna be fun. Briea, you're lucky. You have a nice fur coat."

The lion-shaped lady Knight licked a fluffy paw with her hot purple tongue, winking a yellow eye at her squire. Dain laughed, rolling his eyes.

"Don't worry, Dain," Tryn assured as he paused to make certain his mace was securely fastened to the loop at his belt, "we won't be out in the elements long. Remember that detour I mentioned?"

"You mean we *meant* to come here? Why?"

"Three words: the Listeners."

"Uh… Tryn?" Sal questioned tentatively, "that's two words."

"Shh—I'm a fighter, not a counter."

Kyrin pinched the bridge of his nose, astounded by the display of cheerful idiocy. How in all Alinor could the leader of these questing Knights—the hero among heroes—be content to make himself look so stupid? A fool's life brought no glory.

As the Knights continued their cheery, mindless banter, Kyrin took a moment to glance around. Ahead, through the howling wind and flying snow, a high, white mountain was barely visible against the gray cotton sky. Snow swirled across the ground, glittering dust thrown everywhere by the capricious wind. It was beautiful, if a little uncanny, and very, very white. Snow never stayed pure long in the city, between the polluting mud and traipsing feet.

Kyrin peered over his shoulder to get one final look at the lively, colorful swamp before the party left it behind forever. While it was hellishly humid, smellier than a week-old fish left in the sun, and full of things with a taste for human flesh, there was one upside: the swamp had never made his fingers numb.

An odd shimmer passed through the air, and the fabric of reality over the domain line seemed to ripple and bend. The swamp faded into a vibrantly colored mist that fractured and refracted the slowly dying sunlight, swirling the hues of earth and sky together like paints in some ethereal palette. Greens shifted to reds, brown turned to tan, and the earthy, deep smell of decaying vegetation was replaced by the hard, roasted scent of sandstone frying under the merciless sun.

The swamp was gone, as cleanly and mysteriously as it had come. Tall trees had turned to towering arches of wind-carved stone, banded stripes of blood reds and golden yellows. The pale blue sky was deep and open over the new, rusted waste—not like the cold gray blanket above the mountain snowfield.

A blast of warm air hit Kyrin's face, drying out his eyes

and leaving him all the colder as the pure, sparkling snow assaulted the back of his head. The wind tore at his hair and his clothes, melting snow into the fabric of his shirt to freeze the thief at the earliest opportunity.

As Kyrin stared, the temperature dropped.

He turned back around to see the Knights marching away without him, taking Brysson and his warming magic with them. Clouding the air with a steady flow of muttered curses, Kyrin staggered after them, stumbling through the trail the others had carved through the knee-deep snow.

# Chapter Seven

"How much farther?" In three short words, Dain managed to summarize every thought and feeling within Kyrin's weary heart.

"How much farther?"

Snow pelted their faces, each delicate flake a dagger in the wind's practiced hand. Every uphill step seemed a mile as they trudged up the unforgiving mountain, and any step could easily become a mile's trip downward should balance be lost among the sheer drops and steep cliffs.

"How much farther?"

Brysson's strength was clearly waning, for as he hiked, he had to warm the others. Even Kyrin could see that the Knight would not be able to go much longer without food or rest. His will would fail, he would collapse, and without his warming presence, everyone would die, blood turned to ice on the mountain's craggy face.

"Not far," Tryn repeated for the millionth time, "not far at all. We'll be there soon. Really soon."

But they did not arrive soon. Not until the sun began to sink in the sky to turn the snow to shining, heatless fire did the Knights finally find rest at the Listener's Gate.

While the tall, dark doors would normally have seemed ominous, forbidding, impassable—Kyrin now saw them as the gates to salvation.

Tryn knocked on the door with the handle of his mace. Booming echoes reverberated throughout the mountain, filling the air with thunder.

The Knights waited.

And waited.

And waited.

And finally, after Kyrin had nearly given up hope and resigned himself to leaving life as an icicle, the door swung open, shining a thin ray of light, a yellow beam of hope onto the darkening snow.

"Tryn?" a bearded figure silhouetted against the warm interior leaned slightly into the wind and peered out, "that you, lad?"

"Aye, it's me. I'm here with my flock again to find shelter from the cold."

"Oh, you are now?" The man scanned the Knights' pale faces.

Tryn grinned, "Yep. Been a few years, hasn't it? I'm a Knight, now."

"So I can see. I am very glad for you." The bearded man smiled warmly and stepped aside, allowing the party to pass.

Kyrin's fingers felt like solid fire as they warmed—now that he was in a place of safety, he noticed just how numb his face was.

Brysson collapsed against a wall, exhausted as he finally allowed his incandescent magic to flicker and fade. Briea returned to her human form, shedding needles of ice from her vanishing fur. Sal and Dain began comparing the redness of their hands, and Tryn stood chatting with the bearded man.

Kyrin closed his eyes and rubbed his frozen face with his cold hands, savoring the return to warmth. He missed the ragged coat he had in his wardrobe, and he found himself wondering vaguely whether Mrs. Raph had cleared his room yet, and what she would do with all of the half-dismantled wards he kept lying around when she did. Knowing her, Kyrin guessed the woman would turn around and try to hawk them off for some quick coin— priced as new.

*And Rat—what's he up to? He and his fancy new copytongue partner...* Kyrin wondered if either of them had beaten the other up, yet. Knowing Rat, it was only a matter of time.

*Maybe,* Kyrin allowed himself to fantasize, *this time, it'll be Rat who gets beaten up. Maybe—*

Tryn finished his conversation. The bearded man left, walking steadily down the hallway into the mountain's depths. Tryn approached Kyrin.

"Wrists out, kid."

"What?"

"Wrists out. Now that we're back in civilized company, thief, I don't want you getting any funny ideas."

"Ha. Civilized company. Right."

"Just put your wrists out already, will ya?"

Kyrin almost resisted, but Tryn's expression promised him that arguing was pointless. Gracelessly, Kyrin bared his wrists for Tryn to tie.

And tie them Tryn did, tightly, leaving Kyrin no room to wiggle.

"Is this really necessary?"

"Yep. No sticky fingers here, buddy."

"I'm not your damn buddy, Knight."

"Ain't that the truth."

"And I won't steal anything."

"Oh—so a thief and a liar."

"Shut up!"

"Only if you do."

Kyrin ground his teeth. "I'm not a liar."

"And I'm supposed to take your word for it?"

"Yes. Now shut up."

Tryn chuckled and patted Kyrin's shoulder. "As I said, you first." The Knight stood up, leaving Kyrin to fume while he addressed his compatriots. "Alright, so. I want you all to be on your best behavior, okay? The Listeners are a pretty serious bunch, and they don't much like the loud and rowdy. Get's in the way of their... Y'know... Listening."

"What are they listening for?" Sal piped up.

"I dunno, I don't remember. Something vague and mystic, I think. Universal truth or something. Voice of the gods. Ask Pel when he comes back, he knows better than I do."

"Pel?"

Tryn stroked his chin, mimicking the bearded man's posture and manner, "Guy with the whiskers. He's an old friend of mine."

"Oh, okay then."

From his position against the wall, Brysson let out a tired, nearly incomprehensible moan. "I need sleeeep..."

"Don't worry, Brysson, we'll be here for a few days at least, I think. There'll be plenty of time to recover and plenty of time to rest."

Pel returned, bringing with him a few other people—capable, smiling young men and women with silver hair, dressed all in white. Perhaps it was his exhaustion, but Kyrin was surprised. He had not heard them coming.

Smiling hospitably, the people led Kyrin and the Knights away into the mountain's warm, magelit depths.

Everyone had their own room in the spacious mountain hall. Brysson, Dain, and Briea all found lodging on the left side of the corridor, while Tryn, Sal, and Kyrin each had doors on the right. Although the Knights were valued guests entitled to large, luxurious chambers suited to their lofty social station, in his status as a prisoner, Kyrin was assigned to a room more akin to a closet with a mattress stuffed inside.

*Just like back home*, he noted with a wry half-smile.

The door clicked shut behind him. A key turned in the lock. It was the loudest noise these people had made. Then, silence returned.

Oppressive, crushing quiet, the loudest Kyrin had ever known, filled the room with its rich, impenetrable nothing. Silence in the city was textured, alive with the almost inaudible motions of the wind, the people, the magic, but here—absolute stillness, like death itself. There was no cold whistle from the questing breeze that sneaked through the cracked walls of Kyrin's room to tousle his hair. There were no distant howls from the city Dogs as they chased some unfortunate Guildsman caught halfway up a stranger's wall. No off-key singing from the drunk out past curfew. No arrhythmic snoring from the sleeper next door. No clatter of merchant carts on the cobbled street, no pulsing lullaby of broken wards hiding at the bottom of his wardrobe—no quiet hum of vibrant life gone dormant.

There was nothing—nothing but silence, cold, and darkness.

Kyrin lay on the mattress in the center of the void, wondering if this was how it felt to be dead. At this rate, he would find out shortly. The Knights might fail and he would die. The quest might kill him, and he would die. Or, the Knights might succeed—if they succeeded and subjected him to due process of law, Kyrin would die.

It was pathetic.

Uncomfortable and ill at ease, yet too tired for it to matter, Kyrin tucked his tied hands beneath his head and sank into a chilly, restless sleep.

*The air was gray with rain, hardly drier than the ocean below. Rough waves clawed at the dark dock, growling hungrily as they splashed higher and higher towards Kyrin's legs. Choking back the familiar cry of deep dread, Kyrin turned to run—only to bump into a girl, beautiful and out of place in this realm of fear. Her blonde hair seemed dry despite the rain, and her clear blue eyes sparkled in the dim gray light.*

*"I found you!" she cheered, beaming happily in the face of Kyrin's confusion, "I've been looking ever since we met before. I figured the Knights would come after me, but I never expected they'd bring you along!"*

*Kyrin blinked, only able to stare in dull surprise as the witch giggled.*

*"This is a happy surprise, though! You're going to visit me."*

*"I... am?" Kyrin's voice sounded weak, unused.*

*The witch smiled, grinning her brilliant grin. "You are. You might be a prisoner now, but it won't be forever. Come find me."*

*"How?"*

*"I wait for you at the end of your quest."*

*"But how—"*

*"I am Esmeralda. Come find me."*

*"But—"*

Kyrin awoke to the sound of his door unlatching. Groggy and bewildered, he sat up and squinted at the light that fell from the now open door. A dark-eyed girl dressed in white nudged the door open with her foot, a tray of breakfast balanced on her right hand. Her left hand tucked a strand of platinum hair behind her ear.

Wordlessly, she offered the tray to Kyrin. He stared, trying to clear the sleep from his head.

"Who're you?"

"Tye," she whispered, setting the tray at the foot of Kyrin's mattress.

"What am I supposed to do with that?" Kyrin demanded at normal volume, "my hands are tied." He brandished his bound wrists, displaying his lack of metaphor.

"Um," Tye whispered, "I was told not to talk to you."

"Ah—gotcha. Criminal. Right. Well you know what? That's a load of crap."

"You're not a criminal? But Pel said—"

"Hang that! I'm a thief, not a murderer. You don't need to whisper, and you sure as hell need to stop acting so damn scared."

Tye shrunk back, making Kyrin briefly wonder if swearing had been a bad idea.

"Everyone whispers here," she backed away stiffly, hiding her face behind her snow-colored hair, "we don't want to interrupt the Listening."

Before Kyrin could question, Tye turned and fled, locking the door behind her and leaving Kyrin alone to figure out how a man could eat oatmeal with both hands tied.

Silence returned. Breakfast occupied Kyrin's attention for a little while, but no oatmeal could keep the absolute quiet from weighing on his mind and crushing his spirit. Soon, Kyrin found himself tapping his feet, drumming his fingers, whistling snatches of tunes—even repeatedly thumping his head against the wall in a simple effort to relieve the boredom of incarceration and keep some small noise afloat in the sea of silence.

He was in such a state when Tye returned. She opened the door slowly. "The Listeners request your—what are you doing?"

Kyrin paused mid-thump. "Uh... Obviously I'm softening the wall so I can tunnel out of this dump with my oatmeal spoon."

Her brow furrowed in confusion. "But that's ridiculous, you can't..."

"I was—you can't be—just forget it. You obviously don't understand sarcasm."

Tye accepted this soundlessly, her face as still as the stone wall as she internalized Kyrin's nonsense and moved on. "The Listeners want to see you. Sir Tryn is in audience with them right now. I am to lead you there. Please... Please follow."

Kyrin groaned, pretending not to be overjoyed at the chance to get out of this third cell and look around. "Ugh—what a pain. What do they want from me?"

"I don't know."

"Fine, whatever," Kyrin stood up and straightened his clothes as best he could, "let's just go already. Lead the way—it's not like this is the entirety of my life now or anything."

Tye opened the door wide, ignoring the majority of Kyrin's chatter, "This way, please. Watch your step."

She led him out of his room, out of the guest corridor, and through the silent village of carven stone. Kyrin had little time to stop and gape, but his fleeting impression was of an empty beehive—caves on top of caves, piled around tunnels, littered with the cast off remains of absent humanity. Laundry hung drying here, a game board sat on a table there, and everywhere, great curtains criss-crossed the main tunnel, creating roads and streets and alleys of colorful fabric. No one here seemed to have doors. Instead, each cave-home was shielded from prying eyes by an ornately woven tapestry. Kyrin imagined he saw some of the the tapestry barriers shudder, as if people were spying out from behind them, but he never saw any sign of any inhabitants within.

*This place would be heaven for a thief,* Kyrin mused, *nothing's locked, nothing's warded—everything these people own is there for the taking. If my hands weren't tied...*

Kyrin shook his head suddenly. *No, no, best not to think like that. Not now, not here.* If Kyrin proved Tryn right, he could kiss the last remnants of his freedom goodbye.

A woman emerged from her cave, broom in hand. She began sweeping her front step, and as Kyrin followed Tye past her cave's open mouth, he caught her glare. Kyrin showed his teeth at her in a fierce approximation of a smile—his cold attempt at a friendly greeting. Her child hid behind her skirts, peering around at Kyrin as though fearing he would turn into a monster.

"Good day to you, too," Kyrin muttered, chuckling bitterly under his breath.

Tye led Kyrin through the cavern town, and it was as though a shark had splashed into a small pond. Children ceased their silent games and scattered among twisting tunnels when they saw the pair, and the man coaxing crops from the unyielding cave floor stopped his magic and stared as they went past. It was too quiet—too still. The vast caverns and massive tapestries only made the Listener's mountain seem emptier. Kyrin felt small.

He swore quietly, more to break the silence than from any actual annoyance. "It's too flaming quiet, here."

"It's hard to Listen except in silence."

"Shut up."

To Kyrin's intense aggravation, the pale girl obeyed,

unhesitatingly surrendering the last word.

"You're supposed to fight back, moron."

"But you said—"

"Shut up."

Obviously bewildered and hurt, Tye led Kyrin on, and he followed, feeling sick to his core. It was no fun to hit someone who would not hit back. Verbally abusing this girl was like striking a kitten. At least the Knights, obnoxious as they were, fought back. Picking on the helpless and hitting the weak was... just like Rat.

Clenching his jaw in irritated self-loathing, Kyrin stalked after his guide, hiding his weakness under a thick mask of prideful anger. He did not know what else to do.

Before long, Tye and Kyrin arrived in the Listening Room, the high-ceilinged chamber situated at the top of the mountain. Kyrin's legs ached from the long climb up the hundreds of stairs to the top. His wrists hurt, rubbed raw from the repeated passage of rough rope against smooth skin. However, his pain, his exhaustion, his self-directed bitterness were all forgotten in the face of what greeted him.

A tall, domed white ceiling carved with ancient glyphs of light and warmth and solitude rested above a wide round table made of stone. An open window provided a breathtaking view of the world beyond, wide and wonderful, and Kyrin could see the shifting domains laid out like so many patches on a quilt. Cunning enchantments kept the snow from getting in.

Winged figures adorned the marble walls, part of the detailed relief illustrating the story of the brother gods who made the world. Kyrin had never been a religious man, but the art alone was impressive. One could almost hear the orange-eyed god's delighted laughter as he regarded his creation. One could nearly feel the violet-eyed god's dutiful exasperation as he warned his brother not to break it. Of course, as everyone knew, the warning had not worked. The orange-eyed god had accidentally shattered the world, and then had clumsily glued it back together with magic, vainly hoping that his brother would never notice.

Kyrin wondered absently what the world might have been like if it had never been broken. How would his life have been? On that subject, Kyrin also wondered what had happened to the orange-eyed god when his older brother had learned what he had done. The stories never said. Religion was funny that way.

At the table, fourteen people sat watching him: six old men, six elderly women, Tryn, and his friend, Pel. Tye curtsied and fled the room, her lightly shod feet making less noise on the floor than a feather landing on a cloud.

"Well, uh…" Kyrin began, awkwardly struggling to find his tongue in the face of the apparently important gathering. "You… You need me for something or something?"

*Wow. That didn't sound stupid at all.*

A wizened old man, thin and gaunt like a skeleton clothed in ancient, ill-fitting flesh, looked at Kyrin, analyzing every aspect of him and dissecting him with his eyes.

"This is your criminal, Sir Tryn?"

"Yeah. Well, I wouldn't call him mine, but yes."

A hawk-nosed woman with a face more wrinkled than an apple left out in the sun for a week spoke up as well. "And please, Sir Tryn, refresh me. What are your suspicions about this young man again?"

"I don't know what to think, Lady. The whole event was rather… confusing. I had hoped that you, Listeners, in all your wisdom, might give me your esteemed opinion on this man so that we can know if is he is truly an asset to our quest. We cannot afford to drag dead weight along on such a hazardous journey as this without the assurance that our Gauntlet would normally provide."

"Sir Tryn," another, slightly younger elder raised his finger, gesturing for attention, "one last time, please—elaborate on the circumstance you wish us to evaluate? I would like things to be perfectly clear."

"Of course, sir. This man was captured after somehow breaking our wards and entering our Stronghold," Tryn explained, calm and formal, not at all like the relaxed, lazily arrogant Knight Kyrin was familiar with, "we threw him in a cell, intending to hold him a while until the law could take its course, but a few days later, our Stronghold was assaulted by a witch—a girl with more than one magic of her own. My brother-in-arms, Sir Brysson, later reported that a few hours before the attack, this man had a breakdown, screaming things about how the stones were singing to him."

"Hey, that's—"

Tryn silenced Kyrin with a warning glare. "Then, yesterday, in the swamp, I myself heard his odd claims of detecting strange noises no one else could hear. Perhaps this thief is a madman whom fate humors with coincidence, or perhaps his words hold some truth. I do not know, nor is it my place to judge the circumstance. I surrender him to your infinite wisdom, Listeners. Please, guide us well."

Kyrin frowned. "So I'm just an object again? Bought and sold and given away?"

Tryn shot Kyrin another glare, but kept his polite silence before the elders. One of the old women cackled.

Pel stood up soundlessly. "Come with me, lad."

"What?" Kyrin asked suspiciously, "why?"

"A test."

"What kind of test?"

"The kind of test where you come with me."

A sound somewhere between sigh and a growl escaped Kyrin's throat. "At least give me my hands back."

"No, you won't be needing them."

Kyrin groaned. "Great."

"Now follow." Pel walked to the wall and touched a glyph carved into the stone. A panel swung aside, revealing a hidden door disguised to blend in with the decorative carvings. Pressured by the cold stares of the Listening Council, Kyrin followed Pel into the secret passage.

The short hallway was lit by soft white magelight and decorated with abstract carvings and mosaics made of colored rock, but it ended in a small room containing nothing more than a table and two chairs. Even the walls here were bare and featureless, devoid of the intricate decoration Kyrin had seen everywhere else within the mountain.

Pel pulled out the chair on the right for Kyrin, taking a seat in the chair on the left. Seeing no other option, Kyrin took his seat, eyeing the room suspiciously.

Pel leaned his elbows on the table, giving Kyrin a hard look over his steepled fingers. "What do you hear, lad?"

Kyrin considered the question carefully, then stretched his face into a grin designed to infuriate. "I hear a little devil on my shoulder, egging me on." The woman's reaction on the walk to the council had struck him. She had feared him. That child had hid, as though he were some sort of demon.

"I'm being serious, boy. You know your life depends on your answers—on this test."

Kyrin shrugged, feigning nonchalance, "I'm serious, too. I'm dead either way, aren't I?"

Pel sighed, "Just answer me, please."

"Fine, whatever. I hear nothing but the silence. You happy?"

Pel muttered a spell-word and extinguished the chilly, illuminating magelights on the ceiling. "How about now?"

"You crazy? Light or dark, there's still just silence."

"No—really. Listen to it. Listen carefully and tell me what you hear."

Kyrin scowled in the dark. This man had to be insane—light did not affect hearing, the senses were separate. But… something was different. Something was off. Kyrin could not put his finger on the source of the feeling.

"Now, are you listening?"

"Yeah, but there's still—"

"Don't speak, just listen."

"Whatever."

"Okay, now I'm going to get up, and I'm going to leave the room, and you're going to sit and listen—"

"Like hell I am!" Kyrin leapt from his seat, knocking over his chair in his haste, "I'm not getting left behind to rot in a dark cell again!"

"Don't worry, I'll come right back. Ten minutes, no more—no less. All you have to do is listen."

"What're you—"

"Please, just calm down—"

"I am calm!"

"—and listen to whatever you may hear. This is an important step, lad. For the test to be accurate, you must sit in silence so that you may truly hear. Remember, your life depends on your use to Sir Tryn, so I would advise you to take this seriously." Pel stood up to leave, pushing his chair back under the table.

Frustrated, Kyrin could not resist throwing one final comment in before the man left. "'Cause that'll keep the pressure off," he snarled.

Kyrin got no reply, not even an echo as Pel left the room and latched the door behind him. This small chamber devoured sound, leaving only silence.

Kyrin sighed, fumblingly righted his chair, and sat down, laying his head on the table. The smooth, polished wood was cool against his cheek, his only companion in the quiet darkness.

Kyrin sighed again, venting his exasperation in a puff of aggravated breath.

*Ten minutes, eh? What a pain...*

He sat and waited and watched and listened, but nothing happened. Silence remained silent. Darkness remained dark. No motion broke the stillness. No beam of light signaled the opening door.

*Pel's taking his time*, Kyrin thought as he let go of his anxiety and slipped his mind back into the bored monotony of prison. The funny thing was that this silence *was* different. Kyrin knew that silence was the absence of any noise, but this silence seemed even... less. Something was missing—this silence was... deeper.

Kyrin shook his head, picked himself off the table, and rubbed his face. Maybe the cold or the incident with the kelpie had messed up his ears—maybe he was going deaf. Or maybe he was going crazy. Singing stones, ringing bells, now this uncanny nothing where he apparently should be hearing something... perhaps Rat was right. Perhaps magic was not the only thing Kyrin had been born without.

Ten minutes ticked by, dragging their feet as they limped along from the future to the past. Kyrin almost began thumping his head against the wall again from sheer boredom, but his bruised forehead was saved by Pel's return.

The door opened. The lights switched on. Pel sat down at the table once again, setting a canvas bag on the floor beside him.

"Oh. You're back."

"I said that I would be. Now, as I am back, listen again and tell me: what do you hear?"

Kyrin inhaled deeply, closing his eyes and slumping back in his chair. "This is such a pain," he sighed.

Pel said nothing, so Kyrin had no choice but to listen. A faint ringing emerged on the edge of his hearing—the kind of subtle, unchanging sound impossible to notice until it stops and starts again. This was ordinary nothing—life's ever present background hum. This ringing was the sound of silence.

"Nope. I don't hear anything."

Pel took his turn to sigh. "Are you sure?"

"Yeah—I think I know my own ears. I don't hear anything. Now, what did you do to the room when I left?"

"Excuse me?"

"The room—what did you do to it? You killed the lights and walked out, then things went weird."

"Weird how?"

"Just... weird, weird. Sucking-at-the-brain, weird. What did you do?"

"I closed you in and allowed you to experience absolute silence."

"What?"

"And now we're moving on to the next phase of the test."

"Again: what?"

Pel pulled a strange, elaborately painted crystal orb from his bag, and set it on the table. Glyphs in all colors seemed to float above the iridescent surface, reflecting rainbow spider webs throughout the orb's transparent interior. Kyrin glared at it suspiciously.

"Do you know what this is, boy?"

Kyrin examined the sphere with a professional eye, raising a critical eyebrow as he read the painted spells woven across the quartz ball's glossy face. "Looks like... a water purification device, I think. A really crappy one, though. Did a three-year-old enchant this? Who's idea was it to paint glyphs on a thing that's supposed to go in water? Some of these symbols are half worn off, and the ones that aren't are sloppier than gutter trash. Why the heck did you bring this thing here? These spell threads are junk—if you tried using this thing it'd leak magic all over the place."

"I know." The bearded man tapped a glyph with his index finger, activating the device. It screamed.

"What the—!" Kyrin shouted, hunching his shoulders and pulling at his bound wrists in a futile attempt to protect his ears from the awful, metallic screech, "turn that damn thing off! What're you trying to do—deafen me?"

"You can hear this?" Pel seemed immune to the sphere's harsh squeal.

"Of course I can flamin' hear it! That gods-blasted noise would wake the dead! Now shut that damn thing up!"

Pel tapped a complex pattern out onto the glyphs and gave the orb a clockwise spin, silencing it. Kyrin laid his head on the table.

"Why did you do that?" he snarled.

"I had to find out if you could hear."

"Of course I can flaming hear! You think I'm just—"

"Hold your anger—the Listening Council shall explain everything. I have one more test."

"Hang your tests!"

"You shall be hanged long before these trials are abandoned. Now, relax. Clear your mind, and empty your ears. This test is far more subtle." Pel reached once again into his bag, and drawing out a series of three small cups and a tiny wooden ball carved with minuscule glyphs.

Kyrin rubbed his face with both his hands. "This can't be what I think it is."

"The object of this test is to find the cup under which the ball is hidden," Pel said, laying out the familiar street game.

"You're kidding."

"I am not."

"This is a conman's game!"

"This is a test."

"It's a stupid game of chance!"

"Listen carefully, and you shall find that here, chance is not involved. Let us begin."

Pel set the identical cups down on the table, bottom up, placing one atop the carved wooden sphere. He shuffled them expertly, making Kyrin wonder exactly how many times the man had performed this "test." When he was satisfied, Pel steepled his fingers and looked at Kyrin.

"So. Be silent now, and take your pick. Listen, and you may hear."

"Whatever," Kyrin's usual attitude masked his faint curiosity. Silence fell. Kyrin listened. To his surprise, a faint, barely audible whirring hum emanated from the right-hand cup. Carefully, he lifted it, and was pleasantly surprised to find the ball exactly where he had thought it would be.

Pel nodded, resetting the test and reshuffling the cups. Again, Kyrin listened for the hum. This time it seemed to float from under the cup on the left. He lifted it, and again, he found himself correct.

The sequence repeated a number of times, until at last, Pel was satisfied. The bearded man stood, brushing his hands against his pants in a gesture of finality. "Come with me, now. I have heard enough, and the test is over."

Kyrin swore. He had nothing else to say, and a curse seemed as good an option as any.

"You would do well not to use such language in the Listener's Hall, lad."

Kyrin swore again, unable to relinquish the spirit of contrariness. "I'll do what I want."

"And that is why your hands remain tied."

"Shut up."

Infuriatingly complacent, the man obliged, smiling quietly as he led Kyrin back into the chamber of the Listening Council.

"How'd the tests go?" Tryn asked quickly, fidgeting impatiently as he sat among the dignified elders. Kyrin noted with a flash of mild amusement that one of the old ladies sitting near the Knight kept throwing coy glances his way.

"They went smoothly, Sir Tryn, and I believe I have found an answer to your question."

"You have?" Like Kyrin, Tryn seemed to be bothered by the incessant, excessive formality. It was obviously getting under his skin.

"I believe he is capable of Hearing."

"Uh…" Kyrin intruded deliberately, "No duh."

"Silence." One of the various old men wheezed, waving his gnarled hand, "Continue, Pel."

"Thank you, Listener. As I said, I believe this young man to be capable of hearing magic's imperceptible flow. Without training, the thief is able to detect not only the more obvious noise of our defective orb—in fact, the experience seemed to cause him considerable pain with its apparent volume—but to my surprise, this boy can hear the subtle sounds, all the way down to the resonance of the human soul."

"You are sure?" the hawk-nosed woman asked abruptly.

"No, Listener," Pel answered, "I am not, and I shall never be sure, as the boy's ears are not my own, but—compiled with Sir Tryn's account, I believe that the young criminal indeed has cultivated a natural affinity for our art."

"You, boy." A woman with eyes as blue as the chilly mountain sky raised her soft voice.

"Kyrin," Kyrin snapped an aggravated correction.

"Excuse me?"

"My name, is Kyrin, lady. I'm getting real sick of all this 'boy' and 'thief' crap. I have a blasted name."

"Very well… Kyrin," her eyes glittered with what could have been either anger or amusement, "tell me, are you an enchanter?"

"No." Infinite bitterness hid within the single syllable, staring plainly out from Kyrin's tone.

"And that is truth, Kyrin? I am aware that enchanters often, in their work weaving spells, become attuned to the sounds of magic, as it pertains to their art."

"I am no enchanter." Kyrin stood stiffly, his glare sharp.

"Move closer then, Kyrin. What are you? I cannot hear your soul. Your power is oddly quiet."

"That's because he doesn't have one." Tryn cleared his

throat. "I beg pardon, Listener, but earlier I failed to mention: this young criminal before us... our puppeteer reported after his interrogation that he has no magic, and so far I have seen nothing to disprove her words."

A murmur passed through the elderly crowd.

"No magic? That's—"

"Are you sure?"

"Unnatural—"

"Unholy!"

"Will you all just shut up?" Kyrin stood tall under the disapproving eyes, refusing to accept any more abuse. "I have no magic—big deal! I'm not some sort of freakish monster. I'm not an omen, I'm not a curse—so you can all stop staring at me like that! Enough with the blasted whispers!"

The murmur ground to a reluctant stop. The blue-eyed woman collected her thoughts and began to speak again.

"You have no magic?"

"Did I just say that? I'm pretty sure I just said that."

"No internal power of your own?"

"I didn't realize Listeners were deaf."

"Silence, boy," the woman commanded.

"This actually makes sense," Pel mused.

"It does?" Tryn asked.

"It does." An old man contributed, "One cannot listen except in silence. You see, Sir Tryn, an ordinary man cannot hear the natural flow of magic over the private flow of his own. The sound you know as perfect silence, Sir Tryn, is not true silence at all, but the quiet beat of your soul in relation to the world. As Listeners, we meditate for hours each day to learn to hear past our own magic and detect the sounds of the world outside, but this man—with no magic of his own, he has nothing to inhibit his hearing. It is easy to hear a whisper when one is not shouting."

"I believe I understand, Listener," Tryn lied, doubt plainly visible on his face, "but do you think his listening makes him a worthy asset to our quest—or do you believe it is a skill we can live without? If he has no actual connection to the witch, I do not know if we can afford to carry him onward."

"He has no connection to the witch," the hawk-nosed woman began after a moment's thought, "yet I believe it may be beneficial to have a listener along to assist in detecting the world's dangers. But it is true that a man without magic is as a sword without a blade, and pulling along one such as your criminal here may cause more harm than good."

"So…" Tryn managed, "what would you have me do?"

"Pel?"

"Yes, Listener?"

"How goes your training?"

The bearded man bowed slightly, "It goes well, Listener, I have learned to hear all but the subtlest of sounds, and I feel that my ears grow keener by the day."

"Very good. You shall accompany Sir Tryn on his quest. You are his friend, are you not?"

Pel and Tryn exchanged a quick grin, "Yes, Listener, he is an old friend."

"Then it is decided. Pel, you shall join Sir Tryn and his companions so that he may continue to enjoy the advantage a listener provides to his party, without the liabilities of carrying a cripple and a criminal."

Kyrin's jaw clenched on its own. So even the old and wise considered him nothing more than an arrogant, useless scofflaw… they were no better than Rat, in the long run.

Pel nodded, oblivious to Kyrin's mental rant. "I would be honored to join Sir Tryn in his noble quest, and I am sure that I may learn much, out in the world. Assuming he would have me?"

The question was a mere formality. Tryn grinned, nodding instantly. "I would be glad of your company, Pel. You are a good man, and I am sure you will be an asset on our journey."

"Then it is settled!" A brown-eyed elder said, smiling.

Kyrin's scowl was the only one in the room. Pel was beaming, Tryn was grinning, and all the Listening Council were in various states of cheer.

"Go ahead. Replace me. Not like I helped save your skin back in the swamp or anything, Knight."

Tryn glanced at Kyrin, looking at him as though he had been scraped off the bottom of a boot. "Thief, you are the one who broke our wards, you are the one who allowed the witch to break our defenses, you're the one who let our Gauntlet get stolen, and you're the one who forced us out on this da—" Tryn halted mid-word, remembering his audience, "dratted quest to begin with. Don't try and speak as though you deserve praise."

"Fine. I'm a terrible, horrible human being for wanting to move up in the world. Go ahead, kill me at your leisure."

"Of course I'm not saying that," Tryn countered calmly, "You are an ordinary lawbreaker, and now we can allow you to go and properly face the law, as is fair. We would never kill you without due process, thief. We're Knights, not your Guildsmen."

"Oh, joy," Kyrin muttered, blandly sarcastic, "I feel so loved. Truly, your law is just and good. I never should have broken it. How silly of me."

"And I must say," Tryn continued as Pel bid farewell

to the council and led the outsiders down the stairs to the settlement below, "that typical teenage attitude of yours, thief, is not making it at all difficult for me to bid you farewell. Normally, I might feel somewhat bad about this, but your complete lack of penitence makes this easy for me."

Pel snickered, Kyrin snarled, and the three of them descended the thousand stairs, ready to meet the other Knights waiting at the bottom.

At the base of the long staircase, a bare alcove sat—a lounge for those awaiting the Council and its judgment. Elegant tapestries adorned the walls, and lush cushions padded the unforgiving stone benches that lined the space. Dain and Brysson sat uncomfortably, talking quietly to pass the time as they awaited Tryn's return. Briea napped in the corner, a massive mound of golden fur, rising and falling with the slow pulse of her breath. She twitched a paw, dreaming of some unknowable hunt. Sal lay on the floor as well, leafing absently through a book someone had lent her.

She looked up as Tryn strode down the last few marble stairs, Kyrin tripping in his shadow and Pel walking behind.

"Oh! You're back! How'd it go?"

"Everything's all sorted out now, I'm glad to say," Tryn answered, smiling.

"And?" Briea rumbled, opening a yellow eye to acknowledge her friend's presence.

"Apparently our buddy here can hear magic," Tryn gave Kyrin a nudge forward, making Kyrin stumble, "and more than that, that's what the Listeners do here, too. As it happens, Pel here's a Listener in training. Pel is a Listener in training who has agreed to come with us on our journey and help out."

"The Brother Gods smile!" Dain proclaimed joyfully, "looks like we're gonna breeze right through the rest of this quest! Hail the orange and violet!"

"Don't jinx us, Dain," Brysson chuckled, "We don't wanna spoil our good luck."

Sal chewed her lip, pensively closing the book as she collected her thoughts. "So what'll happen to Kyrin, then?"

"Well," Tryn answered steadily, his offhand manner suggesting he could not care less about the thief's fate, "we don't need him anymore. Time allowing, we can send him back to the city where he can finally be justly hanged."

Kyrin choked, the air preemptively trying to strangle him as he struggled to digest Tryn's statement. "You're kidding. You dragged me all the way out here just to turn around and send me back to die?"

"Well, that's about the shape of it, yeah. We thought you may have proved useful, and now we know that you won't. Plain and simple. There's no reason to drag things out."

"Better a quick, humane, legal death by hanging than a long, slow, painful death by biting fang and tearing claw," Briea bared her lioness teeth as she stretched, flexing her retractable claws as she shook the nap from her fur, "there are things out in the world that would gladly eat you alive, and other creatures that would love to take you apart and show you the color of your own insides before putting you back together and stashing you in the rear of a cave for years on end. There are worse things than a hanging."

"Briea speaks truth. We aren't dragging you all across the world just to have you screw up and get torn to bloody pieces or get lost and die after taking up any more of our time and resources. We can't afford it. Without the Gauntlet, and without magic or training or anything, you're a danger to yourself and everyone around you. Sending you back to face the rope is better than you deserve, thief, and better for everyone, in the long run."

"Not for me it isn't."

"Yes it is. If we hang you, you won't get eaten or tortured. We need to deliver you back to Alinor so the Dogs can take care of the execution all legal-like and whatnot. I suppose technically we do have the authority to carry out the sentence ourselves, but…" Tryn shrugged and looked at his companions, "I feel that once you started dealing death in justice rather than in battle, it'd be rather hard to know when to stop."

Brysson raised a lazy hand. "I'll do it."

"What? No, Brysson," Sal protested, "Tryn literally just said that we weren't gonna kill him, you can't—"

"No, no, no!" Brysson cut her off with an emphatic wave of his hand, "Shut up a second and let me talk, will ya? I meant that I'd play escort. World willing, I can make it back within Alinor's walls, see our favorite little pest hanged, and maybe even find our chimeras and make it back before the rest of you all get too far ahead."

"You wanna go out alone, Brysson? That's practically suicide!" Dain's incredulous voice reverberated against the bare stone walls and bounced off the empty ceiling, "You can't be serious!"

"Oh, but I am. I won't be alone—I'll have him!" the fire Knight joked, jerking a thumb towards Kyrin.

Sal smacked her forehead with the palm of her hand. "I certainly hope you're kidding."

Brysson chuckled. "Only slightly. But I am serious about taking this mission—I can handle it. I trust my luck. Sure, we had some trouble back in the swamp. A bit of bad fortune. But we were all off our game! It was a good wakeup call, and now we can be on our guard. We're the Knights of Alinor, navigating the Outlands is our business. That's what you always say, isn't it Tryn?"

The man seemed uncomfortable having his own words thrown back at him. "Well, yes, but I doubt going alone is wise. Anything that can happen probably will."

"But it's true that we need our chimeras back, and they've been trained to go home. If I can make a trip to the city, I can kill two birds with one stone. Two crooks, one rope, even."

Kyrin winced slightly. Tryn spared him no more than a glance before replying, "Yes, but still. It's not worth you risking your life to—"

"Tryn, without our chimeras, without the Gauntlet, moving forward is already hard enough. If I can make it back, I can find our mounts, catch up, and this whole quest will be safer for everyone."

"But you'll have to fight alone."

"I won't be totally alone. Worst comes to worst, the thief gets thrown to the wolves, the hangman doesn't get paid, and I continue on my merry way. No big deal."

"Brysson, this is stupid, don't—" Dain began again. Brysson cut him off, yawning nonchalantly.

"Dain, you were chosen to be a Knight based off your talent, right? You waved that sword of yours around, and they saw your potential and invited you in?"

"What's that got to do with—"

"See, Dain, I wasn't picked that way. I was picked based off my prior achievement as a mercenary. My proven, established skill at traveling around on my own. Remember that."

"I do remember that—and I also remember you

tripping over your own feet during training, so don't start trying to act all cool and untouchable just because you used to be a half-decent sellsword. It won't work."

Briea shifted her form, stalking over to look Brysson in the eye. "You're adamant?" she asked sternly.

"Yep. This is the best way I can help. The squires depend on you and Tryn to lead them safely, so neither of you can go without endangering everyone else. I'm the only one here experienced enough to survive on my own without a trainee to watch—I'm the only logical choice for the job."

"You're trying to atone for what happened with the kelpie, aren't you, Brysson? You don't have to do that. It could have been any one of us who fell."

"I know—I'm not trying to atone, I'd be volunteering anyway. This is something that needs to be done, and I'm the best man for the job."

Briea stared him down for a long moment, before reluctantly nodding once. "Don't be foolish," she cautioned quietly, "I would rather not lose any more brothers-in-arms."

"'course not," Brysson grinned slightly, confidence pouring off him in waves.

"You all are idiots." Kyrin interrupted, his nerves revealing themselves through his voice, "This is stupid—all of you are stupid! Bravest of the brave, wisest of the wise—I never should have believed that crap. I never should have—"

"Tried to make off with our stuff?" Brysson intruded, winking "that's how I would choose to end that sentence, if I were you."

Ah, a direct verbal attack—Kyrin knew where he stood in a battle of words. Admittedly, it was firmly beside the phrase, "shut up," but it was something to cling to. Kyrin looked Brysson in the eye, setting his face like cold stone to achieve the desired effect. "If you were me, you never would have been able to touch the Stronghold's wards."

"If I were you, I never would have had to bother trying."

"If you were me, you'd be dead at the bottom of the ocean by now, Sparky."

"Who're you calling Sparky, thief?" Brysson's eyes narrowed.

"I'll give you three guesses, pal. Or is that not enough?"

Brysson looked as though he were about to call his flame, but Tryn placed a hand on his shoulder.

"You still sure you want to take him back by yourself? Looks like this guy might drive you up the wall before you've made it a day."

"Yeah, more sure than ever." Brysson nodded, crossing his arms over his chest, "I'll be hanged myself if we keep this guy around with us, what with his winning attitude and all, and no one else can be spared. I'll escort him gladly, and I'll darn well see him done."

Briea stretched her neck and arms, her joints cracking audibly, "If you're certain, you're certain."

"Just don't die in the process, alright?" Dain added, "It'd completely mess up the natural order of things."

Brysson chuckled. "And of course we don't want that."

Tryn waved a hand, flagging down the conversation, "Anyway, if you're set, you're set. One way or the other, though, it's not like you're leaving now. We can afford to rest up a few days before we have to hit the road again. There's nothing in haste but death, so we should take it easy while we can. No knowing when next we'll find a friendly roof to rest under."

On that cheerful note, the Knights went their separate ways, parting to wander the mountain village, or sleep, or eat as they saw fit, and Kyrin was once again confined to his small room.

As soon as the door closed, Kyrin kicked the wall violently, but that only succeeded in bruising his sore foot. Tired, drained, and hopeless, Kyrin sank to the floor and buried his head in his arms, vowing that someday, if he could get just one more chance, he would turn his life around. Kyrin would make things better.

All he needed was one more chance.

The week passed, flying by with the Knights and dragging Kyrin behind like a rag doll attached to a string. For the most part, Kyrin was alone with his thoughts, excluding the occasional visits from the Knights as they checked on their prisoner's welfare, and from Tye as she brought him his various meals. While the Knights would at least hang around long enough to exchange a few insults and fire Kyrin's driving anger with pointed banter, no matter what he said to Tye, the pale, ghostly girl always fled without saying more than a single, nearly inaudible sentence. She reminded Kyrin of the snowflake—colorless, soundless, and prone to vanishing at the faintest sign of heat.

In his soul-dead boredom, Kyrin made it his mission to have at least one proper conversation with her, and finally, on the last day of the Knights' stay in the mountain, a mere hour before Brysson came to escort him away to his date with fate, Kyrin managed to achieve his goal.

Tye came in to Kyrin's cell shortly before the dawn, bearing her usual tray of tasteless breakfast items. Kyrin stretched and sat up, propping himself up against the wall. He rested his bound hands on his knees as he observed Tye's entry. The girl set the tray down on the mattress and turned to leave, but before she could exit, Kyrin stopped her with a word.

"Wait—why do you fear me?"

Something in his voice made her pause. Maybe it was his uncharacteristic lack of anger, maybe it was the strange sadness lurking behind his words, or maybe it was the fact that soon, he would be on the path to death. Whatever the reason, Tye paused and bit her lip, her hand on the door handle as if to flee at any moment.

"You—you and all the people here… what's with the terror? I'm a thief—not a lunatic cannibal killer. Why are you all afraid? My hands are tied—I swear, I'm harmless."

"You are a criminal," Tye whispered, "we have no crime here, and we do not want any."

Kyrin's brow furrowed. "No crime at all?"

Tye shook her head. "The Listeners would not abide it."

Quietly absorbing this statement, Kyrin asked, "But what about those who can't afford to eat? What about the impoverished and the luckless?"

"What? I don't understand."

"What about the people who have no way of getting the money to buy food? When it's steal or die, you can't tell me your people just sit quietly and let themselves starve as law-abiding citizens without doing anything about it."

"Steal… or die?" Tye's tone was beyond bewildered, "I know no people in such a circumstance. Everyone works for everyone. No one eats unless everyone eats, and no one starves unless everyone starves, as is right. Is it not so in the city?"

"No... not quite." Kyrin's mind flew back to Rat, to the Faceless, to the whole of the Thieves' Guild. Their mindset was... different. "The city's too big for people to live like that, I think. Too many bad eggs."

Tye pondered this. "They..." she began timidly, "They tell me that you don't have magic. Is this... Is this true?"

Kyrin nearly swore, but he trapped the words in his mouth in the nick of time. "I don't see why it matters."

"If you don't have a soul—"

"It's magic I'm missing. I'm pretty sure my soul's fine."

"But isn't magic the same as your soul?"

Kyrin gave her a hard look, his green eyes narrowed as his scowl returned. "No, I don't think so."

Tye shrank back under his glare, opening the door reflexively, "I—I shouldn't be talking to you, I'm sorry, I am not supposed to linger. I... I have to do some chores."

Kyrin nodded, turning his gaze to the ceiling. "Very well. Have fun with that."

"Um..." Tye squeaked, pausing as she went to leave the thief with his breakfast, "If you do have a soul, I shall pray that it finds rest in the afterlife." She ducked her head, a frightened approximation of a bow, and ran off, scuttling away through the halls like a rabbit.

Kyrin plucked a piece of dry bread from his plate and tore off a bite, smiling bitterly. "Nicest thing anyone's said to me in a while," he muttered, "Go die, have fun."

Trapped in a web of unkind memories, Kyrin ate his breakfast in silence, waiting for his sentence to end.

Not long after his talk with Tye, the door to Kyrin's cell flew open, revealing a fully-armored Brysson standing in the entryway.

"Up and at 'em, thief. It's time to head out. No more lazing, time to get blazing."

"You're kidding me."

"Nope. Today's the day we strike out for home, and I'm dragging you off, like it or not."

"What? No, you idiot, I meant that line. "No more lazing, time for blazing?' Seriously?"

"What?" Brysson countered defensively, "I happen to like it. Now get yourself up and moving. Come on, I'm not gonna hang around waiting forever. You can walk, or I can drag you. Your pick."

Groaning and rolling his eyes, Kyrin hauled himself to his feet, using the cold stone wall to maintain his balance.

"Lighten up, buddy!" Brysson cheerfully clapped Kyrin's shoulder, nearly sending him back to the floor, "Don't you worry your pretty little head, it'll all be over soon."

Kyrin rolled his eyes and snarled. "I am so reassured."

"Good, ya should be." Pushing Kyrin along before him, Brysson strolled out of the cell, into the empty stone hallway, and down a long flight of steep stone stairs to the massive door where the others waited.

"Brysson! Good luck!" Sal called, running to embrace her friend with an armored clang.

"Yeah, man," Dain added, mimicking Brysson's typical lazy speech pattern, "watch your back out there, all right?"

"Thanks, yeah, I will. Don't worry."

Tryn laughed. "Who's worrying? You're a Knight, we trust you can look after yourself in a pinch. So kill some monsters for me, will ya, Brysson? I'll make sure to slay some for you until you get back here to do it with the rest of us."

"Deal," Brysson grinned, clasping Tryn's hand to seal

the bargain. "And Briea—you make sure to keep a close eye on the squires, all right? I know neither of them is technically mine, but I've grown rather fond of them."

The lioness grinned and nodded, ignoring the protesting words of Dain and Sal's bruised pride. "I'll eat 'em if they misbehave, and eat anything else that misbehaves near them."

Brysson laughed heartily, "Careful! Don't overdo it— you'll give yourself a stomachache, Briea!"

"As if that could happen. I haven't yet met the monster that I couldn't stomach a bite from. You'd be surprised how many of them taste like tuna."

Still chuckling, Brysson shook his head. "Whatever you say, Briea. Whatever you say."

Bidding them all a final, fond farewell, Brysson pushed open the strong stone doors and stepped out into the lightly falling snow. Before Kyrin could do more than blink, his far less dramatic exit was enforced by Briea's firm hand shoving him out into the light of the rising sun.

Kyrin picked himself out of the pure snow, already starting to shiver. He shook pale flakes of ice from his dark hair and squinted into the morning light. Behind him, the solid stone door slammed shut, leaving the mountain barren and lifeless.

"Come on, thief—the others will hit the road in an hour or two, we'd best get a move on. I'm not about to be overtaken by those lazy good-for-nothings. Get walking." As Brysson spoke, the air around his body began to warm, and Kyrin could hear the glyphs on his armor begin to hum as they protected the fire Knight's clothes from spontaneous combustion. Snowflakes melted and turned to rain several feet above Brysson's head, sizzling where they met his body.

"Can't we take it easy, Knight?" Kyrin complained,

"I'm not in a huge hurry to die, you know."

"No can do, I'm afraid. Easy isn't in my vocabulary."

"All right, so when we get back to the city, before you hang me or anything, you're buying yourself a dictionary—because that's a problem."

"No thanks, I don't really care." Brysson began to stroll down the mountain, as carefree and happy as if he were taking a lazy path through a field of flowers.

Without nearly as much panache, Kyrin stumbled after him. "Untie my damn hands, at the very least, will you? I'll go faster if I'm not overbalancing every five seconds, and I'd rather not have to watch my fingers turn to ice and fall off on the way down to the gallows."

"Ugh—fine," Brysson groaned, pulling a small, wickedly sharp knife from his pocket, "As much fun as it is to watch you fall over, I'm morally opposed to delivering damaged merchandise, even if it is just to the hangman. So you're getting off easy, thief."

Kyrin passed the Knight an aggravated glance, "Really—is it truly that difficult for you to remember my name?"

"Nope." Brysson shrugged his metal-clad shoulders airily, seeming happy to be out and about in the world, "It's not that your name is that hard, it's just that I can't be bothered to learn the titles of all the hopeless condemned. I don't consort with criminals. I have more important things to think about."

"Yeah, right. What things are these?"

"Oh, just about anything, really. I could be focusing on watching my footing and not falling off the mountain, for instance. Or I could keep an eye out for monster tracks, or watch the weather, or I could devote my attention to the careful application of magic needed to heat the air without burning myself to a crisp and baking myself alive in my own armor, or—"

"Wait half a sec—you're flammable?"

"Of course I'm flammable—I may have control over an element, but I'm only human. No one's invincible against nature's power. Even the greatest sorcerers of all time can be burned, I think. And drowned. You'd have to be, like, a god or something not to be vulnerable, and there's no way I could claim that title."

"Do you believe in the gods?" Kyrin asked suddenly, his voice apparently detached from his mind as he picked his way around a large heap of drifted powder snow.

"What?"

"I'm just asking. Conversation helps me forget that my feet are numb. Helps me forget for half a minute where I'm headed."

Brysson shrugged. "I won't argue with that. I'm not a devout believer, but it's nice having someone to swear to. I think if you want religion, you need to grab Dain: he's big on that stuff. And Tryn, I think, is pretty strong of faith, even if he isn't a huge fan of the church. I don't know about Sal. And I'm pretty sure Briea follows some Outlands shifter deity. Why do you ask?"

"I told you, because talking—"

"No, I don't want that answer. I was listening the first time, believe it or not. I meant: why ask that question in particular?"

"I was just wondering," Kyrin shrugged.

"Wondering why?"

"Because..." Kyrin faltered, his pale face turning red against the white of the snow and the gray of the sky, "because I..."

"Go on," Brysson prompted patiently, "if you're civil and genuine, thief, I'll be civil and genuine too. I give back what I get."

"Shut up." Faster than thought, the words leapt from Kyrin's mouth.

Brysson sighed, kicking a chunk of black ice down the harsh edge of the narrow gorge beside him. "You know, thief, you are too predictable. I almost thought you were going to surprise me there for a sec, but I guess not. Always the same. No matter what I say to you, I can almost guarantee your response is gonna be—"

"Shut up, all right?"

"And so, you've proven my point."

Kyrin sighed through his teeth, locked in a fierce struggle with his stubborn pride. "Shut up, all right?" he repeated, "I'm trying to... I was just wondering because..."

Brysson said nothing as he picked his way over a stretch of sharp blades made from broken ice, giving Kyrin his chance to speak. Kyrin followed slowly, chewing his lip as he struggled to find his tongue.

"Because... Because I just wanted to know if... Do you think if I prayed, the gods might grant me a second chance?"

Halting in his tracks, Brysson peered over his shoulder at the uncertain figure behind him. "I don't know," he stated after a short pause, "It's not my place to say—I haven't set foot in a church since I left home. It could be that the gods might do it, if they're real. Such a thing isn't in my power though, so they'd have to think of something good."

Kyrin nodded, then coughed quietly. "Whatever. It was a stupid question."

"Not rea—"

"Shut up. It was."

Brysson chuckled and shook his head. "Whatever you say, thief, whatever you say."

Seconds crystallized to become minutes, piling into hours and hours of slow, clumsy hiking down the steep mountain face. Eventually, sheer cliffs and rocky crags turned to long, featureless fields of freshly fallen snow, and while tripping and slipping and sliding became less hazardous, Kyrin found himself falling down far more often. Brysson kept the air warm, but the half-melted slush he left in his wake was difficult for Kyrin to walk through.

In an attempt to keep his spirits up and his mind away from his numb fingers and frozen feet, Kyrin spent his time composing a prayer to ask the gods for help in turning his life around right.

*How does one address a god?* Prayer had never been an important part of Kyrin's life. His father had been far more concerned that his children could recite the principles of enchanting and the elements of magic than he had cared if his sons and daughters knew how to beg the heavens for favors, and then in the Guild, faith was a thing to exploit. There had been a group of professional conmen and vocational charlatans dedicated to preying specifically on the religious.

Lacking any reasonable precedent, Kyrin improvised.

*Uh… Orange-eyed brother in the heavens…*

Was that right? Kyrin hoped so. He had chosen the orange-eyed god because he had looked younger, happier, and a little bit more cheerful than his violet-eyed brother. Plus, if he of the orange eyes had broken the universe, he knew about screwing up and might understand Kyrin's position.

*I'm… er… I know I haven't exactly led the most moral existence, and I'm aware I might not actually have a soul, and I'm guilty of every crime they went and pinned on me and then some, but... All I want is a chance to turn my life around. All I want is another shot—if you give me the opportunity to climb up out of this gutter I've fallen into, I'll seize it. Please, all I ask for is a second chance—just... don't let me go to the gallows. I promise I won't forget it. Um... Yeah. Thanks, and all that.*

"Hurry it up back there, will you?" Brysson called, striding ahead through his stream of half melted snow. Feeling a fool, Kyrin muttered a curse and ran to catch up with the armored space-heater. Prayers would do no good if he let himself fall behind and ended up freezing to death. The gods would only help those willing to help themselves.

The sun inched higher into the sky with every passing hour, but Kyrin could not see it behind the thick blanket of snow-laden clouds. The wind gusted, blowing Brysson's column of snow-melt steam into the open sky.

Kyrin paused, exhausted from the unbroken hours of trudging. The icy gales scoured his face, making his eyes water. His black hair had gone white with accumulated snow, his sharp features were red from cold, and not even the steady, pulsing warmth that flowed from Brysson was enough to thaw Kyrin's pained fingers.

He cleared his throat. "Do you hear that?"

"Hear what? Right now I can't hear anything over the sizzle of evaporating snow." Brysson complained, soaked head to toe in lukewarm meltwater.

"It's not that, it's like... Like a sort of... Whoosh-ey buzzy noise... With kind of a... a ringing, pulsing, magical hum thrown in."

Brysson gave Kyrin a look. "Uh... Could you explain that again? Only this time, try and make sense."

"I am making se—"

The sky turned white. Formless entities with glittering

wings the color of shadows cast on snow darted everywhere. Something bit Kyrin's arm, drinking in the slow trickle of his warm, red blood. With a startled cry, the thief swatted it, beating frantically at the air in his panic.

"Kyrin! Behind me! Now!" Brysson's armored hands sliced the wind, carving swishing tracts of incandescent flame into the frigid winter sky, immolating the creatures that made up the swarm and setting furry white bodies aflame to fall steaming and smoking into the snow. Orange light flashed, painting the thick blizzard with fire.

"What are they?" Kyrin shouted, ducking his head and covering his face with his arms. Tiny creatures, light and fluffy, lacking any eyes or nose or lips, tore at the skin of his hands with pitch-black mouths and needle sharp teeth.

"Snow fey!" Brysson called back, sending his flame dancing through the air to char the translucent wings and blacken the swarm's shifting mass of soft white fur, "Blasted ice fairies! The little demons will eat you alive if you're not careful! They want to drink your blood and drain you dry—mark my words! They're after the warmth!"

"If they want warmth, then give it to them already!"

Brysson grinned, conjuring wall after wall of solid heat with every wave of his fiery hand. "Already on it—hold onto your hair and try not to melt, thief, I won't be holding back."

"Who's melting?" Kyrin nodded, dropping to his belly in the snow and digging in as much as he was able. Perhaps if he stayed low and camouflaged his warmth, the fairies would overlook him, and Brysson could blast them with impunity.

Wave after wave of dry heat rolled over Kyrin as he lay

with his eyes shut on the ground. Dead fairies fell with the snow, a warm, morbidly sparkling rain around his head. A few living stragglers alighted on Kyrin's legs, tearing holes in his pants and nibbling on his exposed flesh so that they could lap up his seeping blood. He shook them off as best he could, and Brysson swept through swath after swath of the swarming horde.

"Hurry it up, will you?" Kyrin peeled a fairy from his arm, wincing slightly as it came away with barely audible squelch. As he held the miniscule bloodsucker in his hand, Kyrin noted with a shiver of revulsion that the fairy's body resembled a child's clumsily made snowman, devoid of all face but a mouth.

"You know how hard this is?" Brysson replied, surrounding himself with a maelstrom fountain of swirling sparks.

"I'm getting chewed up over here!"

"And I'm running out of juice, so chill out!"

"What do you mean you're running out of juice?" Kyrin yelled, raising his head for a moment to shout above the snow.

"There are thousands of the damn things! Now leave me alone so I can do this—I've been playing your damn campfire for the past three hours and what with this blasted blizzard, I'm getting tired!"

"So quit talking and kill them!"

In response, Brysson flared up, encasing his body in a shell of orange fire that hovered an inch from his skin. A brilliant war cry carried the flame out, expanding it into the air to engulf and incinerate the last of the fearful mass. Tiny tufts of smoldering fur drifted down with a rain of fairy glitter, glowing sparks amidst the cotton snowflakes. A dismembered wing fluttered down, brushing Kyrin's frozen cheek with tiny scales of shimmering fairy dust.

Kyrin lifted his head again, wiping the snow from his eyebrows, inadvertently smearing sparkles across his forehead and nose. Slowly, carefully, ignoring the multitude of gently oozing bites all over his body, Kyrin climbed to his feet.

*Is it over? Are they all dead?*

*No—there's one.*

Blackened and bewildered, a single scarred fairy missing half its fur and one of its wings crawled through the partially melted snow. Regarding the creature dispassionately, Kyrin lifted his boot and crushed it, ending its life and its misery.

A sudden wave of compassion washed over him, filling Kyrin with nausea and making him instantly regret his action. The small, pathetic, crippled thing had not stood a chance, but he had crushed it regardless. It had been so easy to kill, so Kyrin had killed it.

*Like father, like son.*

Shoving the thought from his mind, Kyrin walked up to where Brysson lay and knelt beside the Knight in the snow. The man was clearly exhausted—his eyes were dull, hardly open. No warmth flowed from his ashen skin.

Mouth dry, Kyrin prodded the Knight and tried to think up something to say.

"You missed one," the thief eventually managed, "but I squished it for you."

"Oh, you did? Good…" Brysson breathed, "Now, let's get you… Out of this cold… no sense in bringing the hangman a corpse, and… you won't last long… without my fire…"

"Shut up." Kyrin commanded, recognizing the signs of magical overload. He had seen a performer once, a waterworker, who had tried to impress the people of

Alinor with extravagant show at the Fate's Day Fair. After the spectacle, the man had collapsed, and as far as Kyrin knew, he had taken days to wake up again. "Quit talking and just chill, Knight. You overdid it."

"Did not." Brysson's eyelids sank slowly shut. "I'll do... What I want..."

"Listen to me, Brysson, shut your mouth and open your eyes. You need to..."

Brysson showed no signs of hearing. Kyrin poked him again.

"Dammit—Brysson, wake up!"

No response. Kyrin's swore again. This was bad. This was really bad—this was beyond bad. What Brysson said was true—Kyrin depended on him for survival out here in the cold, and with the man unconscious, they would not survive the night. Kyrin had no idea how to get the two of them safely out of the domain by himself.

*Wait half a moment...*

Kyrin moved aside the collar of Brysson's spell-mail shirt, revealing the silver chain that held the Knight's Key. Grinning in relief, Kyrin slipped the pendant over the man's head and held it aloft to read the inscription.

"Know your goal, and I'll show you the way," Kyrin mouthed silently, turning the intricate arrow over in his fingers. The guiding enchantment was simple, yet ingenious. Characters for willpower and courage combined with the glyphs for hero, treasure, and safety worked together to create a spell that would spin the arrow toward whatever place or person the holder kept in mind.

Remembering to offer a quick, heartfelt thanks to the orange-eyed god, Kyrin dangled the Key and pictured Tryn, Briea, Dain, and Sal. Slowly, ponderously, the arrow swung around to point towards the sun.

# Chapter Eight

Placing one foot in front of the other, Kyrin dragged Brysson through the knee-deep snow, leaving a slightly bloody trail in his wake. Physical exertion, continual motivation, the momentous effort of maintaining strength burned Kyrin's mind away and left him with nothing but robotic action.

One foot in front of the other—soon the snow would end.

One foot in front of the other—the Knights would be there.

One foot in front of the other—he could get food and rest.

Until Brysson woke up, until he reunited with humanity, Kyrin's world was one foot in front of the other.

Step after weary step, the criminal hauled the Knight, looking no further than the place his foot would next fall. Things were easier that way. Every time Kyrin saw how far he still had to go, a little part inside of him shriveled up and died. It was better not to look. Things were easier that way.

Every now and again, Kyrin would lower Brysson to

the ground and take out the Key to check their course, but every time he made sure to continue again before his spirit could lose its dead momentum, lose its tired inertia, and let his willpower flag.

Both his life and Brysson's depended on Kyrin catching up to Tryn and the others, so time after time, Kyrin set one foot in front of the other.

When Kyrin finally found the Knights, he was half dead from exhaustion and half sure he was dreaming. Confused faces swam in and out of Kyrin's vision, and his arms and legs felt as though they had been filled with hot lead and left out in the rain. The world seemed to be melting, and Kyrin was tired enough to let it go. He slumped forward, dropping Brysson's prone form as he kissed the snow.

Kyrin awoke an unknowable amount of time later to the sound and feeling of blue. He opened his eyes to see Tryn kneeling over him, a warm hand on his heart and on his forehead.

"Wha're you doin'?" Kyrin mumbled incoherently, struggling to cast off the iron chains of sleep.

Tryn shushed him. "Quiet, I'm healing you. You are going to relax, and then in a minute when I'm done, you are going to explain what exactly is going on."

There was no questioning Tryn's tone. It was an order, and Kyrin did not intend to contest it. He shut his eyes again and let the cool sensation of medical magic wash over him, sealing the fairy bites and soothing his aching muscles.

Tryn withdrew his hands and the magic receded; Kyrin felt energized, awake, and more alive than he had in weeks. He opened his eyes again and sat up, rolling up his sleeve to check the site of a fairy bite.

Nothing remained but an odd, pale ellipse on the skin of his arm, a faint reminder of the terror of the swarm. Kyrin touched the scar lightly. He was completely healed.

"The scar should fade in a few days," Tryn remarked impassively, brushing his hands together and reclining back, "you didn't have any terrible wounds—just a lot of little ones. Now—I want you to explain exactly what happened and exactly how you found us, thief."

Before answering, Kyrin looked around. The Knights had made camp in a dark, coniferous forest on the edge of the snowfield, not at all far from the domain's border. Sal sat within earshot, leaning against a tree's strong trunk as she polished her weapon. Pel tended to the still unconscious Brysson. Briea and Dain were nowhere in sight.

"Well," Kyrin began slowly, "we were walking along, going where we were supposed to go and doing what we were supposed to do, when suddenly a flock of snow fairies comes out of nowhere and tries to eat us. Brysson killed them, but he overloaded himself in the process, so I borrowed his Key and brought him to you. So there you have it. That's the story."

"You took his Key?" Tryn asked sternly.

"Yeah, here it is." Kyrin produced the pendant from the pocket of his jacket, "See? Look at me handing it over peacefully and not claiming it was lost in the struggle or anything. Look at me cooperating of my own free will."

"Why didn't you run off with it?" Sal asked, setting her weapon aside to give Kyrin a penetrating stare, "you could have used it to find anywhere—why did you come back to us?"

Kyrin scowled slightly, "What do you mean, why? Brysson was hurt, I was hurt—I didn't want to die!"

"So you drag him through the snow for miles, just hoping you would find us?" Tryn asked seriously, "That must've taken a lot of determination and spirit, thief."

"Oh, don't make me gag. Would you honestly have healed me if I had left him?"

"Probably not," the Knight admitted.

"So there you have it again," Kyrin concluded. "You happy now?"

"I won't be happy until Brysson is up on his feet again," Tryn stated, "but I'm satisfied."

"When will he be up and about?" Sal asked.

"I don't know. My magic can take care of most physical wounds, but magical overload is a bit beyond me."

"It shall not be very long, with proper care," Pel observed slowly, "and when Dain and Briea return with the herbs I requested, I shall be able to provide that proper care."

"Well that's a relief." Sal returned to polishing her blade. "You sure do know a lot, Pel."

"I spent a great deal of time studying under the Listeners and learning from all who would teach me. The acquisition of knowledge has long been my primary mission."

"Oh, that's nice. I don't know what my primary mission is. I guess it's just to be the best Knight I can be."

Tryn grinned. "And that's why you shall make a fine Knight, Sal."

"What about you, Kyrin?" The brown haired girl tossed the question casually, "What's your biggest goal in life?"

"To live to see tomorrow," Kyrin answered promptly, surprised at having the conversation turned so suddenly to him, "and to live it better than today."

"That's nice. Oh—Mister Pel? Can I ask you a question?"

"By all means, Lady Sal, ask away."

"I never did catch your magename. What do you do?"

Pel smiled. "I am a windweaver; my family has long worked the breeze to drive the landship caravans through the Outland domains."

"Oh, you used to be a caravan runner?"

"Yes, but my control over the wind lacks power, so at an early age, I decided my time would be better spent away from my mother and father and brothers on the caravans. I elected to stay among the Listeners and learn their art."

"That's cool, I guess. I'm glad you did choose that, because otherwise you wouldn't have been here to lend us your aid and everything."

"Indeed. I am glad too."

"So Pel, Tryn… You two knew each other before this, right?"

"Yep." Tryn answered, "We've known each other for years."

"How did you meet?"

"Back in the days when I worked the caravans, we stumbled across Tryn's home village and engaged in some fortuitous, mutually profitable trade. As fate would have it, the Brother Gods saw fit to allow our paths to cross several times since our first meeting, and so friendship was nearly inevitable. The Outlands do not often bring people together, so one comes to treasure the occasion of reunion all the more."

"Yep. And my sheep loved him. And then later on after he ran off to become a monk—"

"A Listener, Tryn, not a monk."

"Whatever. Point is, after he ran off, my sheep would

all try and run off too, to be with him. I've never known two unbound domains to stick so close together, before."

"Wait wait wait—" Kyrin interrupted, staring incredulously at the red-haired Knight, the terror with the mace, "You kept sheep?"

"Yes," Tryn gave Kyrin an amused glance, "I kept sheep. And I was darn good at it, too."

"But—like—sheep? Fluffy, non-sentient, harmless wool puffs?"

"Obviously you've never kept sheep—they're a good bit more than that, even without being shifters. A mother ewe can be properly vicious if she's defending her lamb, for example."

"But *sheep*."

"What's wrong with sheep?"

Sal giggled, "Honestly I couldn't believe you were a shepherd at first, either."

"Is it really that hard to see me keeping sheep?"

"Yes!" Kyrin confirmed, "It kind of is!"

"Would it make it better to know that his sheep were elemental?" Pel offered, hiding his amusement.

"Magic elemental sheep? What did they do—explode?"

Tryn shrugged, "Yeah, sometimes. Or they melted. Except when they hit stuff with lightning."

"You're kidding."

"Nope."

"Your sheep would actually explode."

"Yep."

"I… Shut up. Just shut up. I don't even know anymore."

Sal and Tryn laughed. Even Pel chuckled as Kyrin pinched the bridge of his nose in exasperation.

Before the nonsense could continue, Dain and Briea

returned, bringing with them a bag full of dark, leafy plants the color of emeralds at midnight.

"What's so funny?" Dain asked as he trotted up to join the group, "Did Brysson wake up?"

"No," Briea returned, "but it looks like the thief did."

Pel stood up to greet the pair, "You found the herbs, I trust?"

"Yeah—" Dain brandished the bag, "You were right, I could hear them growing beneath the snow. And Briea had no problem digging them up."

"Good. Bring them here—I shall start preparing the brew immediately."

Dain and Briea handed over the waxy leaves, and Pel began the long and complicated process of creating a medicine from nearly nothing. Sal seemed enraptured by the doctor's art, and Kyrin tried to pay attention at first, but he soon found that the subtle steps and strange machinations of medicine making were entirely beyond his understanding, and he gave up his attempts to comprehend in favor of a good long nap.

"Brysson! You're awake! How do you feel?" Sal's voice cut through Kyrin's sleep like a knife through soft cheese, pulling him out of his dream. He sat up and opened his eyes to see that Brysson had finally done the same.

"What... What happened? What are you guys all doing here?" Brysson mumbled blearily, blinking in the fading sunlight.

"Worrying about you." Briea volunteered unhelpfully.

"I... I thought I was dead." Brysson looked around, taking in his friends' worried faces and Kyrin's still form sulking off to the side. "What happened?"

"You burned yourself out killing snow fey and lost consciousness," Tryn supplied.

167

"Yes, I remember that, but how did I get here?"

Tryn jerked a thumb in Kyrin's direction, "He dragged you here, apparently."

"Wait—what? He... He did?"

"Yep," Tryn confirmed.

Kyrin said nothing, refusing to face the others. It felt wrong, to have saved someone's life. He had not done it for them—he had only done it for himself. He did not want praise, he did not want thanks, he did not want even acknowledgment. Kyrin was a thief, and it was not right.

He could feel Brysson's eyes on the back of his head. He could sense the confusion as his previous role was reconciled with this one, mildly heroic action.

"Oh," Brysson began again after a moment, "alright then. I hadn't expected that."

Kyrin refused to react.

"At least everyone's still alive," Brysson continued. "That's more than I had expected."

"You speak the truth," Pel nodded solemnly, "This could indeed have been much more unfortunate than it is. Now, how do you feel?"

"Honestly?" Brysson stretched as he spoke, "a little bit drained."

"Well, that is to be expected. You may have trouble summoning magic for the next few days, at the least, so I would advise you not overstrain yourself. Your full potential shall return to you faster if you do not rush it."

"Great. So I'm gonna be stuck powerless for a while?"

"I fear that is the case."

"What a pain..."

"Welcome to my life," Kyrin muttered under his breath, not expecting anyone to hear.

Pel glanced at him, but said nothing.

"When do you feel you will be fit to move on,

Brysson?" Tryn asked, ever the leader.

"Actually, now that I'm awake, I feel just—"

"I would advise, Brysson, that you not attempt to travel quite yet. The best course of action would be to wait at least a day until we can be sure you are at least partially back to strength."

"We don't need to wait on me—I'm fine." Brysson protested unconvincingly.

"Listen to the doctor guy, Sparky." Kyrin ordered, staring away out at the falling snow, "I ain't dragging you anywhere else today."

Brysson gave Kyrin a look. "I don't know whether I'm supposed to thank you for what you just did, or punch you for what you just said."

Kyrin shrugged, not in the mood for a debate. The aftereffects of Tryn's magic were wearing off, and exhaustion was once again creeping up on him.

Sal clapped her hands like a schoolteacher, breaking the tension with her forcefully applied joy, "All right, so anyway, I think we could all stand to rest up. I'll start cooking dinner—"

"No!" Tryn and Dain shouted and simultaneously.

"*I'll* make dinner," Tryn stated firmly.

Sal sighed, "Okay, but can I cook tomorrow?"

"We'll see," Tryn conceded reluctantly, "we'll see."


The Knights broke camp at the crack of dawn the next day, ready and eager to face the morning. Kyrin awoke shortly after, just as ready, but rather less eager to confront whatever new danger the sun brought.

He yawned and stretched, and was quite surprised to find that someone had left a chunk of bread and a handful of roasted nuts nearby for him to find. Kyrin looked around. Everyone was busy, bustling around doing other things, yet it seemed unlikely that anyone would leave the food by accident.

Internally shrugging, Kyrin dug gratefully into the breakfast.

A short while later, Brysson approached Kyrin, a stormy look on his face. The flameless fire Knight stood over the thief, his arms crossed over his chest. He cast a dark shadow.

Kyrin raised an eyebrow. "Need something?"

"So I hear you saved my life back there."

"What of it?" This was a conversation Kyrin had never expected to have.

"It means I owe you."

"You owe me nothing."

Brysson considered this. "You're right, there. We'll call it even, then."

"What?"

"You robbed us—well, almost robbed us—and that was a black mark against you, but now you saved my life, and I, at least, consider that grounds enough for redemption."

"Don't joke with me."

"I'm not joking, Kyrin. I'm trying to flamin' forgive you."

"Don't—" his proud, prickly response cut itself short, halted by a thought. Was this not what he had prayed for? Perhaps it was time to let go of some of his hatred. A second chance would, after all, require change.

"Well, don't mention it," Kyrin finished awkwardly, "Th… thank you." The words felt alien on his tongue, foreign shapes, strange in his mouth.

Brysson blinked. "You feeling okay? That fairy dust didn't screw up your brain or something, did it?"

"Shut up," Kyrin growled.

Brysson flashed a grin. "Guess not."

"All right, everybody!" Tryn called suddenly, his strong voice slicing the brisk morning air, "it's time to find your feet and move out! Daylight's wasting!"

Brysson turned, glancing back once before walking away, leaving Kyrin to follow.

Sweet air drifted over the domain's harsh border, bone-white snow ending sharply to give way to the green fields of gently waving grasses and yellow flowers. The morning sun rose slowly, matching the young blossoms and pouring its kindly warmth down into the world below.

Kyrin scowled at the cloudless sky as the Knights and company passed the abrupt transition from winter into sudden spring. Everything was too bright—too cheerful. Kyrin did not know how to cope with the world's intense, ferocious happiness. The flowers waved at him, the sun smiled—it was all too much. The cloying fragrance wafting around the field nearly made Kyrin sick.

The warm breeze whispered softly in his ear, hinting seductively at a lazy, pleasant afternoon stroll. It was almost uncanny, the way words seemed to drift half-formed just beyond the edge of hearing. Kyrin felt almost as if he were trying to eavesdrop on a conversation just out of earshot.

Sal skipped ahead, grinning and spinning in circles out of sheer joy. "This domain is lovely! Everything's so pretty and warm and beautiful—I love it here!"

Briea grinned and shifted her form, exchanging two legs for four to join Sal on a brief romp through the golden flowers.

Tryn laughed, shaking his head at their antics. "If I weren't playing leader, I'd have half a mind to join them."

Pel chuckled, "A lighthearted soul you remain, Tryn, and yet still you always put your flock first."

"Well, some things you just have to do. Anyway, Dain—can you have a word with these flowers and see if they can't give us a heads up on what to expect out here?"

Dain's brow creased as he closed his eyes and made mental contact with the field of endless yellow. "They… won't talk to me," he managed eventually. "I can hear them speaking, but I can't make out the words, and when I ask them a question, they don't answer."

"Well," Brysson shrugged, "no news is good news, right? If they don't answer, then nothing's here."

"Yeah… You're probably right."

"One way or the other," Tryn drew his Key out of his shirt and checked the arrow's direction, "this is the right path, so we have to pass through here anyway, safe and happy or otherwise."

"Indeed," Pel agreed, giving a rare smile, "we should just consider ourselves fortunate that we have been allowed the opportunity to see and traverse such a gorgeous land before our journey's end. I am unfamiliar with this variety of flower, and I am glad to have this chance to observe."

"I'll just count myself lucky if I make it out of this trip in one piece," Kyrin muttered under his breath.

Tryn responded to his comment as if Kyrin had spoken normally, "If you die, thief, you'll die legally at the journey's end. You can count on that."

Kyrin gave a quick, bemusedly puzzled frown. "*If* I die?"

"When you die," Tryn corrected.

Brysson ran ahead to catch up to Briea and Sal as they frolicked. As he passed, he grinned. "You're a thief, Kyrin, but you're our thief now. We won't be letting you get away from us that easily."

The flower field was an ocean of blossoms—nothing but yellow as far as the eye could see. The longer he hiked under the bright blue sky, the more the all-consuming, sweet fragrance made Kyrin want to gag. Thick yellow pollen coated Kyrin's legs up to his knees, clinging to his pants and smearing over his hands and face. No one else seemed to be faring as badly as Kyrin in that respect: all of the Knights had been lightly dusted, but none of them were so thoroughly covered.

Brysson glanced over at Kyrin and sniggered, "You know something, thief? You look almost blond, in this light."

"Shut up," Kyrin commanded, wiping his normally black hair with his hand in a futile attempt to free his head of pollen. He only succeeded in leaving a golden smudge across his forehead.

Sal joined in, laughing, "Seriously though, Kyrin, your hair almost looks the same color as Dain's right now."

Dain, hearing his name, turned around to face the others as he walked. "What about me?"

"We were just commenting on how you and Kyrin nearly match."

"Oh—so we do!"

"Will you all just shut up? Seriously! I thought you all were supposed to be heroes or some crap—is this how heroes act?"

Sal chose to approach the question logically. "Well, we are the Knights of Alinor—or at least squires to the official Knights of Alinor, and that means we are part of a guild of heroes, and this is how we naturally act, so... Yeah!"

"Whatever." To the vast amusement of the other

three, Kyrin increased his pace to catch up to Tryn, Briea, and Pel as they walked ahead.

"Hey—listener guy. Pel. What do you hear?"

Interrupted from his impromptu lecture on botany, Pel sighed and gave Kyrin a look. "Excuse me, boy? What do you need?"

"You're a trained Listener—I want you to tell me what you hear."

"Are you always so disrespectful to your elders and betters, boy?"

"Yes. Are you always so dang condescending? Now just tell me what you hear, will you?"

Pel sighed. "Only the whispering of the breeze, Kyrin. Now, if you are willing, may I continue my conversation? I was midway through elaborating on the various species of sentient plant life I have come across in my studies."

With a glance, Kyrin managed to convey exactly how much he did not care. This was a considerable amount.

"What breeze?" Tryn asked, stiffening slightly and placing a hand on his mace, "I don't hear any breeze."

"Well there's definitely a…" Kyrin looked around. The flowers had stopped waving. The air was still. The whispers continued. "breeze…"

"Knights, to arms!" Tryn roared, his mace practically leaping into his grasp, "Everyone at the ready! Weapons drawn!"

The change was startling. Gone were the happy-go-lucky young men and women—a company of hardened fighters now stood in their place.

Brysson bounded up, his sword held loosely in his left hand. "What's the danger, Tryn?"

"I'm not sure yet," the red-haired man shifted his grip on his heavy mace, "but both of our listeners are on the alert."

Brysson glanced over to where Kyrin and Pel stood, still poised for argument. Kyrin gave an uneasy shrug.

"Dain!" Tryn continued, "What's the status on the flowers?"

"I'm not sure—they're still refusing to talk to me!"

"Blast it," Tryn swore, "I don't like this. Everyone— stay on the alert! I know I don't need to say, but I will anyway: don't let your guard down, and be ready for anything. Literally—anything might happen, and we have to be ready for it when it does."

"Circle formation!" Briea barked the command, "Ears at the center!"

"Ears?" Kyrin growled, concealing his nerves as the Knights made a ring around him and Pel, their weapons bristling out like the spines of a hedgehog.

"She means you," Dain quipped, his blade gleaming silver under the topaz sun.

"I'm not stupid—I kind of realized."

"Then why did you—"

"Just shut up."

"You say that *way* too much," Sal observed, flourishing her sword, clearly antsy and ready to see action.

"So there's no excuse for you not to get the message, girl." Briea snapped, her half-form fur bristling and her clawed fingers flexing, "The thief has said it often enough, and it's true. You need to shut your mouth and pay attention. Focus is the key to survival out here beyond your city walls, and the more you flap your mouth, the more likely you are to get someone—probably yourself—killed."

Sal's voice shrank small as her shoulders hunched apologetically, "Sorry, Briea. I swear it won't happen again. Not until we're all safe and stuff."

"Good. None of us want to have to bury you."

"None of us wants to have to bury anyone," Tryn added.

"Perhaps it would be best if we all walked in silence from this point onward?" Pel suggested, the slight tremor in his voice betraying his calm face.

"There's a thought," Brysson agreed, "I vote we all just shut up for a while. Dain, Pel, Kyrin, if any one of you hears anything out of the ordinary, you know what to do."

"Yes sir, Brysson! As soon as these plants start making sense, I'll let you all know!"

"Indeed, I myself shall stay wary should any otherwise inaudible noise attract my attention."

There was a pause.

"Kyrin?"

"Will you all just shut your damn mouths and let me follow my own blasted advice?"

On that happy note, the Knights shook their heads and adjusted their weapons. As they crept through the endless field of flowers, the brilliant yellow blossoms no longer seemed to possess their pleasant charm.

Pel was the first to fall. One moment, the bearded man walked at the center of the Knights' guardian circle, and the next, he was on the ground, his plain gray tunic nearly hidden by the tall yellow flowers.

Tryn was down beside him in an instant. "Pel! What happened? Are you all right?"

"I... Cannot feel my arms or my legs..." Pel breathed.

"What's wrong?"

"I... I don't know."

"Don't worry, Pel, we'll get you out of here." Concerned, Tryn hoisted his friend over his shoulder and set a new pace, moving quickly to try to escape this frightfully innocent domain at the earliest opportunity.

Not ten minutes later, Sal's legs gave way beneath her as she tried to take a wobbly step forward. It was all Kyrin could do to catch her before she made contact with the terribly solid ground.

"Not Sal, too..." Tryn lamented, his worry showing plainly on his normally easy-going face as Brysson lifted the girl from Kyrin's arms.

"I'm sorry," she said softly, "I'm not sure what happened—one moment, I was okay and then the next..."

"It's all right, Sal." Brysson managed, carrying her carefully, "You'll be okay."

Shortly after Sal succumbed to the pull of gravity, Kyrin fell. As if in a nightmare, he noticed his limbs seeming to grow heavier and heavier as his head seemed to get lighter and lighter. The impossible whispers grew louder.

"Hey, you know," Kyrin began, "I don't feel too... I... I think I might..."

Kyrin's knees buckled slowly. He tasted mud.

Wordlessly, Briea picked him up, set him over her shoulder, and carried him onward.

A hopeless miasma spread over the group as Dain, then Brysson, then Tryn, and finally Briea herself, all followed the other three to meet the cold earth.

*Is this where we die?* Kyrin wondered as he stared blankly at the yellow flowers caressing his face and the blue sky high up above his head. An ant crawled over his hand, but Kyrin could not twitch his fingers to brush it away. He was a prisoner within his own body—trapped once more in the spell of some unseen puppeteer—one who could not be bothered to twitch the strings.

*Did I make a mistake?* Kyrin implored the orange-eyed

god from within the confines of his mind, *did I screw up and waste my last chance?*

Somewhere hidden within the sea of golden blossoms, somebody sneezed. Kyrin focused his willpower and forced his lips to swear.

"You can say that again," somebody—an unidentified voice off to his right—chuckled weakly.

Kyrin swore a second time in wholehearted agreement.

"What do we do now?" A second voice, unmistakably Sal's, gave a plaintive plea.

"Hope and pray, Sal," Pel wheezed, "there's naught left to do but hope and pray."

"And try any other half-plausible idea that crosses our minds," Briea added, "hope and prayer never did much good on its own without action."

A brief silence flitted from person to person, lingering the air until Brysson chased it away with awkward cough.

"So… Anyone have any ideas, yet?"

"The flowers have started to communicate…" Dain offered hesitantly.

"Oh? That's something, at least." Tryn's voice, muffled slightly by dirt, emanated from somewhere off behind Kyrin's left. "They're not getting poetic at us again, are they?"

"No, they're not. They're just… They're laughing at us."

"Oh, again?" Sal said, sighing, "why don't you ever find any nice plants?"

"I do! Remember that cactus back in—"

"Anyway—" Tryn commandeered the conversation before it could get any further off track, "what are they actually saying?"

"It's all pretty hard to make out… Stuff along the lines of… Well… 'wait until you meet the Servants!' and 'wait until you meet the Lord!"

Kyrin swore for the third time. "I liked the poet trees better."

"You're not the only one, there," Tryn agreed, "at least those things made a little sense."

The day faded slowly from brilliant blue to deep, blood red. The silver stars came out, speckling the heavens one-by-one like the first drops of summer rain before a storm.

All attempts at conversation were long dead, killed by overexposure. Sal's cheerful stories had dried up, and when Dain tried to start everyone singing together, no one had been able to muster the heart or will to join him.

Silence reigned. Stillness triumphed. Yellow petals turned to motionless fire in the burning light of the setting sun. Kyrin's eyes began to close of their own accord. His flaming anger had burned down to cold, flat, ash. Seeing no other end, Kyrin reluctantly resigned himself to sleep and to death.

And then he heard the music.

*Boom. thump thump. Boom.*

Hollow, wooden echoes shook Kyrin to the bone, beating a slow rhythm against his heart and mind.

*Boom. Boom. thump thump. Boom.*

The smaller sounds of smaller drums entered the picture as well, pounding quick, complex counterrhythms over, under, and around the massive, mournfully resonating beats. Kyrin's heart fluttered faster, keeping time.

*thump. Boom. thump thump. Boom.*

An inhuman cry rent the air, tearing a hole through Kyrin's psyche. More impossible voices joined the first, changing together in a wild, arrhythmic song.

*Boom. thump thump*—

The voices stopped. Dain screamed.

*Boom.*

A pair of branches shot up from the dark dirt, grasping Kyrin's numb arm in vise-like fingers. Terror chilled his frozen body as another set of grabbing wooden hands—then another and another and another—rose from the churning earth to seize his limp form.

Kyrin cried out, his blood curdling as a misshapen head broke the soil, entering his vision. Knotted branches made a twisted face. Lank, skinny leaves formed a botanic approximation of matted, uneven hair. Mismatched lumps of yellow sap glowed malevolently from among the tangled twigs like cruel eyes, reflecting the dying sunlight.

Kyrin screamed, his voice joining in the chorus of fear as more horrible faces broke free of the soil. Several of the creatures had yellow flowers sprouting from their arms and heads, sinister reminders of the previous peace.

The things pulled their terrible wooden bodies up from the earth, shedding clumps of dirt with every ponderous step. No two monsters were exactly alike; all were different sizes and shapes, grown from malformed wood and marred with a multitude of random protrusions of ancient bone.

Knobby hands and wiry arms lifted Kyrin high above prickly, many pronged heads, and as his own head bounced and lolled about, Kyrin caught fragmented glimpses, nightmarish split-second pictures of the Knights in similar straits.

Two massive plant-things dragged Tryn along, holding his legs and letting the man's head thump unpleasantly along the ground. Kyrin hoped that the crimson gleam he saw was a mere trick of the light and the man's red hair. It couldn't be blood.

A pair of other plant-creatures supported Dain by his arms, pulling the squire roughly along as he struggled to speak with them. Though Kyrin only had a moment to look, he saw the creatures tug Dain in uncomfortable directions, obviously ignoring whatever pleas he made.

A trio of miniature monsters held Sal, carrying the girl along between them like a sack of potatoes. Her wavy brown hair was caught, tangled and knotted around the plants' thorny spines.

Kyrin could not see the creatures that had captured Briea and Brysson, nor could he see how Pel was faring, but from the cries, the shouts, and the screams, he could guess.

The blood red twilight gave way to black night as the plant-men dragged the party further and further into the heart of their floral domain. Slowly, the paralytic agent sealing Kyrin's limbs began to wear off, but the leafy creatures held him tight—Kyrin did not dare to move for fear of accidentally dismembering himself. The wooden fingers gripping his wrists were strong, and the skinny, twisted arms that supported his weight were too firm to fight.

Before long, the stars were all Kyrin could see. There were the silver lights that glowed faintly in the sky above, but the golden stars that gleamed brightly within the tree-beasts' heads were far more worrying. It seemed almost as if the moon was afraid to show her flawless face to view this domain's brutality. Kyrin did not blame her.

Time passed. Kyrin's entire body ached. The strain of being hauled across the domain like an object pulled at his limbs and tore at his mind. His arms were pain, his legs were pain, his midsection was one large chunk of solidified pain. Kyrin closed his eyes and wished to wake up from this nightmare.

Gradually, an eldritch glow, a sickly touch of yellow light began to taint the cold night air. Kyrin's brain began to pulse with the faintly ringing resonance of leaking magic. He raised his head to catch a quick glimpse of the source, and immediately regretted the action. Kyrin could not tear his eyes away.

A great tree towered over the field of flowers like a tumor on the world's face. Glowing bands of sticky yellow sap adorned the tree's trunk, giving its bark a mottled, blistered appearance. Strange dark fruit hung the trees branches. At least, it looked like fruit. A closer glance revealed each lump to be a skull. Kyrin wondered vaguely how many creatures, how many people, had lost their heads to adorn this terrible god of the tree-folk. There were more skulls than he could count.

The savage drums and primal chanting ceased abruptly. The procession came to an halt. A chill crawled beneath Kyrin's skin. The music had been frightening, had set his nerves on edge and jarred his mind, but the silence was worse. It seemed as though the world was waiting, holding its breath for some unknown terror.

Solemnly, ceremoniously, the tree-folk set the humans down on the ground and corralled them into a tight group. Tryn healed what wounds he could, but for the most part the group sat quietly as they were appraised by the lord of the plant-men.

"You have done well, my children," Dain whispered hoarsely, translating the gnarled tree's slow speech, "many heads you have brought me here tonight, and now our soil shall remain fertile and rich—our roots long and strong."

A glad shiver passed among the watching congregation, the rustle of leaves and the faint creak of groaning wood betraying their utter elation.

"Seven, I count. Six shall come to me—"

"Brysson," Tryn hissed softly, "how are those sparks coming?"

"Not good, yet—I'm trying, by the blazes I'm trying, but so far I can't get anything."

"—And one shall remain yours to spread your seed and continue the line, my children." Dain's voice broke as he played the role of translator, his heart revolting against the words his mouth repeated. "Take... take the one you marked as golden. It shall carry your seed."

Dain glanced at Kyrin's pollen-smeared skin. Nauseous, Kyrin stared down at his own yellow-dusted hands. He cursed, spinning around and stealing a dagger from Sal's belt before the girl could blink.

As if on cue, the denizens of the flower field stepped forward to claim their own. Kyrin slashed at them wildly, but his stolen knife was too small to get past their scratching twigs and tearing thorns. The plant-men ripped at Kyrin's skin and clothes, mixing his red blood with their luminous yellow sap. Kyrin snarled, hacking furiously at the plants' leafy, grasping tendrils.

Until his blade broke. The knife jammed into a leering tree man's eye and shattered, splintering into the wood. Four seconds later, both of Kyrin's arms were trapped in the unbreakable grips of two creatures, and another, smaller plant-thing held his legs, keeping Kyrin immobile.

He struggled and thrashed, but the plants were deaf to his curses. Nature's wrath was unrelenting. The Children of the Flowers dragged Kyrin to face their god.

The servants stood woodenly at their lord's roots, offering Kyrin to its mercy. A new tree-man emerged from the waiting crowd. It seized Kyrin's head, sealing his jaw as the great tree ceased tearing at the starry heavens and sent an ancient, gnarled branch to snake down and caress Kyrin's pollen-streaked face with a pale, rose-tinted blossom.

The branch receded slightly, the hum of magic intensifying as the tree's flower shuddered, shedding its petals.

Another plant-man, one taller than the rest, lurched forward on uneven legs, its dark, thorny palms outstretched. The tree-lord shuddered, then bestowed upon the tall plant-man a luminescent seed the size of Kyrin's thumbnail. The priest—for that was what it seemed to be—held the tiny, glowing lump of life up to the sky, presenting its prize to the stars and to the gently swaying tree-people, before slowly advancing on Kyrin.

Kyrin fought to break free of his captor's grasp, but they held him tight—he could not force his mouth open enough to scream. He had no choice but to watch as the plant-priest staggered nearer, brandishing the seed.

His eyes flicked to the Knights. They had been hemmed in, forced back to back within a circle of sentient thorns. At the center, Pel cowered, and Brysson frantically snapped his fingers, struggling to summon a spark.

Paying no heed, the plant-priest halted a mere pace from Kyrin and raised both its hands to the sky. The one appendage held the golden seed, and the other grasped a sharpened stone knife.

Kyrin could not pull away as the priest cut open his shirt and placed the blade's cold tip at the center of his chest. Time seemed to slow. His breath rasped in his throat, ragged with fear.

The gleaming seed flashed, pulsing in time with Kyrin's pounding heart as it bathed the world in nightmarish yellow light, rhythmically heralding Kyrin's death. Slowly, ceremoniously, the plant priest slid the dagger into Kyrin's skin, burying the blade's tip in his flesh and twisting it.

Kyrin screamed.

The Knights shouted, but Kyrin could barely hear them over his own voice. The blood rushing in his ears drowned out their cries.

The plant-thing twisted the knife again, reluctantly withdrawing it.

The seed glowed brighter, a nocturnal sun illuminating the priest's grotesquely solemn face. Shadows danced around the field as the priest raised the seed to the heavens, writhing as the monster slid the point of light into Kyrin's wound and rested its palm atop the bloody smear.

A pulse of corrupted magic surged through Kyrin's body, filling his veins with the bitter twinge of infection. Though his skin knit back together, Kyrin felt as though he were about to die.

A scarlet flash lit up the night. A haze of bitter smoke filled the air. Beneath the chaos, Kyrin heard a lion's roar and the slow-growing crackle of flames, punctuated by crunching wood and snapping bone.

The Knights of Alinor charged. The plant men were too focused on Kyrin. The Knight's assault caught them completely unprepared.

Tryn broke branches, Briea tore through tendrils, and Sal severed stalk after stalk. All the while, Brysson conjured tiny sparks for Pel to fan to strength with his wind magic. Though each could do little alone, working together, the pair coaxed the wooden soldiers to flame.

Their wildfire spread quickly, consuming the yellow flowers and licking at the tree god within moments. The plant people were thrown into disarray, but Kyrin's captors held fast, their glowing amber eyes reflecting the flame with an inhuman hatred.

Hardly pausing, the priest gestured with his blade, signaling the other plant-men to take Kyrin away and hide him somewhere the seed would be safe from the turmoil.

To Kyrin's pain-addled mind, the chaos seemed to slow as the wooden warriors dragged him off, drifting by in nightmare flashes—bursts of fearful lightning. Half-obscured by the smoke, the watery stars seemed to swim and flicker before Kyrin's eyes. Was it just his bleary vision that made the sky seem to ripple and pulse?

The tree-god shrieked. The seed in Kyrin's chest pulsed in time with its lamentation.

One of Kyrin's leafy captors erupted into splinters. Tryn's voice barked some unintelligible order. Flashing swords hacked bloodless hands off wooden wrists. Strong, warm arms took hold, lifting Kyrin down onto a firm, furred surface.

He caught a glimpse of Sal's worried face and Dain's determined grimace as the pair expertly mowed down more of the uncanny horde, their swords flowing like quicksilver through the devilish haze. Sal effortlessly decapitated a particularly tall plant man, while Dain stabbed and dismembered a pair that tried to sneak up behind her.

Kyrin saw Tryn run back, batting distorted forms left and right with his mace as he struggled to reunite with Brysson and Pel. The pair lagged behind, slowed by their efforts to set the field aflame. For every creature Brysson burned, another two rose to take its place. Pel's wind could not spread the blaze fast enough to stifle the swarm. Even as his vision swam, Kyrin saw the swaying sea of botanic murder close around the Listener and the Knight. Tryn was already late.

Kyrin's eyes shut. He nearly slid from Briea's back as the wind picked up its strength, tearing at his hair and face, but he tightened his grip and clung to life regardless. The wind slacked off to the sound of a garbled human scream.

*Windweaver's dead,* Kyrin thought distantly. A flash of orange light seared his closed eyelids. *Brysson, too. I bet they also got Tryn...*

A dark wave of nausea lapped against Kyrin's mind, flipping his stomach and nearly knocking him down behind Briea's pounding paws. The seed in his chest pulsed in time with his fluttering heart, making his blood ache. The black behind his eyes flashed white. The world went muffled, and then mute. Kyrin tasted mud.

# Chapter Nine

Green. Pale, sickly, nauseous green. Kyrin awoke to the sensation of green, although the color was solely inside his head.

He groaned and opened his eyes. The sky was blue. The sun was yellow. Yellow, like the flowers of the—

Kyrin sat up, gasping for air, hideously aware of a constricting pain in his chest.

He looked down, lightheaded, and was sickened. Pale green roots—grasping, earthy tendrils—stretched greedily out from the center of Kyrin's chest, sliding under and over his raw, reddened skin like a needle through cloth. The raised bumps and ridges shone green through Kyrin's aggravated flesh. At the nexus of the vines' sprawl, a vibrant emerald bud erupted from Kyrin's torso—directly over the place where the glowing seed had been planted in Kyrin's body.

His stomach heaved. Kyrin tasted bile.

Ripping his gaze away from his marred form, Kyrin looked around, anxious to see the night's aftermath.

Sal seemed haggard as she sat hugging her knees in the damp grass. Dain paced angrily, and Briea lay on the ground, grooming her fur with her feline tongue. Kyrin scanned the area for Tryn, Brysson, and Pel, and his heart sank—until he twisted around and found them sitting several yards behind him.

At least, Brysson and Tryn were sitting behind him. Pel was nowhere to be seen. Nor, Kyrin noticed, was Brysson's left arm. The scar-faced knight sat despondently in the grass. Tryn crouched beside him, a healing hand on Brysson's truncated shoulder.

"Rest easy now, Brysson. I've done all I can. It's time for you to let your body take over the healing."

Brysson nodded mutely. Tryn patted his back before standing up to face the rest of the group.

"Oh. Thief. You're awake."

Unable to muster a pithy reply, Kyrin took his turn to nod. Tryn stood still for a moment, regarding him coolly. Kyrin could not read his expression.

Dain glanced over. "You see what you've done, criminal? You see what you've done? Those plant things tore off Brysson's arm because of you—Pel *died* because of you—and I want you to think long and hard about—"

"Dain." Tryn's voice was calm and quiet as he stared up at the clear, open sky. "That's enough."

"But—"

"That's enough."

Brysson licked his lips, summoning a soft voice from his dry throat. "I'll be fine, Dain."

"But your arm—"

"It's not worth making a conflict over, here. I can get myself a prosthetic when we get back to the city, alright? I'll be fine. You know I always thought those things were cool."

Dain's face suggested that he was biting his tongue, but he backed off. Tryn stepped forward to examine the parasitic plant embedded in Kyrin's torso. Sal glanced up and joined, rolling her shoulders and shaking her head to shove away exhaustion's fog.

"Are you alright, Tryn?" she asked quietly.

Tryn nodded. "Pel was a good man, but what's done is done. We'll have time enough to mourn when this blasted quest is through."

Sal stood quietly by as Tryn ran a finger lightly over one of the roots growing beneath Kyrin's skin. Kyrin hissed in quiet pain.

"Is there any way I can help?" Sal offered eventually.

Tryn nodded a second time. "Hold his arms."

"Wait—" Kyrin croaked, "what are you—"

"Hold still. I am going to heal you, and I don't need you flailing. Hold him, Sal."

Sal waved a hand, closing her fingers into a fist. Kyrin's arms deadened, his whole body going numb as the puppeteer magic took control and held him still. With movement beyond him, Kyrin became acutely aware of the crawling plant prying its way into his body. He could feel it growing, carving deeper into his flesh.

"My tongue, too," Kyrin managed, made cooperative by pain, "don't let me bite it."

Sal nodded, chewing her lip and pushing back a strand of her tangled hair as she extended her power.

"All ready?" Tryn's voice was flat.

"Yes," Sal affirmed, "I have him."

Kyrin closed his eyes, steeling himself for pain as Tryn laid a cool hand over the grotesque bud and began to work his will.

For a shattered second, the sensation was almost pleasant, a spring breeze blowing through Kyrin's veins, but a moment later the wind tuned ill and Kyrin was blown away with the storm. His blood boiled. His bones creaked. His heart beat as if it were about to burst. Kyrin gasped for breath, unable to scream as Sal held him still. He hoped the pain would fade, would exit his form and leave him healed, but the burning sickness only grew.

"Tryn?" Through the roar of his rushing blood, Kyrin heard Sal's voice waver, "He's getting harder to hold. I—I don't think this is working ."

Tryn showed no sign of hearing, apart from an increase in magical flow.

Kyrin's blood was acid.

"Tryn, I can't—I can't do this—I can't hold him any longer."

"Quiet, Sal. It's working. Just a moment more."

Tryn was wrong, and Sal was right. The last word had hardly left the Knight's mouth before Sal's control broke, leaving Kyrin free to writhe. Tryn withdrew his hand as though he had been bitten, his breath heaving.

Kyrin twitched on the hard ground, whimpering with his eyes squeezed shut as he waited for his body to cease its screaming. The roots pulsed and shivered beneath his skin. Sweat beaded on his brow. Sick, and weak, and angry, Kyrin sat up and forced his eyes open, praying that his willpower was enough to overcome the pain.

In the center of his chest, the green bud bloomed, engorging and unfolding to reveal a broad, pale flower larger than Kyrin's head. Thick, flesh-pink petals tinted with white rested at the center of a web of roots atop waxy, serrated leaves, and the faintly fuzzy eye at the flower's core gleamed a deep crimson—the exact color of blood. Kyrin brushed the center with his trembling fingers and winced. His hand came away red.

"Damn," Tryn swore, "the blasted plant absorbed my magic…"

Sal nodded. "That's what it looks like. What are we going to do?"

Tryn ran his fingers through his hair, sighing slowly. His normally fiery mane was brown with the dust and mud of the road. "I don't know... I'm no botanist. If Pel was here..."

Sal placed a tentative hand on her mentor's arm. "He was a good man. I didn't know him long, but he was a good man."

"That he was." Tryn allowed himself a last sigh before shaking off his grief in favor of duty.

Kyrin nearly blurted out a callous, poorly-conceived comment, but he caught the statement before it could leap from his tongue.

*No reason to make them hate me more...*

"Yeah," Kyrin said aloud, his voice infuriatingly weak, "a good man. Knew a lot about plants. Like the plants that attacked us. Like the plant in my skin right now. Like the plant we now have to deal with. Can we focus on that, again? What are we going to do?"

"I don't know," Tryn admitted, "but what if Dain said is true—"

"What did Dain say?" Kyrin interrupted.

"He spoke to your plant while you were out, and said—"

"It isn't *my* plant."

"Well, it's in you. Regardless, he spoke to it, and managed to gather the revelation that the thing—and those other things earlier, too—are parasites. What they do..." Tryn licked his lips, pausing slightly to emphasize his distaste, "They have a knack for planting seeds in animals. Those plant monsters essentially saw you as a walking bag of prime fertilizer with a built-in trellis."

"Joy," Kyrin muttered, refusing to be sick.

"Yes. And my magic only helped it grow faster. The thing is, we can't pull it off you without... Well, without ripping off half your skin and maybe tearing out a lung."

Kyrin swore under his breath. "Alright... So. You're saying I'm going to become one of those things, right?"

*Remain calm. Stay cool. Deep breaths*—a distressed outburst would do him no good here.

"No," Tryn answered bluntly, "one of those things is going to grow into you and use your bones for structural support while you die a slow and agonizing death."

"Ugh," Kyrin groaned, taking refuge in immaturity, "kill me now."

"We might just have to, thief." Tryn's tone was nothing if not sobering.

"Kyrin," Kyrin corrected, his voice breaking slightly, "My name is Kyrin. I'm not 'thief,' I'm not 'boy,' I'm not even 'Shadow.' I am Kyrin and..." *and I want to live*, "And if you intend to kill me, I will die under my own damned name."

Tryn shook his head slowly, and walked away.

"Wha—where's he going?" No snappy retort? No scathing sarcasm? No pathetically veiled insult? Alarmed, Kyrin forced himself to sit up and watch Tryn depart.

Sal sat down a few feet away from Kyrin. "A walk, I think. He does that sometimes."

"And what are you doing?"

"I'm sitting here. Why—is there a law against it? And don't say yes—I know you want to."

Kyrin bit back the syllable forming on the tip of his tongue, quickly replacing it with another. "Fine," he sighed, not having the energy for a sharpened conversation, "you got me."

Sal offered a tentative smile. "It's not hard to predict when I know you're just as sarcastic as the rest of us. Especially not when I set myself up like that."

"Yeah, you were walking right into that." It felt odd,

Kyrin mused, to speak without bladed words. But, for the first time, he realized: not everyone was like Rat. Not everyone began conversation with the intent to tear him down. Not everyone viewed communication as a means to ensure someone's unpleasant end. Sometimes, talk was just... talk.

Oblivious to Kyrin's internal epiphany, Sal continued her innocent attempt at socialization. "Yes, I was. I'm glad I caught myself."

After such danger, such turmoil, this mundane conversation felt otherworldly. Kyrin could almost ignore the twisting pain in his gut. "It would have been stupid of you not to."

"You like that word, don't you? Stupid, I mean. You sure do use it a lot."

"That's because I'm often stuck in the company of stupid people doing stupid things stupidly."

Sal's expression fell as Kyrin's barbed tone swept away their progress toward civil conversation.

"What I mean to say," Kyrin corrected quickly, wondering what exactly it was that he meant to say, "what I mean to say is that back when I was around the Guild all the time... around that idiotic, illiterate, barbarous horde of half-wit heathens, they didn't understand advanced terminology like 'obtuse,' or 'irrationally irrelevant,' so I had to dumb things down so that they could grasp the full depth of my indignation and be properly offended. And thus, everything became 'stupid.'"

"That's the other thing," Sal mused, halfway chucking, "you sure know a lot of big words for a commoner."

Kyrin raised an eyebrow, his voice regaining a hint of its former flint, "and you should really have more class if you're supposed to be some kind of rich noble's kid."

Sal flushed. "Oh, please. As if you're one to launch a

lecture on manners and grace. Next thing I know, you're going to be attempting to teach me morality."

"Now what's that supposed to mean?" Kyrin narrowed his eyes. The old walls were coming back up. Hostility made its return.

"It means you're a known criminal who robbed us and is only alive because Tryn thought you might be useful. It means that you've proven yourself immoral and can't realistically think yourself good. You've shown me no redeeming qualities."

"Shut up."

"There you go again," Sal sighed, "and for a moment I thought we might actually get somewhere…"

"Shut up," Kyrin repeated, "shut up and stop trying."

"Why?"

"Because it's stupid."

"Why is it stupid?"

"Because I'm dead anyway," Kyrin spat, "Quit wasting your time."

Sal frowned slightly as she brushed a runaway strand of hair from her face. "You can't really believe that?"

"Shut up." Kyrin fumed. He had already said too much.

"No, I won't. I just want to understand, Kyrin. I want to know why you're so angry all the time."

"Because I'm a damned bastard. Deal with it."

"So you believe those words?"

"Shut up."

"Do you want to die?"

"Shut up."

"Maybe…" the soft light of pity entered Sal's face, "Maybe you feel you don't deserve to live?"

"Shut the hell up!" Kyrin's anger flared. He regretted it instantly, as his outburst made the pain in his chest spike.

He doubled over, his forehead nearly touching the grass. "Just go away," Kyrin commanded through clenched teeth, "Leave me."

Sometimes blunt truth hurt worse than any insult. Worst of all, Sal sat there anxiously, devoid of all intent to harm.

"I'm sorry," Sal's gentle apology was another knife in Kyrin's heart, "I should have realized that was the wrong thing to say... Can you forgive me?"

Kyrin lifted his head to look the girl in the face as he painfully clutched at his flower. "It doesn't freaking matter. If this doesn't kill me, you all will. It doesn't matter. I was dead from the beginning."

"That's not true, Kyrin—there's still hope. We can find a way to save you, if only you're willing to change. We hardly know you, but I think you're more than you let on. Please, I only want to help you."

Change... there was that word again. Hadn't Kyrin wanted to change? Did he want to live?

*Yes. Yes I freaking do.*

"I..." Kyrin licked his lips, clenching and unclenching his jaw as he struggled to gain control of his voice, of his will, of his being. "I... I do want to change. By the Brothers, I'm ready to change."

Sal's face froze in surprise, before breaking into a broad smile. Evidently the answer she had wanted to hear was not the one she had expected. "If you're willing to try and change, then there's still hope," she nodded as she spoke, attempting reassurance, "If—"

"Sal, we're setting up camp. I need you to go find firewood. Dain's foraging." Briea's interruption came like a gift from beyond, freeing Kyrin from a conversation he was not ready to face.

"Yes ma'am, Briea." Sal stood slowly, giving Kyrin one

last look. "And you—don't worry, I won't forget this conversation, Kyrin."

"I am so relieved," Kyrin muttered as she left, keeping the spirit of sarcasm alive to the end. It was easier to fall back on the established pattern than it was to embrace the new future.

Which, Kyrin realized, was weak.

He sat in the fresh, clean grass, biting the inside of his cheek as the Knights went their separate ways. Kyrin's finger brushed against the serrated edge of the leaf planted into his chest, his thoughts elsewhere.

*What is strength? What is weakness? Strength is what it takes to survive, and so far I've survived. That means I'm strong, right? That means I'm tough. I can take care of my own damned self, but...*

Kyrin stroked a slightly furred, flesh-pink petal with his thumb, thinking back to his cheap room in the city, his partnership with Rat, and his servitude to the Faceless. Kyrin recalled the long hours spent researching wards and staking out buildings, the sleepless nights spent fretting over money and the long days spent dodging the Dogs and avoiding his debts.

That was no life. It was survival, but it was no life. Kyrin wanted to fly—but sustained freefall was the best he could manage. A heart as cold and hard as stone was just as heavy.

*I'm done surviving. I want to thrive.*

"If I get out of this," Kyrin muttered under his breath, "if I make it, I'm gonna go home and get outta my pit. Been saying that for years, but I'm gonna do it. If I make it home..."

"Sucks, doesn't it?" Brysson's oddly calm voice cut through Kyrin's melancholy, bringing his mind back to the present.

"What?" Kyrin turned around to face the man.

"I said 'sucks, doesn't it?' this whole mess, I mean."

Kyrin paused, then nodded once. "Yeah... Understatement, though."

"Hell yes. I'm beginning to think I might've been better off sitting this adventure out, what with the way my luck's been going."

Kyrin glanced again at the empty space where Brysson's arm used to be. "Only beginning?"

Brysson chuckled slightly, and for a moment, Kyrin saw pain in his face. "Yeah, only beginning. I'm fairly used to hardship, but even as a merc I didn't fare this badly."

"You mentioned before, but I never got the chance to ask... You were a mercenary?"

"Yeah, before I was a Knight. I'd wander and set fire to things for money. Exciting times..."

"You sound like you miss it."

"Like hell I do. The best day of my life was when I met the group that helped me finally chase down the city. If I'd had ended up anywhere like here on my own, I'd be dead, not just broken. It's good to have friends to watch your back. Safety in numbers, y'know?"

Kyrin nodded. "Same thinking in the Guild... A band of thieves gets richer faster and lives longer than a loner."

"I'll bet. But when we nabbed you, your buddy seemed awfully quick to stab you in the back."

Kyrin swore at the memory. "Rat's a bastard."

Brysson laughed, but cut himself off with a wince and a rueful curse. "Tryn's good, but it seems not even his magic can take this blasted pain away..."

"At least you got healed."

Not looking at Kyrin's flower, Brysson nodded. "Yeah... Guess that's true. Gonna take some getting used to here, though. But I bet I'll save a fortune in gloves."

"I'll bet..." the two trailed off into calm silence, until a nagging thought sprouted in the back of Kyrin's mind. He cleared his throat awkwardly, uncertainly biting his lip.

Brysson raised his scarred eyebrow. "Got something you wanna say?"

"Shut up," Kyrin blurted automatically, "I... I... I wanna pay you guys back somehow."

Brysson's other eyebrow shot up to join the first. "Pay us back? What exactly do you have in—?"

"Shut up, I... I don't know, I... Look, I know a lot of this is probably my fault, but..."

"Go on."

"And... well, I'm done. My life ended years ago, but I'd like to start again, if I can get the chance, so... I know a thing or two about enchanting and crap—if I survive this... I can help design you a prosthetic the like of which no one's ever seen."

"Excuse me?" Brysson said, staring blankly.

"I mean it—I've cracked every form of ward under the sun—I know how enchantments work, and I know how they fit together. I could—"

"You're just trying to bargain your way out of a hanging, aren't you?" Brysson seemed almost sad, "You're trying to sell yourself as useful so I'll campaign to help save you, right? Man, I get not wanting to die, but don't—"

"Shut up—I'm serious." Kyrin's face burned, "I mean it. I'm not lying, and... while you're not exactly wrong... I do want to make things up to you all somehow. I... I'm sorry."

Brysson said nothing, allowing a long moment to pass with Kyrin silently cursing his own stupidity. At last, the man's face unfroze, a slight smile cracking through his features. Brysson closed his eyes and lowered himself back onto the grass. "If we make it out of this trip alive, Kyrin, I'll see you get a shot at leveling our debt before the hangman gets ya. So don't worry too much about that."

"Yeah... No problem. Instead I can just devote all my worry to this blasted flower in me."

"Yep. That's about the shape of it. But we'll figure something out."

Before the conversation could progress, the others returned, bringing food and firewood. Brysson moved to help Dain set the fire, and was told to sit back and relax. With Sal's aid, Tryn began to prepare a grim, simple meal, and Briea lounged back in her human form, cleaning her nails.

When preparations were complete and everyone sat around the campfire with their simple, scavenged fare, Brysson cleared his throat.

"So, Kyrin, how 'bout you tell the others what you told me?"

"What nonsense is the thief speaking now?"

"Shut it, Dain," Briea snapped, fed up with her squire's bitterness, "If you have to hate him, do it out of earshot. I would like to relax this evening."

Dain grumbled an assent, poking the fire glumly as Kyrin coughed, suddenly self-conscious. His face burned as he struggled to wrestle his tongue into line.

"Well... I just wanted to say, I... It... I don't know if I had any effect on what happened with the witch thing or not, but... I broke into your place, and you let me live and kept me alive and all I've given you in return is a bad attitude."

"Truth."

Ignoring Dain, Kyrin continued the slow and painful

process of swallowing his pride. "I'm done. As a kid, I always used to dream on going on an adventure with the Knights of Alinor, but now that it's come true, I insisted on making it a nightmare. I don't want to do that anymore. I don't want to make myself and everyone around me miserable, and I'm tired of being dead weight. If I don't go and end up flat-out dead, I want the chance to repay you guys. I can design a prosthetic enchantment—I can fix your lock—whatever. Just… just give me a shot."

Dain sneered. "How do you expect to do that without magic, thief?"

Kyrin bit back an insult. "I expect to do it with that thing called *skill* and that other thing called *intellect*. Ever heard of them?"

"You know, thief—saying things like that after your whole speech about change—hypocritical much? You honestly think that we're going to fall for your sympathy spiel? How dumb do you have to—"

"Both of you, if you don't quit your bickering I'll bang your heads together!" Although her throat was human, Briea's growl was no less than threatening. Kyrin bit his tongue, giving his self-control some exercise.

Tryn spoke slowly, his voice a quiet rumble. "Dain makes a good point, thief, despite his attitude. Where does a Guildsman—especially a Guildsman with no name to speak of—get to learn about designing enchantments? I doubt your Faceless cared to spend the time to educate you, as you are—putting it bluntly—functionally worthless."

"Shut up." The instant response was nothing more than a quick bid for more time to think of something better.

*Change, Kyrin. Remember, you're trying to change…*

"The Faceless taught me nothing. Everything I know, I learned… before."

"Before?" Sal's face held the kind of careful innocence that masked a burning curiosity.

"Yes, before," Kyrin repeated, attempting to keep the condescending irritation to a minimum. "I wasn't always a blasted criminal, Knight. Just like you all weren't hatched from eggs in full armor."

The scar-faced Knight raised his remaining hand, wearing an expression of mischief. "We-ell—"

"Shut up, Brysson."

Dain cleared his throat, apparently determined not to rest until Kyrin had spilled his guts. "This still doesn't explain how you—a… a shadow of a criminal—think you can design an enchantment better than a professional who's been trained from birth to—"

"Don't you get it, Treetalker? I was freaking trained from birth—I couldn't do it because I don't have a flamin' speck of magic—but I learned the freaking trade. I was supposed to be an enchanter, dammit—I was supposed to—" Kyrin bit his lip, cutting off the anger before it could bring tears. This was not the path to change. Kyrin took a deep breath, calming himself enough to continue his sentence. "I wasn't supposed to end up on the streets."

The Knights exchanged glances, preserving a moment of fragile silence. Briea took the moment, snapping it in two with her gruff voice.

"Sounds like you have a story, kid. Care to tell it?"

"Don't call me kid," Kyrin grumbled, "Your puppeteer put all that effort into finding my birth name—now you may as well use it."

"Kyrin…" Sal's kindly expression seemed patronizingly sweet. "Will you tell us about your life?

Please? We've come this far together—you should know by now that we really do have your back, and I should hope I'm not wrong in saying I think you have ours, too. I won't force you this time, but... I would like to hear what you have to say, if that's alright."

The old, bitter voice in the back of Kyrin's mind chuckled. *Have my back? You mean you have my neck, more like.*

Kyrin ignored it, instead heaving a heartfelt sigh. "Fine. You want—I'll sing. Not a happy song, though. Fair warning."

"Hey, you know what," Brysson interjected, forcing a slight smile as he massaged his left shoulder, "I don't know anyone whose song is all happy. I mean look at me—my life was hardly roses all the time, even before I took up arms against the monsters." The man paused suddenly, as if struck by his own words. "Take up arms... Man, I almost feel obligated to make some kind of pun, now."

Sal was the first to giggle. "Only you, Brysson. You're the only one I know who would make a joke like that."

"What can I say? I'm one of a—"

"Guys want me to talk or what?" Kyrin interrupted, self-consciousness making him prickly. Dain looked as though he were about to make some snarky comment, but Sal hushed him.

Briea gave Kyrin a cool, appraising stare. "Up to you, boy. You decide your own fate here, now. How badly do you want that shot of yours?"

Kyrin's mouth went dry. "More than you could ever know."

"Once upon a time," Kyrin began slowly, vacantly prodding the campfire with a stick as he gathered his thoughts, "Once upon a time, there was a very ambitious man named Caesar Spellcrafter, who was bound and determined to move up in the world and see his bloodline head the Enchanter's Guild. He was a cold man, focused and distant, and his work was—and still is—among the best the city's ever seen. I... he used to be my father, though I don't think I was ever really his son.

"See, my siblings, they were prodigies. By age nine, both Kai and Ciannia were already better than most of the wardweavers on the streets, and little Cerra... I remember how proud Father was when he came home to find her chalking spell lines on the nursery floor. But me..." Kyrin trailed off, staring into the darkness beyond the fire, "I was nothing more than a dark stain on his otherwise pure bloodline. I would hear him sometimes— shouting at Mother. Asking her how she could have borne a child with no soul... how... how their union could have produced an abomination like me. If my face hadn't been so like his, I'm sure he would have thrown my mother out for adultery...

"'We're ruined,' he'd say, 'if word gets out that the Spellcrafters brought this taint into the world, we'll be cast down to grovel with the peasants and the scum of the streets. If the Enchanter's Guild hears about him...'"

Kyrin broke off, shaking his head with sudden energy. "My father was a bastard. An ignorant, power hungry bastard unfit to see the sun. But I was the bigger fool—I wanted him to... to be proud of me..."

The Knights exchanged an uncomfortable glance as Kyrin's voice broke, but he had come too far—the dam of emotions had burst, and there was no way to stop the rushing flood of boiling words. Kyrin could only clear his throat and start again.

"I wanted him to look at me the way he looked at

Kai—in his eyes, my brother was potential personified—glowing achievement molded into human form. But me... Father took less notice of me than he did of the shadows in the corners of the house.

"Didn't matter how hard I worked, either. Every day I'd rise with the sun—open my book to catch the first few rays of dawn and study 'til my head felt fit to split. I'd copy glyphs until my wrists were sore and my fingers were raw—I'd memorize all the texts in the library—practice the language until I forgot how to speak Common, then when night fell, I'd go until either the candle melted or I did. I'd dream of enchanting—that I weaved a ward unlike any other, that all my study finally paid off and turned to skill, but when I woke up and tried again..."

Kyrin shook his head again, closing his eyes against the fire's orange glow. The Knights watched, almost startled by this rare vulnerability from their captive.

"He didn't want to see me," Kyrin continued obliviously, "Wouldn't look at me. When my family went out, they claimed I was sick so that they wouldn't have to take me with them, so I studied harder, pushing myself further to try and be like my siblings, yet... One day—it was raining. I was eleven. Cerra and I were practicing together—I was helping her learn her glyphs and understand the symbols, when Father came to us. I thought he wanted to speak with Cerra—I was completely prepared to just fade into the background like usual, but... He smiled. Said we could go together—wanted to bring me working with him like he sometimes took Kai. I jumped at the chance—dreams come true...

"The rain'd turned to storm. It was my first time away from the house. I remember—silver puddles were everywhere, lit by the white hot lightning and the cold, glowing magelights. I couldn't hear the city over the rain's hush. Father walked in front, his hat shaping his dripping silhouette. I followed behind, wet and chilled, but... happy. I was happy, dammit.

"Father led me to the docks—the wooden boats were all slick with water, groaning and creaking with the wind and waves. The air was nothing but salted mist. We were in a world of our own, a little domain just for Father and me... Alone with the ships. We were supposed to go patch up a sea-safety charm that was wearing down, but... Splash. One quick shove off a slippery dock on a rainy night, and all my family's problems were solved. Father knew I couldn't swim..."

Kyrin had to pause, had to sit and breathe and recover his strength. When his voice returned, it was small and distant.

"For a long time, it was just darkness and noise and water. I knew I was dying, but... somehow I found the shore. I woke up on a beach, alone with the salt and the sand. When I pulled myself together enough to drag myself home, I... I saw my family going on an outing. All of them—smiles and laughs. Even little Cerra..."

Kyrin's voice cracked, shattering again as he fiercely scrubbed the dampness from his eyes. Sal moved to place a comforting hand on his shoulder, but he shook her off.

"Don't," he warned, "I don't want your pity—I don't want your sympathy, I'm not telling you this to make you feel bad for me, I... I just want you to understand where I come from. But I don't want your pity."

Sal nodded, biting her lip as she withdrew her hand. Kyrin took a deep breath and resumed his narrative.

"Anyway... after that, I saw I needed to make my own way in the world. Carve my own path or whatever the hell you wanna call it. Tried to find a job, but when you have no trade, no skill, no power, are too small for manual labor and technically too old for a proper apprenticeship anyway... Not much left in the way of options besides falling in with the Guild. So that's what I did. Gave up my name to the Faceless in exchange for a bit of Guild 'protection.' Used all those wasted hours of study to break and enter and take and leave. Can't make wards, but I sure as hell know how to destroy 'em.

"Wasn't worth much, though. Faceless has other wardbreakers. Might not know as much as me, but they aren't freaking cripples. Nameless guy like me—liability. Kept on outskirts with the Guild's scum. Partnered with Rat, the pathetic little bastard. Stole what I could—good half of what I got went to pay the Guild's tax—most of the rest got stolen from me to pay Rat's, and the last bit... Food and rent and... I... I was saving up for a place of my own—somewhere the roof doesn't leak, where I don't have to pay rent. Saving to start a new life in a new place where it doesn't matter if I don't have magic..."

Kyrin lifted his face, addressing all of the Knights in turn. "That's why I busted into your place. Not even so much 'cause of the money, but... Just wanted my name to be worth something. Wanted people to look at me and see a man rather than some soulless shadow. I..." Kyrin broke off again, sighing as he flopped back onto the grass. "I'm an idiot."

His face felt hot, burning with embarrassment and shame as he stared defiantly up at the sky, waiting for the laughter, the derisive chuckles and snarky comments to arrive and stab into his heart alongside the flower's stabbing roots, but the pain never came. Instead, Kyrin was greeted by an awkward cough from Dain.

"You're... Cerra's brother?" the blond squire asked

slowly.

"Yeah," Kyrin propped himself up on one elbow to view the other young man. "What—you know her or something?"

Dain nodded, seeming off balance. "Yeah, she's... a good friend of mine. Once... I remember her telling me about you, actually... she told me that you drowned in an accident."

Kyrin blinked, emotionally numb. "Oh."

"You know," Dain continued, "I thought you seemed familiar... Now that I know you're related... The resemblance is certainly there."

Unsure how to react, Kyrin nodded once. It was as if his world had been shattered around him and glued back together in a different, unfamiliar shape. He could hardly make sense of the new angles and reflections.

Dain nodded vaguely as well, seeming to be in a similar state. An awkward silence took up residence between Kyrin and the Knights.

Sal broke the pause with a bright smile and a cheery handclap. "Well, this is an interesting development," she declared, using her voice to prompt the others back in the direction of social interaction, "our thief is really the long-lost son of one of Alinor's most prestigious enchanters, and our favorite young lord is friends with his sister. What next?"

"Maybe we'll find out that the plant things stole my arm in an effort to magically grow my dark twin," Brysson supplied, refusing to let the air of absurdity die.

Briea ignored him, kicking off her boots as she supplied, "What we do next is recover. We stay put until we're fit enough to get on with our quest, and we'll wait to worry about the rest until we know we'll be around to see it—agreed?"

"Neither of those were quite the response I was looking for," Sal laughed, "but I suppose that works! Right, Tryn?"

The red-haired knight shrugged blandly. "Right. No point guessing about the future until we're there."

"No point fretting about the past, either," Brysson interjected, passing Kyrin a slight, companionable smile, "Last I checked, it was all behind us."

The rest of the day passed slowly. The sun inched by overhead, drifting lazily through the zenith, past the afternoon, and down into a calm evening. As the daylight flared and faded to the cool blue tones of night, Kyrin and the others settled down to sleep.

Though the stars shone brightly and the moon poured its silver light all across the slumbering world, Kyrin slept, locked in a personal darkness all his own.

*Hideous plant men lurched and staggered through a field of yellow flowers, cackling with Rat's voice as they poked and prodded Kyrin's paralyzed form, threatening to tear him to pieces. The world spun nauseously, flipping end over end and lurching in time with the plant people's awkward gait. Every moment brought Kyrin closer to their wooden god.*

*Kyrin's father stood calmly on the stump of the giant tree, his eyes cold and mirthless as he regarded his captured son. Kyrin tried to scream, but his voice was as strong as his magic—nothing passed his lips, save for empty air. Caesar Spellcrafter nodded once, and a plant man stepped forward, its head as smooth and white as bone. The faceless thing lifted a jagged stone knife, and—*

Kyrin sat up suddenly, gasping for air as he pulled himself out of the nightmare and into the waking world. The roots embedded in his chest twinged. Hissing in pain, Kyrin doubled over and cursed all things green.

Dain glanced over, his pale face reflecting oddly in the

orange firelight. "Having a hard time sleeping?"

Kyrin nearly snapped at him with the obligatory demand for silence, but he caught himself at the last moment, choosing to nod instead.

"Yeah, something like that." Casting around for something to say, Kyrin's gaze skimmed over the sleeping Knights. Tryn lay on his back, dead to the world. Briea was a gently breathing mass of golden fur curled up off to the side. Sal rested a few feet away, her hair splayed around her face. Even Brysson seemed to have found easy sleep, resting as he was with his remaining arm folded beneath his head for a pillow.

"So," Kyrin eventually began again, shifting closer towards the fire, "How's the watch going?"

Dain shrugged. "Well, not bad. Same as ever. Dull, really. Though I did see a rabbit about ten minutes ago."

"A rabbit?" Kyrin asked, giving civil conversation his best effort.

"Yeah. Little fellow hopped by in a hurry, as though he were late for something important."

"Off to see the queen, I'll bet."

"Yeah," Dain chuckled, "I'll bet that's it."

The conversation lulled to a gentle halt, the silence friendly for once, rather than awkward. After a moment, Dain cleared his throat.

"So... Kyrin... About earlier—I'd like to... you know—apologize. I was being rather... unreasonable."

Kyrin shrugged, shaking his head. "Nah, I... your angle made sense. I deserved what I got."

"All the same," Dain replied, scratching his head as he carefully avoided confirming or denying Kyrin's statement, "What happened to Brysson—to Pel... Awful, but... I was wrong to blame you."

Kyrin absorbed this in silence, absentmindedly

rubbing at the sore skin around one of the many intruding roots. The treetalker was being civil—friendly, even. Compared to his earlier mood, the contrast made Kyrin wary.

"Is this because of my sister?" Kyrin asked eventually, confident that he had pinned down the squire's motivation, "You mentioned you two were friends."

Dain blinked. "Wha—no, no. Well—kinda… But what I say is true. I was being unfair. The whole sister thing is just… a point in your favor, I guess."

Kyrin couldn't help but give a wry chuckle, though a moment later he wished that he had resisted. Within his chest, beneath his skin, the pale flower's creeping roots revolted at the motion of their host, hurling green wires of pain through each of Kyrin's veins. He sunk to the ground, his forehead touching earth as he gasped for air and held his chest, vainly grasping the fleshy leaves.

In an instant, Dain was by his side. He placed a hand on Kyrin's shoulder, doing what he could to soothe and steady the injured criminal.

"The flower—are you…?"

Kyrin nodded, wiping his mouth with the back of his hand as he forced himself upright. His skin was smeared with crimson. Dull surprise dripped into his heart. Kyrin brought a hand to his lips. His fingers came away red.

"I'm dying," Kyrin observed, oddly detached. "You think I'll live to see the next sunrise, Dain?"

"Okay, look," Dain moved so that he was facing Kyrin directly and took a firm hold of the thief's shoulders, attaining more emphatic eye contact, "you finally convinced me that maybe—just maybe I'd misjudged you. Maybe I was wrong—maybe the reason you haven't betrayed us or sabotaged the quest isn't because you're just a spineless coward—"

Kyrin's eyebrow twitched at this, but he held his tongue.

"—but because you're really just a decent guy in a bad place. Now, I've decide to consider that—so you're not allowed to die until I can prove one way or the other, you hear?"

Kyrin sat still, as if struck, before slowly nodding and wiping his mouth again.

"I hear," he echoed, unused to concern on his behalf, "but... what I want... somehow, I doubt this flamin' plant gives a—wait. Treetalker, this thing is a plant."

"Yes, I can see th—"

"Talk to it."

For a moment, Dain seemed confused. "Wha—but I already did! When you were asleep, I—"

"Do it again."

Shrugging slightly, the blond Knight closed his eyes, focusing his power. Kyrin's ear caught the faint ring of magic resonating in the air. The thick, waxy leaves growing on Kyrin's skin rustled faintly in a nonexistent breeze.

Not five minutes later, Dain opened his eyes.

"Well?" Kyrin asked instantly, ignoring the thick dizziness that swelled to lap at the edges of his psyche, "What did it say?"

Dain blinked a few times, forcing himself to adjust back to the rhythms of human conversation. "It's annoyed. Wondering why it can't feed on your magic. It says that tradition dictates the weakest head joins the garden, but this is disappointing."

"Ha." Kyrin's bitter, humorless bark was only a laugh in name. Twisted though it was, the flower's dilemma appealed to Kyrin's sense of irony.

"It says it's having trouble growing, and it wants you

to go to Tryn again so it can steal the magic that's supposed to be healing you."

"Does it now? Well you tell the little weed that it can shrivel up and burn."

Dain twitched an approving smile, nodding as he closed his eyes to convey the message. In response, the delicate web of roots shifted uncomfortably within Kyrin's body. Dain's brow creased in confusion. Kyrin frowned, concerned.

"What the hell's this thing doing?"

"It... wants you to burn, too," Dain replied hesitantly, "it says it doesn't mind the fire, and... No, I'm not repeating this."

"Tell me."

"Its... No, I can't. It's gruesome and unpleasant and we should leave it at that, alright?"

"No. Tell me," Kyrin commanded, his jaw set. Shrugging helplessly, Dain complied.

"Alright. Well, don't blame me, but the flower... It's going on about how it wants to see your burn—feel the fire's warmth, your... charred flash, seared skin... How it wants to grow over your blackened bones and climb towards the sun... can I stop now? It's going into a lot of detail with some pretty vibrant imagery, and I don't find it terribly pleasant."

Kyrin nodded once, his brain unfortunately full of pictures concerning his own grisly demise. Talk like that... it reminded him of Rat. That man had a love of the details—the more uncomfortable, the better.

Come to think of it, the bastard had a lot in common with this flower: the both of them were awful parasites who liked to get under Kyrin's skin and bleed him dry. Both of them were unwanted and brought unnecessary pain to the world, and both of them made Kyrin angry.

If it weren't for Kyrin's skill as a wardbreaker—

*Wait half a moment...*

Struck by a sudden idea, Kyrin nearly jumped into action, inadvertently sending sharp waves through his body and startling Dain.

"What the—are you quite alright?"

"Shut up—I'm fine. Now Dain, I want you to ask this leafy little demon some questions, alright? And you're gonna have to tell me exactly what its reply is. Got it?"

"Got—okay, hang on a moment—what is this supposed to accomplish, exactly? I don't understand what it is you expect me to—"

"Shut up and listen—I know what I'm doing. I had an idea, just... go with it."

Dain looked skeptical, but when Kyrin added a quiet "please?" he relented.

"Alright. I don't get it, but alright. I guess I'll humor you."

"Good. Thank... Thank you." The last words came out haltingly, awkwardly shaped on Kyrin's tongue. He pushed on anyway, shoving away shame. "So—first question—what's to stop me from leaping into the flame and letting both flesh and flower burn to a freaking cinder?"

Dain shut his eyes, transmitting the question. "It says it—"

"Give me the exact words."

"That's not how it works, Kyrin. Only the really sophisticated plants use real words—most talk using images and feelings and... well—I can't explain unless you're a plant or another treetalker. Please, I'm doing my best here—don't interrupt."

"Fine. Listen, it's... I'm... It's life or death, here, you know? Relaxing ain't easy."

Dain nodded, understanding the unspoken apology. "Anyway, in answer to your question, the flower said 'fire holds no fear, ashes make good soil.'"

"This little freak isn't nearly as inventive as the others, is it?" Kyrin remarked, pulling his lockpicks from his various surviving pockets. By some miracle, none of his tools had been lost throughout the whole misadventure.

Dain watched in mild interest as Kyrin cleaned and cared for his arsenal in the flickering firelight. A pale white moth fluttered by, disappearing into the darkness behind the recovering criminal. "No, it really isn't. Those trees before were far more ancient and wise."

"I'm gonna ponder that later. Now, we know that fire holds no fear, right? Tell the little weed that I'm gonna... I'm gonna go for a swim," Kyrin's voice faltered slightly, his memories of his near drowning unfortunately fresh in his mind, "I'll go swimming—the ocean will tear the roots from my flesh and sweep us both to sea where we can die."

Dain shifted uncomfortably, frowning as he passed the message along. "It's... laughing. 'Ocean waves bring young seeds to new lands. Bodies float.'"

Kyrin nodded, as he twisted the glyphs on his lockpicks around, rearranging the flow of magic around the metal. "I see. So the fire wouldn't hurt it, and the ocean would only further its cause, in a sense. Perhaps, then, I should have you Knights bury me under the earth? On second thought, no. That's stupid and would accomplish absolutely nothing. That's not how I'm going to die. Maybe snow and ice. Dain—you're translating this, right?

"Yeah, but I don't see what threatening suicide is going to—"

"Shut up. I know what I'm doing—just bear with me a

while longer."

"Okay… I don't like it, but alright. Anyway, the plant says that snow and ice don't matter. It's a hardy weed and apparently loves the cold. Though it doesn't seem too happy with the thought of a wasteland… not enough… uh, I can't find the right word, it doesn't translate quite right. Anyway, now it's complaining about you, Kyrin. The plant wants you to wake up Tryn so he can put more magic in your system before you're drained completely dry. Apparently you don't make very good soil on your own. You don't have enough magic, and… iron, or something."

"Wow. I never would have guessed that I don't have freaking—wait… wait! That's it!" Although the others were sleeping and Kyrin had no wish to wake them, excitement fueled his volume, prompting it to grow.

Dain started back slightly at Kyrin's outburst, generally confused. "Wait—what? What's it—it's what? What are you—?"

"The angle! I've found it! It's so simple! Dammit—why didn't I see it sooner?" Kyrin cried, selecting and adjusting two of his prized lockpicks.

"See what? I don't understand."

"Starvation! Hunger! I've found the angle I can take to get this blasted parasite outta me!"

"Slow down—you did what?"

Kyrin took a deep breath, exhaling a sigh laden with repressed excitement. He resisted the urge to declare the Knight moronic. "I just told you, Dain, I found the angle I need to take to extract this flower from my chest."

"You… the questions?" Dain seemed hesitant, lost in the whirl of Kyrin's enthusiasm as he cast around for a handhold.

"Yeah—when you're cracking a ward, the first thing

you usually need to do is figure out the elemental affiliation of the glyphs that make up the ward. Then, when you've got that, you can read the verse and unravel the subtleties."

"Elemental affiliation... you mean like the Prominences?" Genuine curiosity found a home in Dain's voice. Faced with a willing pupil, Kyrin's inner scholar could not resist the call to lecture. Pain be damned—he was going to talk.

"Just like the Prominences. Only while those represent the regular rise and fall of each element throughout the year, in enchanting, well—enchanters take a very scientific approach to magic. While you can just chat with flowers and Brysson can toss around fireballs on instinct, an effective enchanter has to study the behavior of magic to be any good. You can't just draw squiggles on the wall and expect it to act as a ward, you have to truly understand what it is you hope to accomplish, and exactly how you hope to accomplish it."

"Okay, but—"

"Shut up, I'm getting there. In order to get things done and gain this understanding, enchanters ended up dividing all magic into nine basic categories—those are the categories that the Prominences follow. Everything that happens—that could possibly happen—ends up in at least one of these categories, and all the subtleties are just refinements and combinations. Do you follow?"

Dain nodded slowly, his blue eyes glazed—a look familiar to anyone exposed to one of Kyrin's impromptu lectures. "Yeah, I think I get it... So the categories follow the Prominences?"

"No, the Prominences follow the elements. Fire, earth, will, lightning, water, darkness, light, wind, and fate all were figured out first, and then when people noticed that the seasons followed the same pattern, they named the months accordingly."

"That actually makes a lot of sense. Also—while we're doing this—I've always kind of wondered what it meant by 'will,' anyway."

"Will is like... intent. A flower grows to face the sun, but it really doesn't mean anything by it. It's the difference between a man thoughtlessly going about his daily routine because it's what he's always done, and a man actually considering his action and moving purposefully to make some difference in his life. Consider it man's rebellion against fate. Will is also considered the element of soul, and tends to be closely aligned with chaos."

"I see," the blond Knight lied, "so anyway, what does any of this have to do with that stuff you shouted? Starvation isn't an element."

"No, that's where the subtleties come in. You see these?" Kyrin held up one of his lockpicks, gesturing to the rest, "I went and found an expert to enchant them to my design. Each one represents an element, and if you twist this bit here, you can manipulate the glyphs on the surface to get any number of meanings."

"And that works?"

Kyrin paused mid-ramble, raising his eyebrow. "I'm the first to ever break into your Stronghold. I'm the one who unlocked the door to the Anchor Key. I'll give you three guesses before I answer that question, and I damn well hope that you only need the one."

"Alright, alright," Dain raised his hands defensively, "no need to be rude about it—I just don't know much about enchanting, okay? They guard their secrets."

Kyrin stared for a moment, suddenly realizing he had fallen back into his old rut. "I'm sorry," he conceded eventually, pushing back a strand of his dark hair as he uncomfortably lowered his offensive walls, "old habits, you know? Guild life. Hard to break a pattern like that. I'm... yeah."

"Don't worry about it." Dain twitched a smile, shrugging off his defensive pose, "I think I get you—and I can tell you really are trying. Anyway, what were you saying? About your lockpicks?"

Resisting the urge to accuse the treetalker of patronizing him, Kyrin cleared his throat and resumed.

"Well, uh... Right, yes. Hunger isn't an element in the same way fire is, but that doesn't mean you can't call upon it in a spell. Just like... well, lights. Have you ever really thought about the lights back in the city?"

"What—like the streetlights and stuff? Not really."

"Well, depending on the area and the enchanter and such, there are any number of ways you can make those things. Sometimes it's best to just flat out call upon light itself, sometimes you'd want fire instead, sometimes you'd be better off with some twist of will, and other times it's best to just banish darkness. Depending on the scenario, you can use almost any method to accomplish your goal. It's all just a matter of the enchanter's creativity and skill."

"Right," Dain nodded, looking as though he wished he had a notepad and pencil, "So you can do pretty much anything if you only know how?"

"There are a lot of limitations involving material and time of year and... well, there are a lot of subtleties, but almost. Of course, lesser families generally have a harder time handling the more complex elements, and only the best can manage the detail needed for a truly great spellwork, but..." Kyrin shrugged, his lecture losing steam as the roots shifted uncomfortably beneath his skin, "well, yeah. You get a talented enchanter with good blood, attention to detail, and the right dash of creativity, and there's almost nothing he can't do with his craft."

"But the blood is important?"

Kyrin nodded curtly. "Difference between Kai and me. He's a genius. I'm…"

"Also a genius. You know—I actually understood maybe a fifth of that spiel?"

"That's because you're—you're a treetalker," Kyrin swiftly replaced his planned insult with an indisputable fact, doing his absolute best to be civil. "You don't need to know this crap."

"All the same," Dain grinned, giving Kyrin a playful shove, "you're still allowed to banter, you know."

Kyrin swore, giving voice to his sudden pain. Dain winced in sympathy, quickly returning to the topic by way of apology.

"Uh—anyway, I still don't get where you pulled starvation from. Do you mind explaining?"

Kyrin bit his lip, shaking his head to clear out the profanity. "Starvation—hunger—I can pull a refinement of fire, or darkness, or even will, now that I think about it. Here, at least, I'm gonna play with fire. I need will to be the carrot."

"What?" Dain's brow creased in obvious confusion.

"Carrot. Carrot with the stick," Kyrin explained shortly, stowing away all but two of his tools, "fire's hunger is going to serve as the threatening stick, while will is going to stand for the will to live, and will provide the energy as the tempting reward—our carrot."

"Oh. Okay. So how are you actually planning to do this?"

"Just like a ward." Fighting back the pale bloom of nausea, Kyrin lifted his lockpicks and set to work, carefully using the magic-imbued silver to tease the flower's roots from beneath his flesh. He had to guess which roots were weakest and most open to persuasion, because one wrong move would send a dozen wooden stakes into his heart and lungs. Even so, the pain was almost too much to bear. Kyrin gritted his teeth.

Dain watched the slow, agonizing process, obviously sickened by the sight of the roots writhing and warping under Kyrin's skin.

Suddenly, Kyrin gasped, lurching forward as if thrown. His lips gleamed red. The lockpicks slipped from his trembling hands, smeared with a sickly scarlet that seemed to shine in the orange firelight.

One tendril was free. One thin, fragile tendril slithered outside his body, while a whole mess of roots remained beneath Kyrin's inflamed skin. The wound oozed. The stink of blood filled the air.

"I... can't do it," Kyrin whispered, his breath hissing through his clenched teeth, "hurts too much. Hands... won't."

Dain bit his lip, smoothing back his golden hair as he thought aloud. "No point waking Tryn, his power can't help much here, and he... needs his sleep. Sal can't puppeteer plants, and—"

"Dain, please," Kyrin croaked, forcing his glare to meet the Knight's worried stare, "I don't have time. You—you can talk to the thing. Use my picks. I've got 'em set. I'll be fine. Just... a bit bloody."

"Are you sure about this?"

Kyrin choked out a harsh laugh. "Dead sure. Now do it." With that, Kyrin flopped back onto the cold ground, his eyes shut tight and his breath shallow as he fought to subdue his pain.

Dain squared his shoulders. He lifted the gleaming picks out of the grass, opened the mental connection between himself and the world of plants, and began the arduous process of coercing and extracting the flower from Kyrin's chest.

The moment Dain began his work, Kyrin's world became one of darkness and bitter hurt. He could not tell if his eyes were open or shut. He could not tell if the screams he heard came from his own raw throat or from his pain-addled imagination. Kyrin could not tell, and in that hot, dark fog of semi-consciousness, Kyrin did not care. He almost wished that Dain would fail and accidentally send a sharpened root into his heart so that the pain might end quickly.

Hours slipped by, fleeing into the night. Consciousness came and left and came again, and it was not until the dawn—not until the sun broke the horizon and spilled its golden blood over the world—that Kyrin found rest.

A cool hand touched his feverish forehead, closing his half-open eyes. A wash of clean blue light granted Kyrin the gift of peaceful sleep.

Kyrin dreamed.

*He stood on the docks, watching the familiar gray rain fall from gray clouds into the churning black ocean. Water poured down onto Kyrin's head, running through his hair, dripping into his eyes and mouth, and nothing he could do would get it to stop.*

*He took a step forward. One more inch, and the icy sea would claim him. One more twitch, and the ocean would—*

*A soft hand on his shoulder halted Kyrin's progress.*

*"You shouldn't do that," the witch warned gently, "dying in your own dreams won't hurt you, but I'd rather not have to watch."*

*Kyrin nodded silently. Esmeralda smiled. The rain stopped. Kyrin's face grew slightly hot.*

*Bright as the sun, the witch grinned wider. "You know, Kyrin, it's cute when you do that."*

*Kyrin opened his mouth to question, to protest, but his voice made no return. Esmeralda carried on without regard.*

*"I like you, Kyrin. I've seen the dreams you don't remember. I've seen the soul they said you didn't have. We're a lot alike, you and I. They did bad things to you because you're different and they're afraid, and that's not fair. Come to me, Kyrin. Come to my castle and I can set you free. You're so close—only a few days more.*

*Come to me, and we can be free…"*

# Chapter Ten

The intertwined scents of wood smoke and warm food prodded Kyrin's consciousness, dragging him from his dream to rejoin the waking world. The low rumble on the edge of his hearing rose to become the quiet murmur of conversation. Sounds gradually became words, taking on shape and meaning in the new daylight.

"It's been almost two days. Do you think he's ever going to wake up?" Sal's voice, quiet and curious, seemed oddly muffled.

"He should," Tryn replied calmly, his voice seeming somewhat clearer, "the moment he was free of the flower I sent enough magic through his system to reanimate a corpse."

"Wait—you can't really do that, right, Tryn?"

"No, I can't, but it makes a nice picture, doesn't it?"

Sal's skeptical bemusement shone through her voice strongly enough for Kyrin to picture her expression. "No, Tryn, not really. Zombies don't strike me as all that appealing, believe it or not."

"I see your point. Either way, though, Kyrin should be up and swearing again soon. These things just take time."

"Do we have time?" Briea's low rumble cut through

the conversation like a velvet dagger, soft and smooth and sharp. "We've got less than a week until the city goes to pieces. We can't afford to throw any more days away. The thief's proven useful, yeah. Sure, he may prove useful again, but if he remains a burden now... I won't carry dead weight when every minute is crucial."

"Are you saying we should leave him behind?" Sal seemed surprised, but not nearly as offended by the notion as Kyrin might have hoped.

"You know how I feel about that, Briea," Tryn added, 'we are Knights, not dogs or executioners. To abandon him now would be to—"

"Save the hangman a length of rope." Briea's voice was calm and logical. She gave her tone no emotional bias as she spoke, presenting only the facts as she saw them. "Remember, regardless of your personal moral code, Tryn, at the end of the day, he's still a condemned man. Legally and rightly, he's already dead. Would you hold a corpse above all of Alinor?"

Tryn coughed. Kyrin lay still, listening intently from the edge of awakening.

Eventually, the red-haired Knight answered. "He is not a corpse yet, but I see your point. Another afternoon, then we will be on our way."

Kyrin chose that moment to stir. He pried his eyes open and pulled himself into a sitting position, striving against gravity with every thread of strength he still possessed. His whole body ached, but Kyrin refused to let it keep him down. His torso was stiff with wrapped bandages, but Kyrin ignored everything.

"Hey," Kyrin began, his voice cracking as he struggled to think of a good accusation to make his entrance grand, "don't leave me behind."

The others turned to look at him, surprised.

"Oh, eavesdropping, eh?" Tryn chucked slightly.

"Yeah, sure. Not like your talking woke me up or anything," Kyrin retorted, "Now look—I've come this far. Dying now would be stupid. I will see this through to the end."

"Just don't cause that end." Briea's face was impassive. Kyrin could not be certain if she was serious or if this was her own brand of strange, semi-sarcastic humor.

"I'll do my best to keep out of the way," Kyrin replied neutrally, "I did say that I'm gonna try to turn it around, yeah? Flip the leaf or whatever that one saying says."

"Which saying?" Sal asked.

Kyrin gave her a flat look before answering. "The one where you flip a leaf."

Apparently through with the idle chitchat, Briea spoke again. "How soon can we get going? Is Brysson ready to travel?"

The Knight in question woke at the sound of his name, stretching his arm as he yawned. "G'morning. Thief up? Yeah? Cool. Let's hit the… road…." He rolled over in the grass, mumbled something incoherent, then promptly fell back asleep.

Sal shook her head, clicking her tongue in exasperation as she moved to check the bandages around her friend's shoulder. Kyrin scratched at his own bandages, his aching chest accentuated by a faint twinge of envy. The Knights were so close, despite their vastly different skills and backgrounds. A childhood memory—an old dream of knighthood and glory flashed through Kyrin's mind, but he brushed it away. If it weren't for the witch and her offer, the best Kyrin could ever hope to expect was another new beginning as a reluctantly repentant sinner living in fear of the noose. Any greater wish seemed exactly as stupid and as unlikely as his youthful fantasies—and just as out of reach.

Sal fussed over Brysson like a mother hen. Briea left to collect Dain from his foraging duties, and Kyrin was left with Tryn.

At one point, the red-haired giant with the mace had terrified Kyrin—Tryn could smash a man's bones, repair them, and then happily go and smash them again. Now, though, Kyrin looked at Tryn and saw only a tired man with a difficult job.

*Is this what respect feels like?* Kyrin wondered, quietly confounded by the lack of familiar hostility in his heart. The Knights had spared and saved his life. Sure, that was partly out of a desire to use him and partly out of a moral reluctance to let him die anywhere other than at the foot of the Gallows Tree, but all the same. They had spared and saved his life, and he had risked his life for them. And unlike Rat, none of them had once gone to kick him when he was down.

"Tryn?" Kyrin heard himself say suddenly, his mouth moving without his mind's consent.

Tryn glanced up from whatever thought he had been lost in, an unformed question passing his lips. "Hm?"

"I just wanted to…" Kyrin's pride caught up, slamming his voice to the ground, but he fought back, wrestling the truculent emotion into submission. "I just wanted to thank you."

Tryn blinked, his face impassive. "For what?"

"For not bashing my head in that first time when you caught me robbing you," Kyrin answered, shrugging, "for letting Rat go and making me stay. I was angry and afraid, and I can't claim that ain't still at least partially true, but… I'd like to thank you for the fact that I'm still breathing. There've been a million times you could have killed me or left me behind or just not healed me, but…" the flow of words ran suddenly dry. Kyrin coughed, eternally awkward.

Tryn paused, digesting the information, then spared a curt nod. "You should be able to remove the bandages now. The walking wood didn't leave you with much in the way of a shirt, so you have every reason to keep covered if you prefer, but the wounds should be healed enough to manage."

Was Tryn purposefully ignoring Kyrin's rare show of gratitude?

*Fine. Whatever. It doesn't matter anyway.*

Kyrin returned the nod, stuffing his fledgling emotions safely back behind his polished mental armor.

"I'll check later when we stop again," he mumbled.

"Suit yourself," Tryn replied, staring vaguely off into the horizon.

Kyrin looked away, surveying the field as he made the decision to leave Tryn be. If the man wanted to be aloof, he could be aloof.

Hardly a moment later, Briea returned, Dain by her side. Juggling an armful of red, tuber-like vegetables, the blond squire greeted his companions with exaggerated cheer, spreading his most contagious smile. "Hey Sal! Hi Tryn! Morning, Kyrin! Brysson still asleep?"

"How the hell are you so happy?" Kyrin's incredulous query was posed in equal parts irritation and genuine wonder.

Dain's response was equally mystifying. The squire merely smiled and shrugged. "We're all alive here, aren't we? I figure if no one else has the energy to manage a grin, then the job is left to me!"

"You're freakin' crazy," Kyrin grumbled, "you're flamin' insane, simple as that. Completely stupid."

Dain shrugged again. "If this is stupid, I hope to never

be smart."

"You're an idiot, blondie. You're an idiot and well down the path away from intelligence, but..." Kyrin paused to bite the inside of his cheek, incredibly aware of the words hovering behind his closed lips. He forced them out, still struggling to find the strength to change. "But... you did save my life, so... I guess I have to thank you."

Dain grinned, setting down his vegetables to poke Brysson's face.

"Hey, wake up Brysson. You owe me ten silver."

The scar-faced Knight rolled over onto his back, blinking and yawning as he sat up to stretch. "Eh?"

"You owe me ten silver, friend. Our thief remembered his manners."

Grumbling good naturedly, Brysson reached for his wallet and fished out the appropriate coin. "You weren't supposed to thank him, Kyrin. You were supposed to be all stubborn and stuff like usual. Man, now I'm out a full ten coin."

Kyrin sat for a moment, his mouth agape. "You—you two idiots took *bets*? If that isn't the—"

"Hey," Brysson interrupted the budding tangent with a lax shrug, "it passes the time. This is—what—the third random wager we've had today, Dain?"

"I thought it was the fourth."

"Let's see... first we had the one to see if Sal would try to cook again—I got that money. Then you got the money for whether or not you could get Tryn to smile, then I got the cash for you waking up, Kyrin, and—yeah, Dain, you were right. It was four."

Kyrin stared. For a long moment, he sat, treating the two to his flintiest expression, then out of nowhere he threw back his head and laughed until his eyes filled with tears. Dain and Brysson exchanged a confused glance. Neither of them would have bet on this—the possibility would have seemed too far-fetched.

Kyrin laughed until he could not breathe, until his chin dropped to his chest and his sides ached. The Knights seemed almost disturbed by this sudden show of humor, but it felt good to laugh. Kyrin could not care less about the years that had elapsed since his last opportunity.

"You—you two…" Kyrin shook his head incredulously. When he noticed Sal, Tryn, and Briea's stares, he waved his arm to incorporate them into his incredulity. "All of you—you are all the most ridiculous people I have ever met. I thought the Guild was insane— you Knights are freaking crazy! Not bad, though. Crazy and stupid and moronic, but not that bad."

Tryn, busy as he was preparing a meal, cracked a smile. "I'm not sure if we should feel honored or insulted, thief, so I'll choose the former. Thank you, you're not all bad yourself, either."

Kyrin's brain shut down at the compliment, automatically demanding that Tryn shut up as it sorted through its self-conscious embarrassment. Today was a day of impossibilities, and Kyrin could only guess at what tomorrow might bring.

Later, though not much later, the Knights demolished their camp and returned to their trackless quest, Kyrin in tow. Dain laughed and sang, letting enthusiasm take him where tunefulness could not. Brysson told jokes, Tryn told stories, Sal was her usual sunny self, and even taciturn Briea did what she could to keep morale high. For the first time, Kyrin began to feel almost like a companion, rather than a prisoner, and the thought amazed him. He felt warm, as if the sun were shining through his body, lingering in his core. He felt filled, satiated in a way no meal had ever managed. For once, he felt almost... content.

It was... odd, certainly. Almost... comfortable. Definitely unfamiliar, but not altogether bad. For nearly the first time in his life, Kyrin ceased his striving and was satisfied to just sit and enjoy the company of others. He walked behind Tryn and Dain and Sal, listening amiably to the drifting tune of the conversation and the light beat of the group's footfalls. He lost himself in the sunlight, in the breeze—for a moment Kyrin forgot his hatred and his bitterness, his fear and his pride. He forgot his ambition and his desire, and for a moment, he was content to simply be.

Then the grassland domain ended, and a forest realm began. Kyrin still found the line between the domains to be uncanny in its perfection, but he treasured the exhilarated thrill his heart gave as he stepped from the soft green grass to the shade of the looming trees.

As the sunlight died in the high branches, Kyrin could not help but shiver. These trees were dark and tall and proud, never moving and never bending for anything. Coarse black bark led up to waxy black leaves that scraped the distant crystal sky. Wispy grey moss hung from the black branches, trailing grasping fingers through the choked air. Though the Knights entered the forest easily, the daylight had no such luck—beneath the boughs of this strange dark forest, the midday sun was strangled, beaten down into a dim, hazy twilight.

The Knights' bright conversation ended with the fading light. In the face of the unnatural darkness, even Dain and Sal lost their high spirits and remembered their quest's importance.

*Five days,* the wind seemed to whisper through the

trees, *Five days, and then all shall fade and fail.*

"Dain?" Tryn's voice was clear, firm, and reassuringly real, although the frightening new environment had shorn it of all excess emotion.

"On it," the squire replied instantly, his eyes already shut.

Tryn nodded to himself, adjusting his mace and scanning the forest. Briea shifted to her lioness form and smelled the air, her feline ears flicking back and forth to capture every minute sound from the silent wood. Brysson let a spell-flame crackle between his fingers. He might have lost an arm, but he had since regained his magic and was now ready to set fire to any danger that crossed his path. Even Sal was drumming her fingers against her sword's wire-bound hilt.

Kyrin found himself wishing for a weapon and armor; neither his lockpicks nor his tattered clothes were much use in a fight. The realization prompted a sardonic chuckle—his entire existence followed a similar pattern. Kyrin was a specialized instrument, worth nothing to the ordinary world.

"What's so funny?" Sal asked, giving Kyrin a sidelong glance.

Kyrin gave her a purposefully enigmatic smile. "I'm useless."

"What? Why is that—"

A bright, shiny giggle broke from the trees, cutting Sal off. Dain's eyes snapped open.

"Elves!" he cried, "the trees say this is an elf wood!"

"You don't say," Tryn growled, mace already in hand.

Briea swore. Brysson and Sal exchanged a grim look.

"Elves?" Kyrin's voice held the hopeless skepticism of a man who knows he is wrong. "I thought they were just make-believe."

"Make-believe? Yes, make-believe!" a voice called down from a treetop's deeply shadowed branches, "Elves are completely make-believe!"

A second voice joined the first, this one apparently somewhere behind the Knights. "Make-believe indeed! All we do is make believe! Now I believe we may have visitors! What shall we make them believe?"

Kyrin spun around to look for the taunting's source, but Tryn stopped him, placing a heavy hand on Kyrin's shoulder. "Ignore them," he growled, "don't respond, don't argue—don't even try and look for them. They see it as a game. If one of them traps you into playing, you'll be stuck here until either you win or they get bored and kill you—though either might take an eternity."

"Did someone say game? I like games! Come play with us!" a third elf called, "why don't we all make believe together?"

Out of nowhere, the forest shimmered and changed to a beautiful castle courtyard, all polished marble and sculpted stone. A fountain bubbled and leapt, sparkling in the sudden, inexplicable sun. Kyrin's ears rang with the sound of magic.

"The hell?" Kyrin grabbed his head, wondering if he'd gone insane. The random shift was dizzying. The unbearably pure note of magic stabbed at Kyrin's mind.

Sal took hold of his hand and gave it a squeeze, as if trying to alleviate some of the pain. "Elves are illusionists. They mess with perception. It's how they trap you. At least, that's what my books said."

"No duh," Kyrin growled through clenched teeth, "I can flamin' hear."

"You can?"

"You all are deaf as blazes."

Had Kyrin's eyes not been hidden beneath his hand,

he would have seen Tryn and Briea exchange a glance.

The red-haired Knight chuckled quietly. "I told you we would find a use for him."

Briea nodded, giving her tail a satisfied flick. "That you did. Here's hoping it pans out."

Kyrin lifted his gaze to glare at the Knights, making eye contact with each of them as he struggled to block out the false palace around them. "I'll show you," he snarled, delivering his promise like a threat, "I know what you're thinking, and I can do it. I'll flamin' show you."

"Show them what?" a lilting voice tittered from the canopy.

"I think they want us to show them something better!" another voice answered.

The gleaming palace wavered, fading into a vast, terrible volcanic cave. Black rock, smeared and stained with soot, made up the cave's foundation, but it had been twisted—melted by pure heat and reformed into a tortured mass of bulging, billowing curves and odd, sudden drips. Black smoke oozed from the abyss.

Briea hissed. Her tawny fur stood nearly on end. Tryn placed a hand on her shoulder.

"Relax, Briea. Remember, this isn't real."

"It's a dragon's den!" the lioness snarled.

"No," Tryn reminded her softly, "this is only an illusion."

Kyrin watched quietly as Briea regained control, forcing her fur flat and retracting her razor claws as she fought her instinct.

Kyrin raised an eyebrow. Rationally, Briea must know the cave to be a figment of elfin magic, but still…

A chorus of giggles erupted from the dark trees.

"Ooh, that was a good one! Let's try again!"

The scenery morphed again, this time changing to a

glimmering sea shore, all white sand and sparkling silver water that glimmered in the faux sunlight. Kyrin caught his breath. The unbroken horizon was too much—too large and too far and too big. The elves giggled, laughing as he subconsciously stepped away from the rising water. Kyrin bit his lip and set his jaw, closing his eyes to focus on the song of magic and drown out the drone of the ocean waves.

*All a lie. Only a lie…*

"Let's hurry up and get out of here," he muttered. The Knights agreed, and the group pressed in through the blackened wood and its magic mask.

The elves' laughter followed them, haunting their steps with incongruous cheer and unsettling song.

"Our friends don't seem to like the place-game!" One elf mused as the environment shifted again and the Knights forced themselves to take no notice.

"Such a pity," another elf answered, "we should try the face-game!"

Kyrin wanted to punch them.

He wanted to punch them even more when he glanced around and saw three identical Sals following him. The middle one caught Kyrin's eye and shook her head, mouthing for him to ignore the spares.

Kyrin blinked, shook himself, and turned back around, gritting his teeth to repress a tide of creatively foul language.

However, coming face-to-face with his own reflection rendered his effort worthless. Kyrin erupted into volcanic profanity, earning himself a disapproving glare from Briea and a bubbling torrent of elfin laughter.

The not-Kyrin chuckled, giving him a cocky sneer. Kyrin growled at the imposter, giving any shifter's natural animalism a run for its money.

"Seriously?" he asked his clone, "This again? Last time was better."

"Huh?" the illusory Kyrin pouted, looking hurt.

Tryn tapped the real Kyrin's shoulder. "Just ignore him."

Almost simultaneously, a mock Tryn touched the fake Kyrin and delivered the same message.

Neither Kyrin listened.

"What do you mean 'last time?'"

"I mean last flamin' time."

"What was last time?"

"Me, my friends—" Kyrin's tongue tripped slightly when he realized the word had slipped out, but he ignored the heat that came to his face and pushed through his sudden awkwardness. "We've played his stupid game before. Few days ago. We played this stupid game and we freaking won."

"They won?"

"They won!"

"Won what?"

"The face-game!"

Kyrin clenched his teeth, annoyed at the unseeable elves' hyperactive prattle. He glanced at what he assumed was the real Tryn, who shook his head, gesturing for the group to move onwards, away from the chattering doppelgängers.

Reluctant to leave his fight, Kyrin followed.

The black woods were still as the Knights walked. No birds sang, no small creatures rustled in the undergrowth—not even the elves' laughter disturbed the unnatural peace.

"Do you think they're gone?" Dain asked quietly.

Brysson shook his head, placing a finger to his lips as a

sign to resume silence.

Dain seemed unsettled, and Kyrin sympathized. The only sounds in the world were the faint whispers of wind through the trees and the imperceptible hum of distant magic. Such quiet was… frightening.

The forest ended. Sunlight reclaimed the land. Black conifers gave way to coarse red sand and slender waving palm trees. Harsh golden air replaced the pale, dappled sunlight. Kyrin half expected a hot wind to hit his face and carry sand into his eyes, but instead he was greeted by a slow swell in the song of magic.

"Finally," Briea sighed, shaking herself so that her golden fur rippled and caught the light, "this domain could have ended sooner and you'd have heard no complaints from me."

"Doesn't it seem a little too soon, though?" Sal mused slowly.

Brysson shook his head. "Nah, some domains are smaller than—"

"She's right," Kyrin interrupted, "this… this sounds wrong. It's singing too loud to be a natural domain border, and the notes are wrong. I'd bet my life that this is just another trick."

The trees echoed with dozens of voices crying out in good-humored disappointment. The red sand and blue sky faded away, leaving dark trees and black shadows in its place.

"How'd he know? I thought our picture was really good!"

"Our picture was really good!"

"I think he's cheating!"

"Is he cheating?"

"How could he cheat?"

Ignoring the incessant overhead babble, Tryn checked

his Key and led the group deeper into the tangled wood.

The elves tried many tricks throughout the day, setting illusion after illusion and conjuring place after place. Impossible dragons scorched the cool air with imaginary flame. The Knights multiplied beyond the realms of reason. Impossible crowds spawned from nowhere to distract the questers, and vast tracts of forest replicated, drawing the Knights in weary circles. Yet every time, the Knights and Kyrin used what they had to navigate and find the safest path away from the cliffs and the bogs that the elves seemed so keen to steer them toward.

The imperceptible music of magic became Kyrin's world, and listening to the land's slow, ringing heartbeat became his most important function, second only to breathing.

So focused was he on that one duty, Kyrin completely missed the subtle cracking of underbrush behind the shadowed trees.

A dark shape broke from the black woods, charging the Knights in a flash of deep red—a roaring storm of tusks and claws. The group scattered. Dain only barely managed to pull Kyrin away before he was gored by a spear-like tooth.

"What the hell was that?" Kyrin propped himself up on an elbow, lifting himself out of the dirt.

"Sorry," Dain chuckled, offering Kyrin a hand up as he sheepishly scratched the back of his blond head. "The illusion startled me."

Kyrin accepted the hand and dusted himself off, glaring upwards at the disembodied giggles. "Yeah, no, thanks for that. That thing was damn well frightening— what the hell was it?"

Sal shrugged, resheathing her sword. "Don't ask me— none of my books had anything like that in them. Did you see its legs?"

"Yeah," Brysson chuckled as he climbed back to his feet, "All six of them! Did you see the way its feet were? And man, if I had teeth like that..." he shook his head.

"Don't forget the feathers and fur and scales and spines and... all of it!" Dain added.

Sal managed a laugh, stress making her slightly shrill. "Yeah, seriously—it's like the elves couldn't decide what to throw at us so they threw everything all at once!"

Tryn whistled, calling everyone back to attention. "Remember—we're not out of the woods yet; hold your tongues and keep your wits. There's no telling where the next cliff is, we need to be alert."

"Yes sir, Tryn!"

Briea stalked close to the red-haired man, her fur still puffed up and her claws extended as she stepped carefully over the ground. "I don't like this," she murmured softly, "This whole mess feels wrong. This isn't like—"

The underbrush exploded. A hurricane of fangs and spines and unpleasant pointy bits flew from the trees, screeching like a demon. Before Kyrin could even think to swear, Brysson tackled him, roughly shoving him out of the way of the sharp, blood-red tusks and razor claws and reflexively throwing a fireball.

By the time Kyrin could raise his face, Sal, Briea, Tryn, and Dain had surrounded the creature, silent and efficient as wolves coming in for the kill.

Kyrin's eyes were too slow to track the fight—his wits were too heavy to take in more than fleeting impressions of chaotic action. Briea was a lightning flash of claws and teeth. Dain's sword seemed like liquid steel. Tryn was fury incarnate, swinging his mace like a man possessed.

The creature was unfazed. Tooth, claw, sword, mace—every attack from the Knights merely bounced off the creature's patchwork hide. It snapped at Briea, missing her flank by inches, then swatted a heavy paw at Tryn, carving a scarlet swathe through the man's armored chest.

Snarling, Tryn bared his teeth at the beast, ignoring the pain long enough to heal himself in a flash of blue.

Reflecting the magical light, Dain's sword was a sapphire. It arced towards the creature's neck, only to bounce away with a metallic clang. Kyrin tried to push himself up, to rush into the fight, but Brysson kept him pinned.

Through it all, Sal stood calmly at the clearing's edge. Her eyes drooped halfway shut. Her sword dangled loosely in her palm. She did not flinch when the beast batted Briea aside with its massive tail. She made no sound when the monster slashed Dain's leg with its claw. Not even when the creature turned its rage towards her did she break her concentration.

An instant before the monster leapt to claim her life, Sal threw her arms up, palms forward. Her sword fell softly into the dirt. The bizarre abomination froze in its tracks.

"Good one, Sal. You're getting better."

Tryn's remark went unanswered. Sal was lost in the effort of keeping the creature controlled.

Unconcerned, Tryn nodded to Briea. "Help me with its mouth, will you? And Dain—you ready?"

"Yes sir, Tryn!" Dain wiped a smear of dirt from his face. "Ready and waiting!"

Kyrin almost asked a question, but Brysson shushed him. It was safest to stay quiet and let Sal focus as the other Knights completed their duty.

As one, Tryn and Briea pried the monster's mouth open, both grimacing as they faced down its rancid breath. Dain waited, and as soon as the monster's cage-like teeth had unlocked and its two purple tongues flopped free, he thrust his blade point-first down the monster's throat.

Though it screamed in obvious agony, the creature could not thrash or flail. Sal's control was iron, and Dain's sword was steel. Only the tip of the monster's barbed tail showed any life, twitching violently as it died.

The creature collapsed. Dain withdrew his sword and wiped the blade clean on the monster's corpse. Sal exhaled a gasping breath and fell to the earth. Elves tittered. Finally free of Brysson's hold, Kyrin was the first to reach the puppeteer's side.

"Hey, you good?" he asked, reaching down to help her up.

She shook her head slightly, panting. "Tired."

"The creature must've been too big for you, kid. You're exhausted."

Sal nodded in silent agreement.

"Let me see her," Tryn demanded, his mace still in his hand and his front still smeared with his own blood.

Kyrin glanced up. "How 'bout you sit, too? At the moment, Knight, you don't look much better off than she does."

"I'm fine. I'm a healer. I know what I'm doing. Now let me see her."

Kyrin stepped aside, but not before muttering "famous last words."

Tryn ignored him and set to work, checking Sal's vitals and making sure his squire had not overstrained herself. When Kyrin looked around, he saw that Briea was doing the same, checking and congratulating Dain on a clean kill.

Trying not to feel left out, Kyrin wandered over to talk

to Brysson. The scar-faced Knight stood by the fallen monster, examining it and occasionally poking it with the end of his sword.

Kyrin cleared his throat. "Thanks, Brysson... I'm... You saved my life. Again. You've been doing that a lot, and I just wanted to... thanks."

Brysson looked up. "Huh? Oh—don't mention it. You save me, I save you—we watch each other's backs, out here. That's how the Knights work."

"Only I'm not a Knight."

"Eh, well, you're out here with the rest of us. If you weren't a criminal, I'd honestly say you'd stand a shot of earning a place in our ranks, what with the good you've done."

Kyrin's heart sank slightly in an unexpected disappointment. "If I wasn't a criminal?"

"Yeah, you've pulled through for us a fair few times, and you've done a lot of good. But you've also done a lot of bad. Robbed us. Started this whole mess off, even if that was indirect, as you claim. Don't think I've forgotten being bound and gagged in my own damn basement, too." Surprisingly, Brysson's voice held no malice. "But— even so. This quest has been messy. I know I earned my squireship for dealing with less. Really, it looks to me as if things could swing either way. It all depends on how the trial will go."

The word 'trial' sent Kyrin's already sunken heart scuttling for cover beneath his stomach. If the law did not have him hanged, he would soon wake up with a slit throat and a missing tongue. The Faceless would never suffer his secrets spilled—even what few that Kyrin knew.

Seeing the look on Kyrin's face, Brysson shrugged. "If it were up to me..."

"Shut up. It's not up to you, and it doesn't matter."

Furious with himself for feeling so hurt, Kyrin turned his face away. *Why should I care how the Knights see me? I have no reason to. No reason to care and no call to worry. Esmeralda shall take care of everything. I might even...*

Kyrin shook himself, ending the thought before he could think it. The notion that he might someday be happy was almost too strange to bear.

Brysson gave him an odd look. "You alright?"

"What? Yes. Shut up—I'm fine. Let's just hurry up and get out of this blasted forest. All these illusions are giving me a headache, and the actual monsters only stand to make it worse."

"I'll second you on that!" Brysson laughed, calling over the other four. "Tryn! How's Sal? She good to pick up and run?"

Tryn stood, sighing as he nodded, "Aye—she could use another minute, but we've rested long enough. She'll be fine."

"Awesome. And you?"

"I'm fine."

"Alright! Briea? Dain?"

The lioness shifted back into her human form. "Set and ready to move."

"Then let's get out of here!"

Following Brysson's example, Tryn took his place at the front of the group, leaving everyone else to follow behind, still maintaining a fighting formation in case of another ambush. Briea and Dain took up the rear, leaving Kyrin in the middle with Brysson and Sal.

The girl's brown hair was a bird's nest of tangles and twigs, her face was muddied and her shoulders stooped from the magical exhaustion, yet for all her stress, she smiled.

Kyrin kicked a small stone from his path.

"You're happy," he remarked quietly.

"Of course I am! I've never stopped something that big before!"

"Really?"

Sal nodded, finding some hidden reserve of enthusiasm. "Really! Before now, I've only ever stopped people-sized things. Or large shifters, sometimes. I can even manage two, if I'm really focusing, but even then— people are easier. It's the difference between throwing cotton and throwing knives—people are sorta fluffy because they have so much going on, intent-wise. Animals, though—especially the monster kind—are so... strong, and single-minded, it's really hard to keep a hold on them."

Kyrin blinked, finally understanding how others felt during his lecture on enchanting. The only response he could muster was a rather stupefied "what?"

"Puppeteering! People are fluffy, monsters are sharp, and I just did something big!"

"Right... er—congrats, I think."

"Thank you and you're welcome! That thing was more than a little scary—I've never seen anything like—"

A small gesture from Tryn silenced the chattering squire. She bit her lip. Kyrin gave a questioning glance, but Sal only shook her head, nodding at the healer at the front of the party.

Tryn stood, still and silent as the tall black trees, his closed fist raised in a call for quiet.

A group of twenty elves sat in a small clearing directly in front of the Knights, all staring with eerie intent.

Brysson and Kyrin both swore, almost in sync.

A few of the elves chuckled. None of them were larger than children—the tallest, had she been standing, would have stood roughly level with Tryn's waist. All of them had long hair, dark and tangled like the growing trees. Their skin was painted black and green to blend with the dappled sunlight. The only specks of white on their childlike forms were their unsettling silver eyes and their gleaming pointed teeth.

This in itself was frightening, but Kyrin's horror only grew when he realized that every elf—male and female—was clothed in an awkward mess of skin and scales, of fur and feathers that could only belong to the kind of six-legged monstrosity the Knights had only barely managed to defeat. They appeared as demons clothed in the cast-offs of abomination, the darkest twists of nature's untamed heart.

One of the elves, a tiny female with a necklace of assorted teeth and the shadows of cobwebs painted across her brow, stepped forward. Kyrin guessed from her ornamentation that she was some sort of leader, and from her confident gait and mischievous smile that she meant trouble.

Tryn stepped forward to meet her, Briea by his side, supporting him.

"What do you want?" the Knight demanded, fingering his mace uncomfortably, "why won't you leave us be? We mean you no harm."

This earned a group-wide laugh from the elven gathering.

"No harm, he says? No harm at all?"

"He says no harm—but his stick says otherwise!"

The cobwebbed elf grinned, waving her hand to silence her friends' rambling.

"You mean no harm, yet you came bearing arms."

"Nine arms!" Another elf piped up.

"And four weapons, twenty claws, and probably about

a hundred and fifty teeth!" A different elf added to a chorus of laughter.

Kyrin groaned. "Shut up—there's nothing funny, here. Nothing at all."

The elves let their laughter die. Each and every one of them turned to stare at him. Kyrin's skin crawled.

Tryn risked taking his eyes off the leading elf just long enough to shoot back a glare. "Kyrin, if ever there was a time you needed to follow your own advice and shut up, this would be it."

Before Kyrin could respond, one of the elves pointed at him. "Look! Look at him!"

A murmur passed through the small crowd of tiny people. "He has no soul!"

"No soul at all!"

"Not even a little drop!"

Kyrin flushed, gritting his teeth against his rising anger.

The elves exchanged glances and pointy grins, before collectively raising their arms to work their magic.

Nothing appeared, but the song of their casting rang out through the forest, seeming to well up from every black tree, to drip down from every dragging wisp of hanging moss—to pour into Kyrin's head like a flood of icy water, cold to the point of pain.

Kyrin screamed, clapping his hands over his ears. The Knights started at the sudden shout, but the elves giggled.

"He *is* a cheater!"

"No fair! No fair! No fair!"

The elves chattered excitedly, and the clamor of magic grew louder. Kyrin felt that his brain would soon start melting if the ringing in his ears did not stop.

A heavy hand came to rest on his shoulder, and Kyrin got the impression that Tryn was speaking, although he could not distinguish the words beneath the roaring waterfall of bell-like notes.

Then, suddenly, the onrush of sound ceased, and Kyrin was left in silence. He lifted his hands from his ears just in time to catch the cobwebbed elf's disapproving ultimatum.

"A cheater may not pass through our woods unpunished. Every man, woman, and beast among you must stay with us and play with us for the rest of forever."

"Hey—wait half a minute," Brysson interrupted, stepping forward despite Tryn's contrary motion, "No one here cheated. We never volunteered—no one gave us any rules—"

The elf waved a tiny hand, and her people stood. Brysson fell silent. The elf smiled, toying with her necklace of teeth.

"What is it your people say, Knight of the Lonely Arm? Ignorance of the law is no excuse—the stupid man comes to harm."

Kyrin nearly swore, but he resisted the almost overwhelming urge. The elf woman gave him a disapproving stare regardless.

"He is a cheater, so he must stay—here in our realm to always play." She said the phrase once, then twice, then a third time, and the other elves took up the chant. Delighted by this new game, they grew louder and louder, clapping their hands and whooping in their feral joy.

The Knights shifted uneasily, their hands never leaving their weapons.

Suddenly, a voice spoke in Kyrin's head—a light, cheerful voice he knew only from his half-remembered dreams.

His eyes widened, then narrowed in suspicious surprise. "Esmeralda?" he whispered, his lips hardly moving.

"Yes! I found you! I've been trying to get this silly glove to work nearly forever, and I finally got it!"

"What?"

"The glove I got from the Knights! I figured out how to shift the domain close enough to talk to you when you're awake!"

"So it wasn't just a dream…" Kyrin murmured under his breath.

"Of course not, silly! Well, it was—but it was halfway real, too. Now hurry up and get clear of the Knights—I'll come and get you if you can escape a little bit!"

Kyrin's heart leapt, fluttering on hope's confused wings, yet he smacked it down, refusing to be misled by euphoria with his life on the line.

"This isn't a very good time," Kyrin muttered beneath the elves' frantic chanting.

"Of course it is!" the witch giggled, "I've arranged the domains—now is the only time we have! Now I'll meet you in a little bit, okay? I can't wait to see you in person!"

"Hold on a second, don't—" Esmeralda was already gone.

Briea passed Kyrin a cautious glare, her mane of hair practically bristling as she prepared for battle with the cheery elves. "What did you say, thief?"

Kyrin gritted his teeth and took a deep breath. He had spoken louder than he had intended. "I said that you should all hold on for a second and kindly refrain from doing anything intensely idiotic for half a flamin' second," Kyrin said, summoning all his disdain to bolster his failing nerve.

Briea narrowed her eyes and flared her claws. "Stop talking, thief. This is no time for your squawking," she commanded.

"Shut up."

"He is a cheater, so he must stay—"

"Shut up." No. No more chanting. Kyrin was done with that.

"Kyrin, stop. You'll only—"

He shook off Sal's sensible hand.

"—here in our realm to always play!"

"Shut up!"

Tryn looked back. "Kyrin. Stop. We can't afford to—"

"No! You stop! Everybody—just shut the hell up!"

For once, the world listened. The black forest fell silent. Kyrin was the center of attention. He took a deep breath, willing his voice to be stronger than his shaking legs, and spoke, struggling to forget his screaming sense of self-preservation.

"You want me to play with you? Fine. I'll stay. I'll stay and play all flamin' day. I'll play all the games you want, if..." Kyrin licked his lips. His mouth was drier than dust. He forced himself on, pushing through an uncomfortably true lie to a believable performance. "If you just let my friends go free."

The Knights' shocked silence was louder than all the elven laughter,

Dain blinked. "Did you just..."

Brysson threw his arm in the air. "The world is ending!"

Kyrin shot him a glare. "Shut up, you Knights—you lot are heroes every day. Now..." He paused a moment to lick his lips again. "Now you all need to step back a moment and give me a shot."

Tryn looked at him, a quiet gratitude in his eye, even as he shook his head. Kyrin felt like a crook. A filthy liar. Even as his twisted humor reveled in the notion of fooling the Knights of Alinor, the atrophied little bird that was his conscience beat at the bars of its cage.

Kyrin shushed it.

"This is not your call, Tryn. This is between me and the people I have supposedly wronged." Kyrin looked at the elf chieftain. "Right?"

The diminutive lady seemed to consider, before nodding and flashing her pointed teeth in what could only be called a grin. "One for all or all for one—the cheater's chose—the deal is done."

The elves whooped and cheered, leaping up like so many leaves cast upon a fearsome gale, and the scenery changed. The slow knell of magic called forth a vision of distorted colors and swirling shapes. Kyrin could barely keep his balance, much less his focus, from his place within the eye of the imaginary storm. He dreamed for a moment that he heard the Knights call out to him, but not a moment later, the colors faded and the waking world returned. His companions were gone, vanished with the declining hum of magic. Only the elves remained.

"What did you do with them?" Kyrin asked, his throat dry.

"Nothing!" One male elf laughed, a wide smile splayed across his sharp features. "Nothing at all!"

"But we did something to them!" Another elf chimed in, apparently delighted by this grammatical technicality.

Kyrin's heart went cold and his anger flared. "You told me you would let them go." His voice was an icicle, pointed and deadly.

"We did!" A female called, "we let them go right into a monster nest! They'll be taken care of. The monsters are very hospitable."

"Very hostile, too!" Another elf added, before the group of them burst into happy laughter.

Kyrin shut his eyes and clenched his teeth. The Knights could look after themselves, right? They were strong. Kyrin just had to worry about himself, now. If he could just last a while longer, Esmeralda would come for him. Assuming he had not fallen prey to a hallucination, or... *gods*...

Kyrin swore under his breath, biting his lip until it almost bled. Had he really just bet his life that the voice in his head was genuine? Had he really made the gamble that Esmeralda's message wasn't some trick of the elves?

Had he really...?

Kyrin swore again.

Now, his best chance for survival was to stall for time and pray to the gods.

"Hey!" he called, shouting to get the mob's attention, "How 'bout we all play a game! That's what you like, right? Playing games?"

The elves continued to giggle and titter, but they quieted down a bit, moving into a circle around Kyrin. He pretended not to mind the closing ring of gleaming eyes and pointed teeth, preferring instead to imagine himself some great hero returning home to his fan club.

His deadly, sadistic fan club...

Kyrin shook himself and stopped imagining. That road led nowhere good.

The cobwebbed elf stepped forward, led by her grin. "The cheater wants to play a game—the cheater wants to win some fame. He thinks we must be stupid fools because we follow all the rules. Shall we show him how he's wrong? Let's make him deaf to magic's song!"

On that signal, the sound rose, and Kyrin had to shout to hear himself over the headsplitting peal.

"No—no! I'm sorry, okay? I didn't mean to cheat or whatever—I'll play by the rules this time!"

The sound continued to swell, almost to the threshold of pain.

"Stop! Please, stop! I—I thought of a game I can't cheat at!"

Green eyes met silver in a desperate plea for human sympathy. The sound died down slowly.

"What?"

"A riddle contest," Kyrin explained, nearly tripping over his tongue as he hurled the words, scrambling to hide behind them. "An honest contest of wit and wordplay—just you and me. Does that sound fair?"

Slowly, the elf nodded, spreading her thin lips in another too-wide grin. A chill swept down Kyrin's spine, freezing his blood and lingering in his bones.

"Riddles sound fun," she laughed, "You tell first. I'll guess."

Kyrin licked his lips, cleared his throat, and scoured his memory for some confounding rhyme. This gambit had not been properly considered. He had simply thrown out the first idea that had sprung to mind.

"Um... what flies high in the sky except when low to the ground—cannot be touched even when all around?"

"Cloud."

"Dammit."

The elven female had not hesitated—her answer flew as quickly as Kyrin's curse. A cold sweat began to bead on the young man's forehead. His already racing heart quickened.

"My turn to tell," the cobwebbed elf stated slowly, allowing her voice to drift down to a low, sibilant, singsong tone, "above and beyond the blue of the sky, persisting long after all mortals die—this thing creates life and oft heralds death—we go with its flow from our first to last breath.

"Listen to the singing stones,
Hear it on the sighing breeze
The voices speak, each one alone,
Through heat, through spring, through winter's freeze."

Kyrin had no answer.

"Uh…" he stammered, his mind floundering as it struggled to race, "Maybe…" he couldn't think over his throbbing pulse, his panicked breath, the whirring portion of his brain unfortunately dedicated to noticing the elves' gleaming teeth and pale eyes. This was not like enchanting, where—

*Wait…*

Kyrin took a deep breath, closing his eyes to better imagine the twisting glyphs of spellmaking. He traced the invisible curves and whorls with his hands, sketching the patterns for analysis.

"Above the sky—after we die… transcendence of time and space," Kyrin muttered, twitching his fingers as if to disable the imaginary ward, "creating life and bringing death—something beyond mortality… something we flow with—something that *sculpts* mortality… evident in the stones and the wind and the… voices of… everything…"

Kyrin opened his eyes again, pride lending him confidence. "The answer is magic."

The elf woman nodded, and a whisper of disappointment passed among the gathered crowd. Focused as he was, he had not noticed the elves press close around him and their leader. He cleared his throat awkwardly.

"Okay, so… my turn to ask…"

Kyrin paused to consider. Now that he was thinking again—truly thinking, rather than just floating through a compliant mental fog, perhaps he stood a chance.

"When all else moves," he began slowly, composing the riddle as he went, "this thing stays, though people may go their separate ways. Although not alive, it is far from dead, and it has no neck beneath its head."

The elf did not frown, but Kyrin was delighted to catch a momentary flicker of uncertainty behind her eyes. He had guessed correctly—although her knowledge of nature was likely unparalleled, the elven lady was no expert on the affairs of man.

After a long pause, the elf woman spoke up. "The answer—it is the city—that place you humans call Alinor."

Kyrin nodded, flicking a dark strand of hair away from his face as a grin twitched at the corner of his mouth.

The triumph of the moment was so sweet to savor— Kyrin nearly missed the beginning of the elf's next riddle.

"Many suns shine in day's night after the fading of the white."

Kyrin blinked, his arrogance fleeing as quickly as it had come.

"What?" he managed after an uncomfortably obvious pause.

"Many suns shine in day's night after the fading of the white," the elf repeated helpfully.

Kyrin swore.

"Is that your answer?"

"What? No! Hell no! Give me a minute!"

The woman backed off, a faint, smug grin sneaking across her face. Kyrin squashed the desire to berate the audience for giggling.

Instead, he repeated the phrase again to himself, turning the words over and over in his mouth.

"What the hell is day's night?" he wondered aloud.

The elf merely smiled.

Kyrin went through various different puns and symbols, until a thought finally struck him. "Shade... and then—" he glanced up at the shadowy treetops, then down at the earth around him. "—if the white is... snow, yes—snow, then... many suns shine in the shade after the snows melt—the answer would be yellow flowers blooming under the trees!"

The disappointed hiss from the gathered elves assured Kyrin that he was right. He allowed himself to indulge in a triumphant smirk as he composed his next puzzle.

"Faster than the blinking eye, deeper than the sapphire sky—flies with arrow-like precision, yet wanders off on simple missions—what soul provides, yet life does not, the answer to this rhyme is..." Kyrin trailed off, cutting his words short before he could inadvertently spill the answer into the flood of rhyme and rhythm.

The elf pondered for a moment, before bobbing her head in the semblance of respect. "That is a good riddle. You, boy, are not a bad riddler."

"Do you know the answer?" Kyrin knew he sounded disrespectfully abrupt, but he was too caught up in the game to care. *This will be a fine adventure to brag about later.*

The elf waited another moment before speaking. "I've had time to think, and like as not, the answer to your rhyme is thought."

The only thing that kept Kyrin from cursing was his eagerness for the next riddle.

"Okay, so now it's your turn to tell."

Gracefully, the elf agreed.

"When valleys are high and hills are low, when stone is fast and river slow, when—"

A familiar rising tone interrupted the elf, welling up and drowning out her soft voice.

Kyrin shook his head, as if the motion could serve to lessen the distraction. "Uh... say that again?"

The elf woman obliged, but Kyrin heard even less than he had the first time.

"Is this some trick?" He could barely hear his own voice over the bell-like note.

His opponent frowned, and Kyrin could see a murmur pass among the elven gathering, even if he could not hear it.

The volume jumped higher. Kyrin clapped his hands to his ears.

"Stop it—stop it! We agreed! We agreed to play a game! Stop this noise—please!"

Whatever reply the elves may have had was lost beneath the ringing torrent. Kyrin shut his eyes. He felt as though his head were about to explode from the pressure of the sound—and he almost wished that it would. At least then he would have silence. Were his ears bleeding? This noise—this unbearable, high-pitched wail kept getting louder and louder—seemed to be emanating from everywhere, all at once—seemed to be...

Silent.

Kyrin opened his eyes. The elves were gone. No trace remained, but for a single cord—the necklace of monster teeth belonging to the elven leader. Kyrin picked it up, his fingers numbed by the sudden surreal stillness. He felt deaf and blind—as if the sheer volume of the bizarre magical song had somehow deadened his perception of reality.

A soft giggle broke the silence, shocking Kyrin partway out of his stupor. He whirled around, just in time to see Esmeralda fade into the scene, a golden ray of sunshine miraculously existing among the dark trees. The missing gauntlet was on her arm. It gleamed in the sunlight.

"Kyrin!" She ran up and gave him a hug. "It's so nice to see you in person!"

Kyrin's tongue was a small sack stuffed with sawdust. His mouth was a dry stone.

"You—you're really here. And they... What happened to them?" he asked, mildly surprised when a puff of dust failed to fly from his throat.

"To who?" The witch's barely suppressed giggle showed that she knew quite well.

"To the elves."

"Oh, them? I chased them away."

Kyrin nodded quietly. Her answer made as much sense as anything.

"I was winning, you know," he managed to mumble after a moment.

"What?"

"The elves, I—we were playing a game. I was winning."

Esmeralda blinked. Apparently that line had no place on her internal script.

"Well," she began again, after she had taken a moment to collect her thoughts, "maybe now that we're together, we can play some games too, Kyrin. I'm sure you'll win some of those."

Kyrin looked down at the pendant in his hand and found that he was numbly tracing the various monster teeth with his fingers. "Yeah..." he answered absentmindedly, "I guess you're right."

"Now come on, Kyrin! Let's go back to my castle!"

The lost thief's head shot up, his attention well and truly caught. "Castle? You have a castle?"

Esmeralda nodded, a playful grin flitting across her fair face. "I have a castle."

Kyrin felt his own face stretch to fit the unfamiliar shape of a smile, and he slipped the pendant over his head. "Well, what are we waiting for? I want to see this castle of yours."

The delight on Esmeralda's face made Kyrin's heart stop and his face glow. When she offered him her hand, he took it without question.

The world faded away.

# Chapter Eleven

Kyrin was blind and deaf and dumb. His only sense was touch, but he felt nothing beyond the witch's fingers entwined with his own. Nausea rose, along with panic and a bizarre dread.

Then the world returned.

Gone was the forest of darkness, and gone was the fading sunset sky. Kyrin stood with Esmeralda at the shores of a small river, under a canopy of silent stars. Thin silver trees dotted the hillside around them, almost mirroring the twisting boughs of the distant constellations.

The sky was black, though one spot in particular was blacker than the rest. As Kyrin stared at the starless shape, he realized that the space he had initially taken to be void was actually a towering fortress that loomed up from the earth to block the light.

Kyrin's breath caught in his throat. Esmeralda squeezed his fingers.

"Welcome home, Kyrin,' she whispered softly.

"That's... that's your castle?"

"It's yours now, too. Our castle."

Kyrin had to pause for a moment as his brain

absorbed the witch's quiet words.

"I can't believe it."

"Well, it's true."

Another small silence slipped past before Kyrin found his tongue. "This... it feels like a dream—but... even if it is, I think it's the happiest one I've ever had."

Esmeralda's smile was barely visible in the dim starlight. "I know."

Hand in hand, the pair of outcasts approached their happily ever after, and Kyrin nearly forgot his place with the Knights of Alinor.


"So, how long have you lived here?" Kyrin asked, his hands stuck awkwardly in his pockets as he strolled along the elaborately sprawling corridors of Esmeralda's castle.

"Oh, almost forever," the girl answered cheerily, "ever since my village chased me away. They were scared of me and my power, I think. It's nice, isn't it?"

Kyrin paused to examine a particularly interesting glyph painted on the ceiling. "You don't even know."

"What do you mean, Kyrin?"

"This place—it's amazing. Whoever lived here before you left this place a haven protected from almost everything—fire, flood, pestilence... See that glyph there?" He pointed upwards. Esmeralda gave the symbol a cursory glance.

"Yes?"

"That one—it's at almost every doorway, in every hallway... Basically everywhere, here. I've never seen it before in the city, but if I'm right... It looks like a powerful spell to keep away strangers. Not even the king himself would be able to get in without an invitation."

"Oh, really? You're so smart, Kyrin."

That comment caught him off guard. "What?"

"You're so smart. I'm really glad I brought you here. You know so much about magic, even though you can't do any."

Kyrin's jaw clenched automatically, but the look on Esmeralda's face made his anger fade. She meant no harm. She had intended to compliment him.

Somehow, Kyrin managed to force out thanks. Esmeralda seemed oblivious to his twisted-up emotions. She was like a puppy with a new toy, leading Kyrin around the castle and showing him every little treasure along the way.

Some of her treasure were fascinating, like the room of broken glass, fractured mirrors, and glyphs half-erased by time. It seemed, to Kyrin's eye, like some bizarre chamber designed to predict the domain's uncontrollable shift. He could have easily spent the day examining the shattered orbs and eroded magics, studying the unfamiliar techniques and learning the new subtleties, but Esmeralda, did not have the patience to wait for him.

She dragged him on from one confounding treasure to the next, showing him room after room of ancient glyphs and broken furniture. She brought him to an echoing chamber deep underground, and the two of them shouted and laughed at the walls to hear their distorted voices bounce back. They marveled together at the ancient, time-blackened chain tethered to the floor and took turns imagining what purpose the broken iron might once have served.

Esmeralda showed Kyrin chambers filled with gold, with coins, and with all manner of valuable art lost to the centuries, and then at last, she brought Kyrin to a small, circular room in the center of the castle. Inside sat the Anchor Key, the glue that held domains together and allowed the city of Alinor to exist as one cohesive whole.

Kyrin wanted to stop and study it again, but Esmeralda insisted on finishing the tour.

"Come on—I have one last thing to show you."

"But—the Anchor Key—"

"It'll be there when we get back! You can poke it all you want later! Now come on!" She fled up the stairs to the tallest tower, and Kyrin had to stop to shake his head and laugh before following. Esmeralda's enthusiasm was contagious.

When the pair reached the tower's top, Kyrin had to pause for breath. His legs ached and his throat felt raw. However, Esmeralda's beckoning smile was all it took to convince him to step out onto the high, narrow balcony.

The view was worth the pain.

The world below was a painting, beautiful and surreal. The stars were a rain of liquid light, frozen mid-fall. Beyond the castle's dark walls, silver-wooded beech trees grew tall, reaching up as if to pin the heavens in place. Through the night's clear darkness, Kyrin could almost make out the distant patchwork of the neighboring domains—shadowy mountains wavered and faded as he watched, replacing themselves with vast, mysterious canyons and unsailed seas. A faint breeze blew in from who-knows-where, carrying a faint, spicy odor and tousling Kyrin's hair. The wind was cool against his skin.

The word 'breathtaking' sprang into Kyrin's mind. He cast it aside. It was not strong enough.

Esmeralda took Kyrin's hand and gave it a gentle squeeze. "What do you think?" Her voice was hardly louder than the wind's whisper.

Kyrin licked his lips, desperate to let his heart speak words. "I've never seen anything comparable in my life, except maybe…" Kyrin's eyes darted to Esmeralda's face, but he cut himself off with an awkward chuckle and a shake of his head. "Never mind. I don't know what the hell I'm trying to say."

Esmeralda flicked a windblown strand of golden hair from her face, but the breeze pushed it back, heedless of her perfect smile.

Without consulting his mind, Kyrin's hand rose to guide the lost lock behind the girl's ear. His fingers brushed her cheek. Her soft smile grew a little bit sweeter.

Kyrin felt his face grow hot, and he snatched his hand away, mumbling incoherent apologies. Esmeralda laughed and waved his apologies away, then turned her gaze back over the railing to the world below.

Kyrin did the same, all the while aware of the witch's arm against his.

Not a single word in Kyrin's expansive vocabulary seemed to fit the occasion. Joy and terror seemed the same. Wisdom and folly were indistinguishable. Every emotion that Kyrin had long kept buried as fuel for his anger seemed to want to escape at once—to explode into the night like a shower of fire beneath the stars.

Oblivious to Kyrin's tumult, Esmeralda stood still—a stone before the breeze. A soft sigh carried her contentment. Kyrin did his best to clear his mind and share the moment of peace.

Before long, Kyrin found his eye unconsciously drawn to a subtly shifting shadow down below—a vague hint of movement that was almost beyond perception.

"Do you..." he began uncertainly.

Esmeralda nodded. "I see it, too."

Hidden by darkness, the Knights crept along the ground, hoods pulled over their heads and their armor blackened—undoubtedly by Brysson's fire. Their camouflage was not bad, but from his high vantage point, Kyrin could watch their every move.

Esmeralda bit her lip. "I won't be able to fight them as easily this time."

"What?" Kyrin turned to her, confused. "What do you mean?"

"My powers. I spent the last of my fire on my way back from Alinor, and the last of my teleportation went towards bringing the both of us here—that's why it took me so long to come get you. All I have left is mindtalking, and a little bit of flight for emergencies."

Kyrin blinked, unable to reconcile her statement with the known laws of magic.

"What?"

"Kyrin—did I ever tell you my magename?"

"No. I assumed you were like me and didn't have one—on account of your multiple magics." His voice was calm. Controlled. Carefully casual.

"Well, I do have one. And I do only have one magic. One real one, anyway. I'm a Soultaker, Kyrin. My power is to steal other people's powers."

She looked so scared—so frightened that Kyrin might reject her based on her admission—he couldn't help but laugh.

"You don't hate me?" She asked, passing Kyrin a guarded, careful look.

"No—actually, that answers a lot of questions I'd had. I don't understand what this has to do with them down there, though."

The Knights…two weeks ago, Kyrin had feared and hated them. Now…

Unaware of Kyrin's prickling conscience, Esmeralda continued her explanation. "You see—it's hard work, stealing souls. I can only actually hold about five or six at once before some of them start vanishing on me. And those five or six—I can only keep them so long and use them so often before I can't hold onto them any longer and I need to find new ones."

"Find new ones?"

"Yes—sometimes I get lucky, and some inhabited domain comes near or some deranged exile wanders by, and I can collect their souls."

Kyrin had to absorb this comment in a moment of silence. It was one thing to abstractly conceptualize the theft of magic, but it was quite another to envision Esmeralda creeping through a village in the dead of night to steal souls as the people slept.

"What... what happens to the people after?"

"After what?"

"After you take their magic."

"Oh, I don't know. I never stick around that long. Usually they just go to sleep. I think maybe they die."

Kyrin's stomach twisted, but he was not sure why. Logically, her position was no different than his. Both of them survived at the expense of other people.

Esmeralda must have seen something in his expression, because she grinned. "I have an idea! Kyrin— I'm sure if you and I work together, we can beat them! Then—if I get the chance to take their magics, I can share one of them with you!"

Kyrin blinked, his qualms forgotten. "You can do that?"

The witch nodded.

Kyrin grinned.

"What do I have to do?"

Although the stars provided ample light, Kyrin found the path from the castle to the wall to be surprisingly hazardous, dotted with thorn bushes and pitfalls that had been invisible from the tower. By the time he had reached the gate, Kyrin's face was smeared with mud and his arms burned with a multitude of tiny scratches. He felt he must look like some lost wraith, or some deranged ghost left to wander the world—clothed in bandages, a mess of knotted hair and tangled scars held together by bad intentions.

He felt like something the Knights might hunt.

Shaking the thought from his head, Kyrin edged nearer and nearer to the gate, until he was within earshot of his former companions. Kyrin was surprised how glad he was to hear their hushed voices.

"—definitely in there," said Tryn.

"Now we only need a way past this damn gate." Briea's growl was as harsh as ever.

"I might be able to melt the lock," Brysson offered, his hand glowing faintly.

"That would be too dangerous," Tryn murmured, "we don't know what wards might be in place." He turned to address Dain. "Have the plants told you anything yet, Treetalker?"

"Only that the witch has returned—and something about another new pet, or something. The trees aren't being very clear."

"Oh, wow," Sal laughed, "the trees aren't being clear. What has the world come to? I'm shocked."

Kyrin heard what sounded like a collective snigger, before Tryn spoke again. "Let's hold the sarcasm until after we've got the Anchor Key and my Gauntlet back in our hands. We only have a few more days until Alinor drifts apart—we can't waste any more time."

The sobering announcement brought a moment's silence, eventually broken by Sal.

"I bet if Kyrin was still here, he'd be able to get us in."

"Yeah," Brysson agreed, "say what you want about the

guy, but he was good at what he did."

Tryn cleared his throat. "Yes, well, he isn't with us anymore. He and Pel both gave themselves up so that we could continue our quest, and we need to make sure their sacrifice isn't in—"

Kyrin could not bear to hear anymore. He stepped out from his cover and put on his best approximation of a smile. Although he tried to think of some witty line to make his entrance complete, all that came to mind was the simple, "I found you."

Nevertheless, the Knights were impressed. Sal nearly screamed.

"It's a trap—" Briea cautioned, "another illusion meant to lure us to death!"

Kyrin treated her to his best flat expression. His heart pounded too loudly in his ears for him to focus enough to form a retort. "No, Briea," he eventually managed, "no matter how much you might wish otherwise, it's really me. Turns out I suck at self-sacrifice."

"But how?" Sal asked incredulously, "and how did you get here ahead of us?"

Brysson nodded. "The elves didn't seem too keen to let anyone go—least of all you, Kyrin. And with a present, no less," he added, nodding to the necklace of teeth around Kyrin's neck, "What happened?"

Kyrin shrugged, his mouth dry. "Well, after you guys left—"

"You mean got dumped in the middle of a monster nest."

"Shut up and let me talk, Dain. After you all left, I played a game with the elves, and I won. That's how I got the thing. But then the witch apparently thought you all were in the forest there too, so she came and attacked. The elves fled, and she took me captive. I picked the lock—and thank the gods I ran into you here."

The Knights exchanged a glance. Brysson shrugged. "That's good enough for me."

Tryn, however, remained quiet. He gave Kyrin a long, hard look. The boy felt transparent, as if all of his lies were written upon his face for the world to see.

To Kyrin's relief, though, Tryn seemed unable to decipher the metaphorical glyphs. The man nodded once.

"Open the gate, Kyrin. I want to wrap this up and go home."

Shirking slightly at the word 'home,' Kyrin nodded, using the ward on the gate as an excuse to lower his face. Every admission of faith—every trusting expression and honorable tone squashed his heart and made his stomach curl. Every time the Knights said his name, Kyrin wanted to curl up into a ball and confess. He hated it—he hated this—he hated them—he hated himself.

Kyrin took a deep breath and attacked the ward. He knew the secret to opening it—all he had to do was invite the Knights inside—but that did not stop him from bringing out his lockpicks and taking the spell to pieces. The single-minded focus necessary to wardbreaking calmed him.

When the spell was in shambles and Kyrin's pulse was again normal, the thief stood, rolling his shoulders. He took a step back.

"There. That should do it. Come on in."

One by one, the Knights of Alinor entered the witch's castle. None of them noticed the slim figure pull the gate shut behind them.

Kyrin and the Knights picked their way over the castle grounds, keeping a careful eye out for traps similar to those in their own garden. Thankfully, the ground was bare of everything more complicated than a few long-neglected familiar-summoning wards from days gone by, and the ghost dogs the wards conjured, though immortal, were easy to outrun and easier to outsmart. Even when Kyrin had been stuck with Rat as his partner, he hardly would have considered the creatures a threat. With the Knights by his side, they were nothing.

When everyone reached the door, Tryn cleared his throat and began giving hushed orders.

"Alright—we don't know what's waiting for us in there. We don't know what to expect. Obviously, if she took Kyrin, she knows we're on our way, and it's only a matter of time until she realizes he's escaped and let us in. When that happens, we need to be ready for hell. We can't get taken by surprise like we were back home—we knew the place, then, and she still got the best of us."

Everyone nodded, and Briea took over, offering her strategic insight.

"I say we split up into two groups of three. That way, we can search more efficiently without overly weakening our combat potential. Dain and Brysson—you two are with me. With any luck the Anchor Key and the Gauntlet still smell like home. Tryn, Sal—if you take Kyrin, he might be able to hear the magic or whatever it is he does. Sound like a plan?"

Kyrin nodded mutely along with the others. The plan was perfect—with the Knights divided, he and Esmeralda could conquer. This was a dream come true. The fact that the Knights had accepted him into their number as more than just a liability only increased the surrealism.

He banished the unwelcome emotion from his heart—this was no time for introspection: the Knights were already moving on.

"Are you sure this is the right way, Kyrin?" Sal asked after a little while of wandering, "I don't like the look of this passage. It's too... twisty."

Kyrin shrugged, glancing back over his shoulder at his two companions. "This sounds right. Before I got lost and found you guys, I did a little poking around and started to get the feel for this place. Unless I'm mistaken, there's a library or something up ahead. I remember hearing something over this way, and more importantly, I think I remember seeing a map in there. I didn't get a good look at it the first time. I was trying to lay low."

Tryn raised a skeptical eyebrow. "Does it sound right, or do you remember hearing something?"

"Both," Kyrin lied, "I'm hearing it now, but I remember it being stronger further ahead."

Tryn nodded skeptically.

Sal chewed her lip, glancing at Kyrin with something akin to worry. "You said the witch came and captured you when you were still with the elves?"

Kyrin nodded. "That's what I said."

"She didn't hurt you, did she?"

"What?" Kyrin asked, suddenly remembering glowing fingers on an exposed neck—cries of pain and demands for treasure. Sal still had a faint, hand-shaped scar. "No, uh—no... She didn't hurt me. She just... she made it clear that she would if I tried anything funny. I think... I think she was curious about me... about my lack of magic."

"Good. I already want to kill her enough. If she'd hurt you, too, on top of everything else..."

Kyrin almost stopped in his tracks, but he caught himself at the last moment, barely stumbling. It was almost disturbing, hearing Sal make threats.

"Shut up, will you? I'm trying to listen, and it isn't easy

when you're talking to me. Just keep your eyes open or whatever, alright?"

He did not look back to see the girl's reaction. He did not want to know what she was thinking or how she felt. Kyrin did not want to see anything that might make him begin to doubt.

The trio walked the rest of the way to the library in silence. Each quiet footfall seemed magnified by the stillness. Kyrin swore that he could hear everyone's pounding hearts.

The mercilessly short corridor twisted to an abrupt end before a massive, ornate doorway. The ancient slab of black wood was carved with bizarre animals contorted around each other to form glyphs of strength and protection. Kyrin nodded to Tryn, and together, the two managed to push the heavy door open, inch by inch.

Kyrin nearly choked on the smell of old paper. The place was a forest of books. Shelves took the place of trees, stretching up to meet a cathedral sky hung with orbs of magic light. Books lay open all about like strange, pale flowers, their semi-translucent leaves fluttering vaguely in the faint draft. Pages pulled free from broken spines and took to the air like strange, flat ghosts, ethereal in the dim, dusty magelight. Faintly flickering glyphs grew up the walls like vines, deepening the shadows and making the whole room sing.

The quiet music gave Kyrin a headache. He glanced suspiciously at the spaces between the dark shelves, forcing himself to remember that ambush was the reason he had come here, and not some threat he needed to fear.

"This way," he said aloud, avoiding eye contact with Tryn, "I believe it was over here. We can figure out our next move after we find it."

"I'm not moving until you tell me what's going on,

Kyrin." Tryn stood tall, mace in hand and expression firm. Sal stood beside him, her sword drawn in a similar manner.

"I don't know what you're talking about," Kyrin claimed, knowing full well what the man was talking about.

"Don't play dumb. Ever since we picked you back up, you've been different. Shifty, almost. I'm not an idiot, thief—I know when someone's hiding something."

Kyrin barely suppressed a curse. "What the hell would I be hiding? I haven't stolen anything, if that's what you're thinking."

"I wish I could believe you. Sal—" the Knight nodded to his squire, "hold him. Just because we can't trust him doesn't mean we can't use him. I want you to keep him listening and keep him telling the truth."

"But Tryn—what if—"

"If he's telling the truth already, we'll apologize later. Now do it, Sal."

Sal stepped forward, and her eyes met Kyrin's. Once again, her will replaced his own.

"You don't have to do this," he managed, fighting for one final lie before Sal stole his tongue.

"I'm sorry, Kyrin." Sal seemed surprisingly genuine, "We can't be sure. But the easier you make this, the faster we can trust you again. Now please, tell us honestly what you hear."

Kyrin almost resisted—almost fought back for the sheer principle of the thing, but a flicker of motion among the shadows of the shelves caught his eye. At that moment, a familiar ringing filled the air. Kyrin flinched at the sudden volume.

"I hear... I hear the witch."

"What?" Squire and Knight exchanged an alarmed

glance. "Where is she?"

Kyrin looked Sal dead in the face. "She's right behind you."

Sal moved to turn, her mouth forming a question. A golden hand burst from her chest in a spray of yellow light, fingers clasped around a small orb roughly the size of an apple.

The noise was intense as the magic holding Kyrin broke.

Tryn swung around, shouting wordless concern. Sal fell to the floor. Her eyes were wide. Her lips were still halfway parted in an unfinished cry.

Behind her, Esmeralda stood triumphant, smiling as the golden glow faded from her hand.

"What did you do!" Tryn shouted as he rushed at the witch. He swung his mace, missing Esmeralda by inches. "If she's dead, I swear to both Brothers above—I'm gonna—"

"Silence." Esmeralda waved her hand, Sal's soul shining faintly through her fingers.

Against his will, Tryn stopped dead in his tracks, his tongue a stone. The hate on the man's face made Kyrin sick.

Averting his eyes, Kyrin sought comfort in Esmeralda's features. The girl beamed, her eyes locked on Tryn.

"Thanks for helping me, Kyrin! This would have been a whole lot harder without you!"

"No problem," Kyrin muttered vaguely, all too aware of Tryn's burning eyes.

Esmeralda's hand began to glow again. She seemed almost nonchalant as she thrust her arm through Tryn's body and extracted his soul.

Tryn's eyes lost their life. He toppled, his armor

clanging against the hard stone floor.

Kyrin could not force his gaze away.

He cleared his throat softly, fighting the confusing mess of emotion welling up from his stomach. "Are they dead?"

"Hm?" Esmeralda glanced up, midway through stowing the souls in her front left pocket. "Dead? No, just lifeless. And so long as we keep their magic far away from them, they'll stay that way, so don't worry! Those bullies won't bother you ever again."

Kyrin absorbed the statement silently. "We can't just leave them here…"

"You're probably right. When they do die, it'll smell. Will you help me carry them to the—wait—no… I have a better idea! We could use them as bait to catch the other three!"

Kyrin stared at her for another moment before responding. "You have a plan?"

She nodded, winking. "I always have a plan!"

"I don't like this plan," Kyrin murmured as Esmeralda bustled nearby, positioning Sal and Tryn on the ground around him.

"Don't worry so much, Kyrin! Just play your part, and everything will fall into place."

*That's not reassuring,* the voice in the back of Kyrin's mind whispered. He ignored it.

"Just be ready to bail me out," he said aloud, "the moment the others catch on, my head's gonna roll. I came all this way to meet you here—I'd rather not have to say goodbye just yet."

Esmeralda smiled softly. "Don't you worry, Kyrin. I'll be there long before that happens. I'm not letting you leave me. Just relax. Do your thing, and then the two of us will have all the time in the world."

Kyrin nodded. "I'm not worried. I'm just saying."

"I know." Esmeralda knelt down next to Kyrin and leaned in, gently brushing her lips against his cheek. "And I'm just saying. Hang in there, and everything will be okay."

She gave Kyrin one last, lingering smile before letting her magic carry her up through the ruined ceiling of the corridor—up to the place from which she would keep watch.

Kyrin closed his eyes and let his head thump back against the wall. His face burned and his heart pounded, but he was oddly happy. Things would work out. They had to work out.

This was his second chance.

Kyrin opened his eyes and stared at the opposite wall, avoiding the dead stares of the unconscious Knights. Soon, Kyrin would be free from everyone who had ever hurt him. He would be free from the law and free from judgment. All he had to do was this one little thing...

Time passed. Kyrin could not tell the minutes from the hours. As one blended to the other, Kyrin was certain he saw the vines on the opposite wall growing—slowly creeping upwards to catch the faint starlight. In his head, Kyrin cheered them on, willing the plants to someday leave the shadows and find the sun.

Finally, just as Kyrin feared he might fall into an unwelcome sleep, he heard the faint clatter of approaching footfalls and the soft clink of metal armor moving against metal armor.

Kyrin's heart took flight on wings of panic, but he forced his body to remain still as he feigned unconsciousness.

The footsteps grew louder. The clinks came closer.

Kyrin heard three familiar voices gasp their alarm. Next thing he knew, someone was shaking him, calling his name and lightly slapping his face. Kyrin let his eyes drift open.

Brysson was there, the picture of concern. Before Kyrin could blink, the man turned and called to Briea and Dain.

"Kyrin's awake! Are the others?"

"No—" Briea called back, "Tryn won't move!"

"Dain—how's Sal?"

The squire was too busy shaking his friend—too busy calling her name to respond.

Kyrin cleared his throat softly, doing his best to sound pained. "The witch—she... she stole their souls."

Briea came into Kyrin's field of vision, Tryn supported on her shoulder. Her face was grave.

"Tell me what happened."

Kyrin licked his lips, collecting his thoughts before he launched his lie.

"We... the three of us were walking—searching this corridor for any sign of anything, when..." He trailed off. A faint ring—a familiar quiet noise hung in the air, distracting him.

"When?" Brysson prompted, deaf to the sound.

"...when she appeared out of nowhere. Before we could react, she'd..." The noise unnerved him—disturbed him, even, though he could not place the tone. It did not sound like Esmeralda. "She'd stolen Sal's soul. Tryn attacked her, but..." Kyrin shook his head, using the motion as an excuse to scan the room. "But it wasn't enough." Dain knelt in the corner by Sal's body, stiff in his distress. "Next thing I know, she had his, too." Unless it wasn't distress... he was staring fixedly at the wall—at the vine on the wall, almost as if...

*Dammit!*

"I…" Kyrin tried to finish his story, but he could feel his whole body tense. His heart beat faster and his blood chilled. "I tried to… but she…"

"They're… working together?" Quiet though he was, Dain's mumbled words hit Kyrin with the force of a bomb.

Both Knights turned to look at the squire. Kyrin's fingers closed around a chunk of masonry.

"What?" Briea asked. Kyrin shifted his weight to stand.

"The vine—it says… I can't quite… It says a fight happened here. I think… Kyrin and the witch are working toge—"

Kyrin leapt up and struck Brysson. The one-armed Knight fell, unable to keep his balance. Kyrin threw himself at Briea. She toppled, her clawed hand catching Kyrin's face as Tryn's weight pulled her to the ground.

Kyrin let momentum carry him to Dain, but the element of surprise was gone. Dain drew his sword and swung towards Kyrin's neck. The thief was only barely able to duck and roll away from the blow in time.

A feline snarl and a chime of magic signaled Briea's shift. When the lioness leapt, Kyrin was certain that he would find his death on the ends of her dagger-like teeth.

Suddenly, Esmeralda dropped in from the ceiling, her blonde hair whipping about her head like the corona around the sun. She barreled into Briea, saving Kyrin's life and stealing the Knight's soul in one well-timed swoop.

Dain cried out in anger as his mentor fell, her body fully human in its lifeless state. He charged the witch, but Kyrin could not stop to watch their fight.

He scrambled to his feet, setting himself eye to eye

with Brysson. The scar-faced Knight held his sword in his hand.

"Why?" Brysson demanded, stepping nearer as he let his flame play up and down the steel of his weapon. "What the hell were you thinking, Kyrin? Man—you really had us going—thinking you were a good guy in a bad place. You really had me fooled, you flame-ridden bastard. I guess I wanted to believe. Hah—to think I almost called you comrade, when this whole time you were just gonna let Alinor burn." Brysson advanced slowly, his sword trained on Kyrin.

The words stung, but instead of calling anger, Kyrin met the other man's gaze, retreating until his back came up against a wall.

"I'm sorry."

Brysson growled and raised his fiery sword. "Sorry ain't gonna cut it."

The sword fell upon Kyrin like a guillotine, but instead of flesh, the blade met metal and stopped mid-swing.

Brysson staggered, unbalanced. The fire surrounding his sword went out. Dain grimaced as his arm moved to strike Brysson on Kyrin's behalf.

Esmeralda laughed as Kyrin ducked away. "Being a puppeteer is such fun, once you get the hang of it! I should have tried this ages ago!"

Kyrin attempted a chuckle. "Or at least a few minutes ago. I was sure Brysson was gonna kill me."

Esmeralda beamed, her eyes still intent on Dain's movement. "Don't worry—I would never let that happen. But look—I can make them fight!"

The witch waved her hand, and Dain raised his sword again. His movements were slow—it was clear he was fighting Esmeralda's magic with all of his strength, but he was powerless against her will. Brysson only barely managed to deflect his clumsy strike, new as he was to fighting one-handed.

Kyrin had come so far beside these two—he had watched them defeat monsters straight from the realm of nightmare—seeing their combat so far degraded was almost comical.

He glanced at Esmeralda. She seemed enthralled by her new toy. Kyrin let her smile push away his worry.

"Just don't wear yourself out, alright Esmeralda? I hear puppeteering is difficult work."

"Oh, of course! I'll be careful!" The witch replied, still enraptured by her game. Kyrin found his eyes drawn back to the fight.

Dain's attack, though clumsy, was enough to keep Brysson too busy to risk a shot at Kyrin or Esmeralda. However, Brysson's defense was slipping. Every blow Brysson blocked seemed as though it would knock the sword from his grasp—every dodge Brysson pulled looked as though it might be his last.

Yet Dain kept coming. Esmeralda allowed him no rest.

It wasn't until Brysson finally succumbed to wounded weariness—until the strength left his arm and his sword fell—until the knight himself lay sprawled upon the floor with Dain's blade at his throat that Esmeralda finally let her puppet show end.

She approached the defeated pair, her control unwavering. Kyrin followed, a shadow at her heels.

"Don't let him up," the witch commanded, making Dain hand Kyrin the sword. Kyrin nearly dropped it, barely managing to keep the weapon at Brysson's throat. He could hardly stand to look the Knight in the eye.

A flash of magic preceded a soft groan and a thud. Esmeralda stepped over Dain's body and gave Kyrin a cheerful smile.

Although Kyrin did not dare to take his eyes off Brysson, he caught the concern as it flashed across Esmeralda's pretty face.

"What's wrong?" he asked.

"Your face... doesn't it hurt?"

"What?" His left cheek stung where Briea had scraped it, but he had given no thought to the pain.

"Never mind—just keep the sword in place. I'll take a look at it in a minute, okay?"

Kyrin nodded, growing more aware of the pain with every passing moment. His cheek hurt, but he was almost grateful. This was something to think about—something to focus on aside from Brysson's expression.

He tried to keep his mind on the pain as Esmeralda extracted Brysson's life. He tried not to see the way the man's eyes dulled, the way his head listlessly bumped against the marble floor. He tried not to notice the way Brysson's breath gasped to a sudden halt, but despite all his effort, Kyrin remained painfully aware of Brysson's soul passing into Esmeralda's palm.

Esmeralda rose from her crouch. Kyrin let the sword fall to the floor. He touched a numb hand to his cheek. His skin was slick with scarlet blood.

"Here—let me see." Esmeralda took Kyrin's chin in her hand and turned his face towards her.

"Briea... when I had to make a move, she—"

"Shh, just let me look."

She turned his face this way, then that way, then she made him sit.

"Those are some ugly cuts... I'm gonna try to heal them, alright?"

Kyrin nodded, still numbed by conflicting emotion. His eyes swept the room, taking in the sprawled forms of the Knights of Alinor.

"I can't believe... they're the bravest of the brave—the strongest of the strong—the wisest of the wise... yet we took them down."

"Obviously, the two of us are braver, stronger, and wiser. Now keep still—I've never used this form of healing before."

Esmeralda wiped the blood from Kyrin's face. He closed his eyes, letting the blue light wash over the wounds and knit his flesh back together. The cool magic soothed the pain in his face, but for some reason, the stolen power made his stomach twist.

Kyrin cleared his throat. "Thanks."

Esmeralda bit her lip. "It's... not perfect. I fixed the cuts, but... Well, at least it doesn't look *that* bad. They're pretty thin, and you look like a proper adventurer now."

Kyrin raised his eyebrow. "Scars?"

The girl nodded. Kyrin shrugged, for once hardly caring how he looked.

The witch noticed his detachment. She seemed almost desperate to bring him back to reality.

"Oh! I almost forgot! Kyrin—here." She took one of the golden orbs from her pocket and offered it to Kyrin. A tiny flicker of orange flame seemed to shine from its center.

Esmeralda beamed. "Now you have a magic all your own, Kyrin! You can be a whole person, and the two of us can live together—happily ever after! No one from the city will ever bother either of us again!"

*The city... Alinor... Everyone is going to die if I go through with this...*

Kyrin closed his eyes and remembered his home—his childhood—every dream he had dared to chase and every goal that had slipped beyond his reach. The years of anger, the guilt, the pain... the sneers and jeers and betrayals… He had wanted so badly to be normal, then. His heart still ached to make the world see…

*You will never amount to anything.*

But the Knights… They knew the way to glory.

Kyrin opened his eyes and smiled at Esmeralda, taking her hands in his as he climbed to his feet.

"You're right. There won't be anyone left. Here's to a happily ever after." He put his arms around her. She put hers around him.

Kyrin's heart pounded. Esmeralda blushed. Together, they leaned in and shared a kiss. Kyrin closed his eyes and slipped his hand into her left front pocket. His fingers closed around the smooth orb inside. It was warm in his hand.

He and Esmeralda drew apart. Kyrin met her soft smile with a look of sadness.

"Esmeralda, I'm sorry."

Her worried frown broke Kyrin's heart.

"What? What for?"

He broke away and stepped back, holding Sal's soul up as he willed the witch to be still. "This."

"You—no. You didn't—" There were tears in her eyes.

"I did. I'm sorry." Kyrin's own eyes felt dry and hot. "I wish things could be different—"

"Then make them different!"

"That's what I'm doing. That's why I have to act. I'm sorry." The rest of Kyrin's focus and energy went towards keeping Esmeralda immobile. How did Sal do it? The effort of holding Esmeralda still and simultaneously trying to function gave him a splitting headache and made his muscles shake. He wanted to collapse—the pain the magic caused him was almost enough to deafen Kyrin to Esmeralda's raving sobs. He was almost blind to the hurt on her face as she begged him to change his mind.

Every word she spoke was a knife in his heart, but that did not stop Kyrin from binding Esmeralda's wrists and ankles with a length of rope from the Knights' supplies. His fingers shook, and his vision began to blur as he secured the last knot. Just as he gave the rope its final tug, his hold over Esmeralda snapped. She pulled at her bonds, cursing Kyrin as she tried to find flaw in his knots.

Kyrin listened, nodding along with her insults as he searched her pockets for the rest of the stolen magic. The tears on the girl's face might as well have been blood from his own veins, her curses echoed his own inner thoughts, but... Despite his heavy heart, Kyrin's conscience was clear.

*Esmeralda... If she hates me, she hates me. If the Knights condemn me... Well, at least they and the rest of Alinor will survive to see me hang in peace. Second chance be damned, I won't have their blood on my hands. ...Not even I'm that selfish.*

Locating the Knights' magic was the work of a moment. The hardest part was facing Esmeralda's broken, half-sobbed curses. When Kyrin lifted the last stolen orb from her pocket, her voice was nearly a scream.

"No—you can't take them from me!" She wailed, cursing Kyrin and everyone who had anything to do with him, "you can't take them—I—no! I won't let you!"

Before Kyrin could reply, the souls in his hands began to vibrate, and the terrible, jangling music of magic entered the air, just as it had that night in the Stronghold. Kyrin threw Esmeralda a panicked glance, but the girl's eyes were squeezed shut in fearsome concentration.

The wards on the walls and the ceiling began to ring. One of the spheres—a leftover white-tinted orb that Kyrin could only guess contained some poor bastard's power of flight—evaporated suddenly with a burst of noise that popped several wards.

Kyrin screamed. Esmeralda was releasing her magic—destroying the souls so that they could never be restored.

Frenzied and panicked, Kyrin leapt into action. His muttered prayers were lost beneath the rising tide of noise. He floundered through a sea of sound, fighting exhaustion as he struggled to reach the prone forms of the Knights on the floor. The song was intense—it seemed to block out all other senses. Kyrin could not see—could not feel—could not breathe. He knew nothing but the sound. The ear-splitting, blood-freezing sound.

Somehow, Kyrin managed to locate Dain. He fumbled with the orbs for a moment until he found the Dain's shimmering green soul, which he set down on the Treetalker's chest. It dissolved into a cloud of tiny lights and entered Dain's body, passing back into the skin over his heart.

Barely pausing, Kyrin staggered away. The next nearest Knight was Brysson. With fumbling fingers, Kyrin sent the flickering orange soul back to rejoin its body, then moved on.

The noise intensified. The world seemed to swim. Kyrin tripped over Briea's body, accidentally dropping the remaining souls. They rolled away in all directions across the smooth marble floor. The sound swelled. Kyrin could barely make out the scattered spheres through his fading vision, but he could see them shaking on the verge of explosion. He knew his head was probably doing the same.

Crawling along on his hands and knees, Kyrin snatched up the souls.

*One, two, three, fo—*

One of the spheres burst in his hand. Kyrin felt his brain go with it, impaled by the high-pitched noise.

Three left. Kyrin prayed they all matched with the Knights.

He held one of the orbs up in front of his face and squinted at it. *Briea...* He rolled it back to her, then pushed himself up enough for his watering eyes to find Tryn. The two souls left in his hand vibrated to the point of pain.

Three different Tryns lay on the ground, wavering in and out of sight. Kyrin rolled the cool, blue-tinted orb to the middle one and hoped for the best.

The man reabsorbed his power. Only Sal was left.

Kyrin could barely keep her soul in his hand. It burned, stinging his skin—a swarm of irate bees bound together in a tiny storm of solidified magic.

Sal sat slumped against the other side of the corridor where Esmeralda had positioned her. Kyrin could barely distinguish her pale form from the rest of the dark gray wall. The world was too much of a blur. The blood in his ears did not help.

He dragged himself along the floor until his legs gave out beneath him. He pulled himself further until his numbed arms refused to move.

The noise—the pain—the guilt—the grief— compounded with the unfamiliar magical exhaustion and the all-too-familiar physical strain... The chill that numbed his body and deadened his mind came as a relief. Death meant no more hurt.

He rolled Sal's soul the last few inches to her, uttering a wordless wish that she survive. Success was now in the hands of the gods. Kyrin's world was consumed by screaming shadows.

Silence fell. Kyrin fell with it.

# Chapter Twelve

*Icy rain, rushing—rushing—hissing—cold on his skin—screaming against his skin.*

*Dark pier—silver waves—pointed teeth—jagged—chew and swallow. Lapping waves—howling storm. Rushing rain. Puddles on the pier. Screaming. Drowning.*

*Turn around—gold figure. Smiling teeth.*

*Turn back. Silver. Chew. Swallow.*

*End of pier. Last look back. Golden smile—false gold. False future.*

*End of pier.*

*. . .*

*Splash.*

Kyrin swam back to consciousness with all the grace and ease of a fish trying to walk over tar. When his head finally broke the surface of sleep's black waters, Kyrin sucked in as much air as he could get, rocketing himself back to awareness.

It was then that he realized his hands were tied.

Yes, his hands were tied, his back was to the wall, and the Knights sat around a table in front of him, speaking in low, strangely muted voices. Evidently, they had moved the group to a new location in the castle—a derelict meeting room of some sort.

Kyrin looked around. Esmeralda sat propped against the opposite wall, bound as Kyrin had left her. The Knights had added a gag.

"Alright," Tryn was saying, though his voice seemed distorted, "if we found the Gauntlet over there, the Anchor Key will likely be somewhere in the vicinity."

Briea tapped her claws against the wood of the table. "I'll take Dain—we'll cover the search. I recommend that you, Tryn, stay here with Brysson and Sal to guard the prisoners and keep the Gauntlet in our hands."

Tryn opened his mouth to speak, but he was interrupted by a voice Kyrin only barely recognized as his own.

"It's in the room at the center of the castle—right next to the room by the stairs to the tallest tower. Follow the third hallway to the left from the great hall, then go right when it forks."

Everyone turned to look at Kyrin.

"Why should we trust you?" Brysson's tone was bitter.

"By rights, you shouldn't. But what have you got to lose? Believe it or not, I'm the reason you're still alive. Worst I could do right now is waste your time, and I don't know any way I'd profit from that."

"It could be a trap. More importantly," Briea's voice was harsher than usual, and her hands kept shifting back and forth between human fingers and lion claws, as if she were imagining ripping out Kyrin's throat. "how would you know? Give me one reason to believe you're telling the truth."

Kyrin nodded to Esmeralda. "She told me. Showed me, actually. Now I'm telling you."

"Why?" Dain, too, seemed hurt and wary.

"Because. This is how I choose to spend my second chance. I could have chosen to let you all die, steal your powers and live the rest of my life happy with the girl of my dreams, but…" he risked a glance at Esmeralda, then shook his head. "That's what Shadow would have done, and I'm not him anymore. You hanged him, and hell if he didn't deserve it. I'm tired of hating myself all the time, and I'm tired of doing things wrong. You dragged me all the way here so I could help you find the Anchor Key, right? Well that's what I'm doing. Now go get it."

There was a pregnant pause. Briea sighed. "Dain, let's go check it out."

"Wait—so we're trusting him?"

"No. We're checking to see if we can trust him."

"But what if—"

"Not now."

The pair left, Knight leading squire, and Kyrin was left with nothing but an awkward silence between himself and the people he had betrayed. He cleared his throat awkwardly, acutely aware that the quiet was deeper than ordinary.

Something was subtly wrong. Kyrin had been feeling it since the moment he woke up, but he was only beginning to grasp the cause of his discomfort.

"Tryn?"

The Knight's stare was humorless. "Yes?"

Kyrin cleared his throat again. "Let's pretend for a moment that when Esmeralda found out that I didn't plan on staying with her, she got angry and tried to destroy the souls she'd taken. Let us continue to pretend that exploding souls are incredibly loud…"

"What are you getting at?"

"She blew out my hearing. Can you fix it?"

Tryn sighed and ran a hand down his face. Kyrin

watched, biting the inside of his cheek as he waited. The red-haired Knight got to his feet wearily to lay a hand on Kyrin's forehead. He summoned his magic, and the subtle layers of music returned to Kyrin's world.

Kyrin sighed his relief. "Thanks."

Tryn waved his hand, dismissing the gratitude. "Don't thank me until we decide if we're hanging you or not. You stepped out of line, and we all nearly died—and nearly failed to save Alinor."

Kyrin bit his lip and tried to find a proper reply. "I may have stepped out of line, but I also saved your lives and your quest. You can't deny that. I'll thank you if I damn well want—one way or the other, I want to get my life turned around before I lose it."

Tryn shrugged and returned to his seat. The man leaned back in his chair and laced his fingers over his eyes. "We'll make our decision when Briea and Dain return."

Kyrin blew a strand of hair from his face, trying not to imagine the rope tightening around his neck. "Fine. I can wait. There's no hurry…"

An hour elapsed, driven on by quiet, muttered conversation among the Knights and continuous glares from Esmeralda. Brysson and Tryn both kept casting suspicious glances in Kyrin's direction, and even Sal seemed wary of him. When Dain and Briea finally returned with the Anchor Key between them, Kyrin was thanking the gods.

The Anchor Key was found, the witch was captured, the Gauntlet was back on Tryn's arm, and all that remained in the quest was the Knights' journey home.

Kyrin wondered vaguely if this was triumph or tragedy.

"Well?" he asked softly after the Knights had taken their time to discuss. "Are you going to hang me? Or can I have my hands back?"

The Knights exchanged glances. Brysson said something inaudible to Sal. Briea nodded. Dain snickered. Kyrin gritted his teeth, fearing the worst.

Sal stood and drew her sword. Kyrin's heart was a drum.

She raised her blade and cut his bonds.

The walk back to Alinor was short. Tryn activated his Gauntlet, manipulating the elaborate enchantment and aligning Esmeralda's decrepit castle with Alinor's vast anchored domains. The Knights followed their Keys, and within a few hours of leaving the castle, the group was back amidst the familiar green of Alinor's orchards. Kyrin had never imagined he would be glad to see the high, forbidding walls that had once held him captive.

He was exhausted. Physically, mentally, emotionally... Kyrin was tired to the point where one more surprise, one more interruption, one more dirty look from Esmeralda might break him. Never in his life had Kyrin longed so deeply for his old, battered mattress in his drafty little room on Aspen Road.

Kyrin and the Knights staggered through the city gates just as dawn broke the sky. The birds chirped, the magic hummed, and the familiar city bustle was just waking up. The people on the streets waved and smiled at the returning Knights, shouting their thanks and congratulations to the heroes who kept the city safe.

"Do they actually know what we did?" Kyrin whispered to Dain after a woman handed the golden-haired squire a flower.

Dain managed a small smile and shook his head. "It

doesn't matter. They know what we stand for."

Kyrin shook his head and sighed. He was a stranger here in the dawn among the Knights. The shadows had always been his home.

He followed the group to the Doghouse, where Tryn and Briea turned Esmeralda over to the city law, along with specific instructions for keeping her confined. Kyrin kept his head down, hoping to avoid the Dogs' notice and evade the girl's hateful gaze.

When their prisoner was secure, the Knights made their return to their Stronghold to restore the Anchor Key to its rightful place.

Kyrin followed them up the road to their gate, where he stopped. Only heroes could step beyond the threshold. He sighed. Everything looked so different now. Here in the daylight, he hardly recognized the place he had robbed with Rat.

The Knights were already halfway up the path to the front door. Kyrin cleared his throat.

"If you need me, I live in Mrs. Raph's boardinghouse in the alley on Aspen. Assuming she hasn't given my room to someone else... Anyway, just... let me know when you want me to come back and fix what I broke. I'll start working on designs for your arm, too, Brysson."

The Knights turned around.

"What are you talking about?" Brysson lifted his scarred eyebrow.

"Isn't this where we part ways?" Kyrin's voice cracked slightly.

Briea snorted. "You think we'd let you go just like that? You betrayed us and almost brought an end to the civilized world, kid. We're not letting you out of our sight."

"Yeah, after that mess, we fully intend to keep an eye

on you, Kyrin!" Sal laughed. "You did some pretty remarkable things out there. Both good and bad—I wanna see what you'll do next!"

"And if we can steer you towards a path that's a bit more beneficial to society as a whole," Dain added, "there's a chance we can use you."

Kyrin blinked, his eyebrows furrowing. "I don't understand."

Tryn sighed, running a hand through his dark red hair. "It's not uncommon for civilians who get sucked into our quests and respond with bravery to be rewarded with a title and a place in our ranks."

"That's what happened to me," Brysson interjected.

"Though your situation was a bit different, Brysson. Regardless, we can pass you off as a civilian, Kyrin. You can get a fresh start with us, so long as you can pretend that we picked you up in some Outlands village or something. We've discussed it, and we decided to give you one last chance to atone. Think of it like... like parole, or probation or something."

Kyrin nodded, hardly daring to believe what he was hearing.

*I'm dreaming... this can't be real. It has to be some sick joke, or—*

Tryn coughed quietly. "The point is, while your methods may have been... less than ideal, you did come through for us in the end, Kyrin. You betrayed us, but then you came through anyway, saving us and Alinor even though you had everything to lose and nothing to gain. If you're serious about making this change, we think you could do a lot of good working beside us. It's about time Brysson got himself a squire, anyway."

Brysson flashed a grin. "Don't you worry, thief. I'll get you straightened out on the straight-and-narrow. Play your cards right, and the hangman never has to know."

Kyrin felt a slow smile spread across his own face. "I swear—if you guys are pulling my leg…"

"No, Kyrin, we mean it. You're one of us, now. Welcome to the Knights of Alinor."

# MARA MAHAN

# ABOUT THE AUTHOR

Mara Mahan lives in Virginia with her family, her dog and her army of loyal minions. She spends most of her time writing, and spends the rest of her time juggling, reading, playing video games, and occasionally even sleeping.

Follow her on Twitter @MaraMahan, and check out her website for news about upcoming books and other random ramblings.

*www.MaraMahan.wordpress.com*

Share your opinion! Show your support! Don't forget to leave a review on Amazon.com and Goodreads!

Now, read on for a sneak peek at Mara's upcoming book, *Windswept,* available 2017.

"Guinevere, will you marry me?" Gale sighed and smoothed back his straw-blond hair, restraightening his threadbare canvas shirt for what felt like the hundredth time. "No, wait, that's not right…"

He fixed the angle of his cracked shaving mirror against the rocking of the ship, looked himself in the eye, and tried again. "Guinevere, I'd be honored if you'd see fit to marry—damn it, that's wrong, too…"

The ship groaned as if in agreement. Gale sighed again and reset his mirror to try another tone.

"Please, Guinevere—"

"Shift's up, Gale. Final turn's yours to… what are you doing?"

Gale dropped his mirror face down and leapt to his feet. "Blazes, Crawford—y'damn near scared me to death!"

Crawford raised his eyebrow and leaned forward, glancing skeptically from Gale to the upturned mirror. "Aye? And what has you so jumpy?"

"Ain't no business of yours." The two men stared each

other down for a long moment, then simultaneously burst out laughing.

"Ain't no business of mine? Ain't no business of mine? Blast and becalm me, Gale, I drop a pin and you're jumpin' outta your skin—hell if that ain't my business, mate. All the years I've known you, I don't think I've ever seen you strung so taut."

Gale gave a rueful smile. "Aye, I s'pose you're right. It's Guinevere, Crawford. I'm... I'm gonna ask her to marry me."

Crawford froze. "Guinevere? Guinevere Syren, the shipwright's daughter?"

"Aye," Gale said, nodding, "I'm gonna ask her to be mine as soon as we make port. Way I see it—sweet thing like her... If I don't man up and propose, I'll go ashore one day to find that some other man made his move while I was busy waitin'."

"Aye..." Crawford nodded slowly. "I s'pose you're right... one way or the other though, Gale, you got a wind shift to run. Better get on that, or the captain'll keelhaul us both."

Gale laughed. "Aye, but then he'll be out the two best windworkers in all Alinor!"

Crawford grinned. "Fine then—even worse than keelhaulin'—the captain might dock our pay."

"Aye, now, there's a penalty to fear! Gods know my wallet ain't already loose enough. Catch you later, yeah?"

"Yeah, now get out of here, 'fore I kick you up that ladder myself."

Gale laughed again, giving Crawford a cheery salute as he swung himself up the ladder and onto the deck.

Out under the sun, the ship bustled. Sailors went about their work with the ease and efficiency of long practice, shouting orders and singing shanties as they filled their nets with shining silver fish. A gull flew down and landed on the deck, turned into a man, and pointed out a new school of fish to another sailor who promptly jumped overboard, shifted into a dolphin, and swam away to herd the school towards the ship. Likely they'd be asking Gale to push the ship that way in a few minutes so they could scoop up the school before any of the other ships could reach it.

Gale leapt into the rigging and climbed his way to the top of the mast, where he took his place beside Harisin, the lookout, in the crow's nest. Down below, the signal man made a broad gesture with his left hand, sweeping it outward with his palm facing up, then bending his elbow at a ninety degree angle. Gale nodded to himself and called the magic in his blood, summoning a stiff breeze from the sea to push the ship further out into the wide blue world—right up to the edge of Alinor's domain.

The ship pulled within a hundred yards of the edge before Gale stopped the wind, manually becalming the ship. The other men scurried about, raising the sails and readying the nets again, and Gale leaned himself on the low handrail to await his next order. Occasionally he would divert a stray breeze conjured by some other ship's windworker, or readjust his own power to account for a shift in the world's wind, but the tasks left his mind with plenty of time to roam.

Though he tried to be attentive and watch the signalman, Gale quickly found his gaze wandering out over the open ocean, away from the distant shore and the innumerable masts and sails of the other assorted fishing boats. The light in the waves—the color in the water—it distracted him like little else could. The deep, beautiful murky green of Alinor's home water shimmered comfortably next to the brilliantly sparkling blue over the domain border—that unnaturally straight line in the sea that no ship dared to cross—and beyond that, the world was a patchwork of blues and greens and silver-greys, all the way out to the horizon.

The waves gleamed, swelling and ebbing with the breath of the world, and the waters shifted, sea blurring with sky and vanishing, giving way to foreign patches of water as the domains of the oceans disappeared and reappeared to the gods' chaotic design. Gale's eye drifted lazily over this tapestry of constant motion, eventually coming to rest on the single spot of color that did not ever move or vanish. One narrow band of red-tinted water stretched out beyond the bounds of human sight, reaching all the way to the distant shores of Mikare—Alinor's only trade partner.

"What d'you think it's like out there, Harisin?" Gale eventually murmured to the lookout, "sailin' on the Rose Line, I mean."

"Eh? Hard and dangerous," the older man replied, running the back of his hand across his nose, "May as well call it the ocean's throat—she'll swallow you soon enough without temptation. Sure, the brave idiots who come back get paid a fortune, but I've known too many good men gone down to think a trip more than a fool's risk. Now put the thought out of your head and attend, lad—the signalman's wavin' us home."

Gale glanced down sharply. Sure enough, the man on deck swept his hand downward and gestured towards the shore.

"I'd have thought we'd be out here for a good hour or two more," Gale said, calling up a landward breeze.

The lookout snorted. "What, you lose track of time with your head in the clouds, Gale? Ain't much time left 'til sundown, now. Don't know 'bout you, but I'd like to be good and drunk afore curfew falls."

"Aye," Gale laughed, filling the newly-unfurled sails with wind, "that plan sounds right enough! Have a drink for me, will ya? I won't be able to make it tonight."

"Goin' after your girl, are ya?" Harisin snickered.

"That I am," Gale replied, grinning as the ship turned her prow towards port, "it's worth staying sober if it means I get to see her smile."

That made Harisin laugh. "Aye, an' soon enough you'll be drinkin' just to forget her scowl, if I know anything 'bout women. Mark my words, Gale. It ain't worth the time or effort chasin' 'em."

Gale chuckled and shrugged, commandeering a wisp of a breeze to sweep his hair from his eyes. "If that's what you think, Harisin, I don't reckon you're chasin' the right women."

Three quarters of an hour later, the ship made land, and every able-bodied man was back in human form and working to bring the ship home safe. Even Gale, once he had blown the ship to its destination, had to help haul lines, move cargo, and see the ship docked safe. When that was done and the massive barrels of fish had been signed over to the dockworkers, Gale received the three shiny silver coins that made all five days of hard labor at sea completely worthwhile.

Swaying happily with the motion of a ship that was no longer beneath his feet, Gale pocketed his pay and strolled away, down towards the dockside market.

The setting sun lit the sky and the sea on fire with a bright orange light, lending a warm glow to the narrow market streets. The black-pebbled beaches, the low stone buildings, everything looked as though it had been painted gold by some divine hand. Even the people looked happier than usual—the normally sullen dockworkers bustled cheerfully among the ships, the sailors fresh off their boats wandered happily from tavern to tavern, and even the cutpurses and pickpockets seemed to be going about their evening work with a particular odd glee.

Gale shouldered between the lot of them, greeting everyone he met with a grin and a friendly "good evening," albeit with his one hand guarding his wallet and his other hand resting over his knife. He had a plan, and to pull it off, he would need every coin—

The door to Gale's favorite tavern, the Sunrise Blue, swung open as he strolled past. Warm firelight spilled into the street, energetic music danced through the air, partnered with happy, raucous laughter.

Gale paused. Maybe he could spare one coin—just enough to get a quick pint and a hot meal, or—

No, no… Gale shook his head and strolled past the beckoning door. Best stay on task. Guinevere was waiting.

The thought brought a dreamy grin to Gale's face. One glance from her made his heart beat faster than the most vibrant music—one kiss from her was better than the finest wine.

Gale couldn't help but hum to himself as he strode past the taverns, past the fishmongers and the fruit salesmen, past the warehouses to the little shop in the back alley off Palm Street where the specialty silversmith worked.

Gale pushed the door open. A little bell chimed, announcing his presence with its cheerful little welcome. Missus Smith looked up from her book.

"Are you back again, Gale, y'old scoundrel? I hope you have some coin in your pocket, this time. You know

I won't work for free."

"Aye, you old sea witch—I've got the coin, if your dry old bones still have a drop of magic left in 'em. I ain't payin' 'less the job gets done."

"Rascal. I don't have to take that kind of talk from you. Come here." The old woman stood and spread her wrinkled, tattooed arms. The silver beads at the end of her many, tight-wound braids clinked together with every motion she made, and her wizened, shrunken face shone with a sort of hardened, weather-worn vitality.

Gale grinned, embracing her warmly. "It's good to see you again, ma'am. Been too long since we last spoke."

Missus Smith cleared her throat, giving a few gruff coughs to hide her own affection. "Wouldn't have been so long if you'd have come back sooner, boy."

"Aye, well, you made me swear not to return 'til I had the coin for the job or the sense to forget about it, and I've yet to grow any more sense into my skull. I do have the brain, though, to recognize that you didn't raise me to go around breaking my word."

The old woman clicked her tongue and chuckled. "Boy, I reckon I didn't raise you so much as I ruined you. I figure it as a wonder you grew up at all."

Gale laughed. "Ruined me? Gave me life, more like. What manner of man would I be if you'd never have brought me to the sea? A kitchen boy? A lawman? A clerk?"

Missus Smith reached up and lightly cuffed the side of Gale's head. "A whole lot politer, that's what." She paused, staring up at Gale's face for a long moment, examining the cast of his features and appraising the light in his eye. "A kid with magic like yours... Couldn't stand the thought of knowing your talent was rotting away in some children's home. The Brother Gods hate waste, and

I ain't about to offend them. But that don't mean I did it for you—I'm a selfish woman and I wanted your power on my ship, and you better not forget that. But... I s'pose you coulda turned out worse."

Gale nodded amicably. He'd heard the speech hundreds of times before—nearly every time he stopped by to visit. Sometimes, when he wasn't paying attention, he found himself mouthing the words along with her. Now, though, he called a grin and his own original reply. "I turned out fine. I'm doin' fine, what I've got suits me fine, and I'm gonna thank you whether you like it or not, Missus Smith."

"Aye, everything you are is thanks to me," Missus Smith agreed, nodding as she returned to her sturdy cedar chair, "I done you too many free favors, boy. More than my share, Gods know why." Though she frowned, Missus Smith's stern look did not reach her smiling eyes.

"Well, don't you fret, ma'am, you won't be workin' for free this time. I wasn't spinning tales when I said I had the coin, this time." Gale opened his wallet and upturned it next to Missus Smith's book on the low wooden counter top. Silver and copper coins spilled forth, rolling every which way. Missus Smith's eyes widened. Gale grinned.

"There you have it, ma'am, twenty silver. You owe me a necklace for my lover."

Missus Smith muttered something incompressible, herding the escaped money back into one neat pile. She counted the coins out for a moment, separating and sorting them, then sighed. "You must be serious about this girl, Gale."

He nodded. "Guinevere means the world to me. I'd save a thousand times over if that were the only way I could show her my heart."

"Guinevere, eh?" Missus Smith looked up sharply, rolling one of the silver coins between her scarred fingers. "This wouldn't be Guinevere Syren—that shipwright Markus Syren's daughter—would it?"

"Aye, the very same. In all my life, I've never met a girl so—"

Missus Smith cut Gale off with a gesture. "She's from old money, Gale. Old blood. I hope you ain't expecting this one pretty bauble to impress her overmuch. She probably owns pieces twice the worth of any of the best pieces I can throw together."

"Firstly, ma'am, that ain't true—your smithing is some of the best in all Alinor. Secondly, that's not the point. I love her, ma'am, and I'm fair certain she loves me. We've been talking for long enough now—I want to show her how much she means to me. How much I mean this. I aim... I aim to ask her to marry me."

Missus Smith chuckled. "You're a fool, boy. A blasted sun-baked fool. Does her father know?"

Gale gave a lopsided grin, smoothing back his salt-stiffened hair and shifting his weight from foot to foot. "Know I'm a blasted sun-baked fool, or know I hope to marry Guinevere?"

Missus Smith let out a single barking laugh. "The second option, boy, the first point is plain enough for anyone with half an eye to see."

Gale scratched at his cheek, shifting his weight again and shuffling his feet. "I haven't quite told him my plans, yet, but I'm fair certain he knows Guinevere and I have been talking."

"Gods know what he thinks of that notion," Missus Smith said, shaking her head slowly. "I'll do the job I said I'd do as best I can, but I pray you don't end up getting yourself sore disappointed."

Gale shrugged, plucking a stray thread from his shirtsleeve. "A man's gotta dream, ma'am. And then a man's gotta have enough steel in his soul to chase that dream. Fish can't fill the nets you don't throw—aren't you the one who told me that, ma'am?"

"I swear, boy, if I weren't retired, I'd give you the hiding you deserve. I swear, throwing my words back at me... Hah! Who do you think you are? 'Cause to me, you don't look like nothing more than a young fool." Missus Smith sighed, suddenly exchanging her harsh edge for an air of strange wistfulness. "Don't ever get old, Gale. I tell you, it ain't worth it."

"I'll try, ma'am," Gale chuckled softly.

Missus Smith sighed, then clicked her tongue in mock disapproval, shaking her head as she collected Gale's money into her hands. She gave him one last appraising glance, then stepped out into her shop's back room to gather her materials. Gale crossed his arms and leaned himself against the wall to wait.

A few minutes later, Missus Smith returned, carrying a heavy-looking toolbox with both of her frail-looking arms. Gale stepped forward and offered to take it, but she shooed him away, thunked the box down onto the counter, and gestured for him to pull up a stool and sit.

"So. Let's go over again: what is it you wanna get, Gale?" Her hard, flint-brown eyes stared firmly into his soul, all business.

"A necklace for Guinevere," he answered immediately, "Something silver—maybe a sea flower—with those delicate leaves and vines and such. Oh, and I'd like this in it, too, maybe as a centerpiece."

Gale reached into his pocket and pulled out a small drawstring bag, which he opened to reveal a large, slightly misshapen pearl and five tiny blue-green stones. "I found these on the beach over the course of these past few months. I thought if you could work them in, it'd make the gift more… personal, I guess."

Missus Smith took Gale's contribution, examining the stones and testing the pearl beneath her fingers. "I guess you really are serious, boy. I'll throw something together for you. You go and show Guinevere what a lucky girl she is to have your heart."

Gale grinned and nodded, and Missus Smith opened her toolbox, withdrawing several lumps of dark metal from the various little compartment boxes. As Gale watched, she carefully selected one, set it aside, then examined another, and then a third. When she found a lump that appealed to her, she would click her tongue and add the piece to the tiny pile. Elsewise she would shake her head so all her beaded braids clicked together, and she would return the lump to her toolbox.

When she had found four—five bits she deemed satisfactory, Missus Smith clicked her tongue again and cracked her knuckles as she always did when calling her magic. On cue, the lumps of silver began to shine and shimmer and look almost alive. They shuddered, and one-by-one started to morph, birthing tiny glimmering beads that pulsed and shivered with the gentle rhythm of Missus Smith's breath. She closed her eyes, and the beads ran together, creating tiny puddles on the counter top. The puddles then stretched and became strings in different shades of silver, and the strings all wove together to create an intricate braid of living metal.

Gale watched as shapes began to form across the surface of the shining braid. The brightest color of silver pooled in the center, forming a brilliant sphere of iridescent white. The sphere inflated, then exploded, blooming into the perfect image of a sea flower. The metal seemed almost more alive—more real than the living plants that grew by the shore. Missus Smith opened her eyes and carefully pressed Gale's pearl into the flower's center, where it stuck. She set the small blue stones at equal intervals all along the braid's length, and the metal moved to accommodate and encase them.

Sweat beaded on the old woman's brow. The metal grew brighter, the patterns became more intricate, twining around and coming together to form delicate leaves and elegantly curving vines. Finally, Missus Smith exhaled, and the bright silver faded back to its more normal hues. Gale exhaled as well.

"Ma'am—you've outdone yourself, and I don't think I'll ever be able to thank you enough."

"Start by promising me you'll keep that head on your shoulders where it belongs, Gale. You get pretty stupid when you let it float off into the clouds."

Gale nodded, gently scooping the necklace up from the counter and stowing it away in his safest pocket. "On my honor as a windworker, ma'am. I'll keep my idiocy to the bare minimum."

"Good," Missus Smith said, collecting her leftover materials and returning them back to her toolbox, "That's a promise I expect you to keep. And you'll start by takin' this." The old woman extended her hand. Five pieces of silver and three copper coins rested in her palm.

"What? What do you—"

"Just take it, Gale."

"But you made me swear I'd have the full cost when I came—you insisted I pay full price—"

"Aye, that I did. And then you did. And if I know you, you didn't keep so much as a single copper back to save for yourself, and you probably haven't eaten. I didn't take you outta that home just to watch you starve yourself to death over some girl."

Gale smiled and clasped her hand with both of his, accepting the money and pulling Missus Smith into another hug. "I owe you too much, ma'am. Someday I'll find a way to repay you—just let me know if you ever—"

"Oh, belay that gushing, boy—it ain't proper."

Missus Smith could not hide the grin in the corners of her mouth. "You paid me with cold hard coin like everyone else and there's no call to be gettin' sentimental. Stop wasting time with these old bones and go find your girl. She's waiting, aye?"

"Aye!" Gale clasped Missus Smith's hand again, unaware of the faint breezes his joy was stirring up in the room. "Aye, that she is! Thanks a million ma'am—I'll stop by again 'fore I set to sea! Until then, wish me luck!" Gale gave a small salute and a wide grin, then he turned and fled the shop, taking the restless breezes with him.

He ran all the way down Palm Street, through the market, past the docks, and into the shore-domain residential district. He cut through the slums to reach Molly Street, then followed that further into the city before he took a left on Keller Road and headed back seawards. From there, Gale just had to hop one wall, climb down another tree, sneak through a back alley, then he was throwing pebbles at Guinevere's window. The sun was down, sunk well below Alinor's high walls, but Gale knew Guinevere would still be awake.

Sure enough, after only three pebbles, she opened the window and her smile lit up the world.

Gale felt his heart trip. His breath caught in his throat. Guinevere held up one finger, mouthed something inaudible, and disappeared from view.

Gale crossed his arms and leaned up against the nearest tree. His smile was wide enough to make his face hurt, but he didn't care.

Two minutes passed. A faint breeze rustled the sleeping flowers in their neatly-ordered beds. Crickets chirped in the manicured hedge.

Guinevere reappeared at the window. She had put on a jacket, and had braided her long brown hair down her left shoulder.

Gale smiled and blew her a kiss, sending a light breeze to ruffle her bangs. She laughed quietly and blew a kiss back, before swinging her leg over the windowsill and climbing down the ivy trellis to meet him.